Purple
Moon

<small>BY</small>
TESSA EMILY HALL

PURPLE MOON BY TESSA EMILY HALL

ISBN978-1-64526-029-5
Copyright © 2019 by Tessa Emily Hall
Cover design by Ken Raney: www.kenraney.com
Book design by kateink.com

＊

For more information on this book and the author visit:
www.tessaemilyhall.com or write: tessaehall@gmail.com

Scripture quotations are taken from the HOLY BIBLE NEW
INTERNATIONAL VERSION r. NIVr Copyright c 1973, 1978, 1984
by International Bible Society. Used by permission of Zondervan
Publishing House. All rights reserved.

Library of Congress Cataloging-in-Publication Data
Hall, Tessa Emily
Purple Moon / Tessa emily hall 2nd ed.

Printed in the United States of America

Praise for *Purple Moon*

Purple Moon is a story of redemption as powerful as any I've read. Selena's story is one of deep brokenness and healing—the same story that can be found in so many teen hearts today. Tessa Emily Hall, a talented debut author, is one to watch. Writing for her contemporaries, Hall understands the delicate social lives of teens and the need to strike the right balance between role model and reality.

~ **Laura Anderson Kurk**
YA author of *Glass Girl* and *Perfect Glass*

Purple Moon is a story of ache and courage, of hunger and hope. Selena's unflinchingly honest voice will keep teens flipping pages well into the night.

~ **Stephanie Morrill**
YA author of *The Revised Life of Ellie Sweet* and *The Reinvention of Skylar Hoyt series*

Purple Moon radiates with a light of its own, offering YA readers relatable characters and an inspiring message to encourage teens everywhere to shoot for the moon—and never stop reaching.

~ **Betsy St. Amant**
YA author of *Addison Blakely: Confessions of a PK*

I enjoyed reading this book immensely. Tessa Emily Hall is a very gifted new author. The book deals with actual issues for teenagers today, and I think the youth will be able to identify themselves with Selena. I know I did! The message is very deep and moving. This is the first book that really brought tears to my eyes since reading Nicholas Sparks' *The Notebook*. All I can say is a big THANK YOU and AMEN to the author's writing.

~ **Rebecca Maurino**
freelance writer

Tessa Emily Hall writes with an authenticity that is both compelling and original. I very much enjoyed this new voice in YA fiction. Hold on to your heartstrings—Selena will tug them all over Lake Lure!

~ **Rachelle Rea**
freelance editor

Purple Moon is truly an inspiration! The easily relatable protagonist, Selena, will have each reader feeling as if they are in her shoes every step of the way in this journey. Such a great underlying message, and the writing style of author is outstanding! Hard to put this book down without finding out what happens next. A must-read for all ages!

~ **Tara Hall,**
Hillsong NYC youth leader

Purple Moon is a breath of fresh air. It can warm your heart, take your breath, and provoke your thoughts all in one chapter... The characters are lovable, but not without fault: they're real. There was suspense, laughter, love, sorrow, and everything else you could imagine in a book or in life. Every time the story looks as though it's headed down a predictable road, there's an unexpected turn, and you know you just can't put it down. *Purple Moon* is an unexpected beauty not only in its story and characters, but in the spiritual lesson that melts its way into the reader's heart. Word to the wise: Don't start reading at night, you absolutely won't be able to sleep!

~ **Jennifer DeViney**

Purple Moon is an awe-inspiring story of faith and the reality of being a teenager. After finishing this book, I was left feeling refreshed and inspired. Tessa tells such a wonderful story about the beauty of endings and new beginnings. She gracefully tackles the challenges of being a teen, and the hurdles you face as a teenage Christian, while not shying away from the issues. The importance of grace and redemption is evident all throughout this book.

~ **Kaylie Lazarek**

Tessa Emily Hall tells a believable tale with memorable characters that teens can relate to, even if they don't share the same backstory. The author also has an amazing way of letting the reader into the story. I had to stay up all night in order to finish it. *Purple Moon* was an incredible story.

~ **Kathleen Powell**

Absolutely an amazing book! I'm not much of a reader. In fact, reading is one of my least favorite things to do. So it's not likely for me to sit down and read books, besides the Bible. But the author was able to catch my attention, and as I ended a chapter, I would have to keep reading to find out what happened next! Very good story! Loved how the story was written to Glorify God!

~ **Joshua Biggar**

I enjoyed this book very much. The characters are complex and realistic...The story is touching and the message behind the story is even more so.

~ **Ashley Carr**

Purple Moon brings a realistic teenager to the reality of Christ. Just because you're a Christian, doesn't mean bad things won't happen to you—but because Christ lives in you, you have the power to overcome all things, all situations. I believe this book can help teens who may be confused about church, or what it really means to accept Christ and live life according to God's plan.

~ **Jessica Netzler**

Purple Moon depicts a teenager's world in a very real way. Beautiful story!

~ **Katie Lake**

I thought that Purple Moon was a very well-written book for young adult Christian readers, or even for those that are questioning Christianity and what it means...Much of the book even seemed spot-on with things that I have experienced in my own life and walk with God.

~ **Emily Imdieke**

This is a story of redemption, where God takes one life—with all its scars, fear, and pain—and turns it into something beautiful. In *Purple Moon*, we peer into the life of a teenage girl who once had beautiful dreams, but poor choices (not only her own) left them shattered. A summer at the lake turns her world upside down, and she finds hope—not a fairy tale hope that will never come true, but the hope of a reality in which God writes a story worth living and a true happy ending.

~ **Katy Kauffman**

I loved *Purple Moon!* There truly aren't enough good books written for Christian teens...It is a fantastically written and inspiring book, and I look forward to more books from Tessa Emily Hall.

~ **Amy Victoria**

Dedication

To Mom, who would write my stories down for me when I was a toddler; who would put up with my begging to publish them when I was a kid; who has gone with me to every writing conference when I became a teenager. I could never repay you.

Acknowledgments

This book could not have come together without the support and help of several others. I would like to thank my parents, who have always encouraged me in pursuing my dreams. If not for your support, I would never have gone to my first writing conference at the age of sixteen, which is where I met my publisher. It is because of your support that I have persevered, and it is because of your faith in God that I also believed in the gift that He has given me. Also, thank you, Aunt Penny for all of the critiques you gave me in the beginning stages of *Purple Moon*.

A very special thank you to Eddie Jones, the Acquisition Editor for Lighthouse Publishing of the Carolinas. You believed in *Purple Moon* from the very beginning. Thank you for the patience you have had as the perfectionist in me kept wanting to make it the best it could be these past few years. Thank you for giving me this opportunity to allow my dream to come true.

Thank you, Elizabeth Easter—my first editor, and the best one I could ask for. You have also had patience with me as I kept wanting to tweak *Purple Moon*. Thank you for believing in this story and for making it a better read.

Thanks to my best friends: my older sisters, Shannon and Tara; my cousins, Jeremy and Josh; and Erica. You all have always had faith in me. Thank you for supporting me throughout my writing journey.

Thanks to the Kauffmans, who I met my first year at Blue Ridge Mountain Christian Writer's Conference. If it wasn't for you instructing me on how to make appointments and meet with editors, I never would have been offered a contract.

Thank you to the amazing teachers I had growing up—Emily Nunnery Valentine, Rosemary Emory, and Jennifer Wilson—for the faith you had in my writing even when I was young, and for helping me grow in my writing at an early age.

Thank you to my prayer warrior grandmothers. I would not have the relationship with God that I have today if it was not for your faith in God, as well as your prayers.

Most importantly, thank You, God, for giving me this gift of writing, and for allowing my dream to unfold so early in life. Thank You for putting this story together in the way that You did. May every word that I write throughout my writing journey be a reflection of You and only You.

Prologue

"**O**nce upon a time, there was a beautiful little princess named Selena."

One of my favorite childhood memories is of my dad tucking me into bed one night. He sat on the edge of my bed, stroking my hair. The room was dark, the only light coming from a princess night-light plugged into my wall.

I allowed my heavy eyelids to close. Tugging my blanket to my chest, I let Dad's soothing voice paint a story in my head, just as it did every night.

"Selena was an incredible artist, always drawing pictures of her horse named Fairy Tale."

I squinted my eyes open slightly, catching Daddy glance at the wall behind me where I had taped up every picture I'd drawn. "She was definitely a daddy's girl, too. Took after him a lot, including her nose—"

He reached over and pinched my nose between his fingers as I giggled.

"—her brown eyes, and even her brown hair. Selena hardly ever caused trouble. She was definitely the perfect little child. And even though she's a bit small for her age, I know that God is going to use her to accomplish big things in life. As long as she continues being His best friend."

I smiled as Daddy leaned down to plant a kiss on my forehead. The bed squeaked when I felt him stand up.

"Daddy?" I rolled over, wishing he didn't have to leave. Wishing that he could continue stroking my hair, telling me fairy tale stories as I drifted off into dreamland.

He turned around. "Yes, Selena?"

"You didn't mention the part of a Prince Charming. Will there be a Prince Charming in my story, Daddy?"

I held onto my blanket tightly, watching as the corners of his lips rose before he came back to sit on my bed. "As much as I don't like to say this, yes. There will be. You're much too beautiful not to have a Prince Charming in your story." His hand returned to my face, stroking the side, like one would a pet puppy. "But until then, little Miss Selly, you are mine and mine only." He held up his pinky. "Promise?"

I released my blanket to connect my pinky with his.

Sealing a promise that my dad was to break just two years later.

Chapter 1

When I consider your heavens, the work of your fingers, the moon and the stars, which you have set in place, what is mankind that you are mindful of them, human beings that you care for them?

- Psalm 8:3-4 (NIV)

"Why couldn't you just leave me alone in our apartment for the summer, Mom? I'm sixteen. I'm responsible. Mostly mature."

Our Camry swerves as we turn into Lakeview Estates. Three-story homes span the landscaping that stretches for acres then tucks into the bordering lake.

Families visit here every year for summer vacation. The majestic mountain peaks that outline the water of Lake Lure offer a refuge of seclusion to escape the stress of hectic lifestyles. No words describe the beauty of this place.

Yet I shut my eyes and sink further into the seat, trying to wish myself away. Somewhere else. Maybe to the fairy tale land that I used to imagine when I was a kid. I would even welcome the idea of turning around and driving all the way back to Brooklyn.

Anywhere but here.

"You trust me, don't you?" I'm tempted to add, *It's not like I don't practically live by myself already,* but bite my tongue instead.

Although the familiar, pale yellow house that Mom and I lived in eight years ago is hidden by trees, I recognize it instantly and let out a huff, forcing myself to unbuckle.

It takes way too long to drive through the Huiets' winding driveway, yet not long enough.

A knot in my stomach tightens as the car jerks to a halt. I'm sure Mom is dreading this just as much as I am.

Without even a glance toward my mother, I step out of the passenger seat and slam the door behind me. The heat from the blazing sun beats down, reminding me that I should've brought more summer clothes. I attempt to inhale a deep breath of fresh mountain air but am smothered by the humidity—or maybe it's the sense of dread that overwhelms me. The only beauties I find in this situation are the two butterflies that flutter away as I open the car trunk.

Everything else just doesn't make sense.

"I honestly do not see the point in this." I sling my suitcase over my shoulder and reach for my sketchpad in the trunk.

Mom shuffles a few of her own bags around, obviously to delay facing her sister. She turns toward me; her touch on my shoulder is just as unsure as the look in her eyes. "Selena, I trust you. But you know I can't just leave you in New York by yourself for practically three months. Besides"—she slams the trunk shut—"you may be here longer than just the summer."

A bee buzzes around my head. I'm not in the mood to shoo it away. "What?"

Mom applies lipstick to her chapped lips, the only makeup I've seen her wear in eight years. "Sweetie, I'll be staying at a rehab center. They may not let me go until I've completely recovered from my alcohol addiction. You know what a mess I am, Selena. I can't guarantee it'll just be for three months." She throws the lipstick tube back into the black shoulder bag she calls her purse. "We'll just have to see how things go. You do want me to do this, don't you?"

"Well, yeah." And I mean that, too. I'm sick of my mom leaving me constantly to go out and party with her friends. I'm tired of having to remind her what happened the night before as she rolls out of bed with a hangover that forces me to be her nurse for the day.

"Well, do this for me, okay?" Her puppy dog eyes have no effect on me. I can see right through her intentions. "I know you may not care for Aunt Kori and Uncle Ben, or even Whitney. But please try to perk up and be thankful that they're at least allowing you to stay here again. Besides, it'd be much more comfortable living in their lake house for the summer instead of our cramped apartment anyway. Don't you think?"

I nod. Sure, that part is true. But is it really worth staying with Mom's snobby sister who never even tries to get in touch with us? It's obvious that the only reason Aunt Kori keeps offering her home for us is to remind Mom how much better Kori's life is than ours. She just likes to shove in my mom's face the fact that she and my uncle are still together and have successful careers.

A black cat prances past Mom and me as we walk between the rows of white lilies leading us to the Huiets' front porch. I feel an urge to turn and run, but instead follow behind Mom as she goes up the porch steps, one step at a time.

"You know that we both need this time away from each other. Not to mention some time away from our bad habits." Her frizzy waves bounce as she glances at me before ringing the doorbell. "Don't forget about our little agreement, now."

Of course I couldn't forget about that. Mom agreed to check herself into rehab only if I would also stop drinking and smoking while I'm here. It's worth it to me.

I'm just not sure how long we'll be able to keep our deal once we get back home to Brooklyn.

Mom plasters a grin on her lips, waiting for her sister to answer the door. This smile translates, I'm trying to look like a perfect mother, but deep inside I'm hurting and far from perfect.

"Who knows?" she says through her forced smile. "This may finally be the new beginning we've both been searching for."

Oh, I'm sure it will be. Just like all the other times you've said that.

The door swings open. "Jackie!" My aunt throws her arms around my mom. If she hadn't said my mom's name, I would've probably wanted to check to make sure that we were at the right house. Aunt Kori looks strangely younger than she did eight years ago.

"Goodness, it's been so long!"

"Oh my, Selena." She looks at me now. Her bright red lipstick, matching red hair and low-cut top make me almost sure that she is now taking fashion advice from her daughter. Or perhaps she's just borrowing her clothes. "Look how beautiful you have become."

Yes, same to you, Auntie. I absolutely love your new nose ring. It goes so well with that tattoo of whatever that creature is crawling up your arm. Oh, and congratulations! I see you've grown a chest over the years just like I have. Well, except mine is actually from natural growth.

"Hi, Aunt Kori." I quickly put on my fake smile. This one

is called the you-can't-fool-me grin. Or I-secretly-hate-you. Same difference.

The mixed scent of cigarette smoke and strong perfume overwhelm me as Kori attempts to give me a hug. I decided on the way here, though, to be fake only through my expressions. Unlike my mom, I don't have to be affectionate if I don't mean it.

So I give Aunt Kori a one-arm hug and quickly pull away.

Great. Now Mom's giving me "The Look".

"So is Whitney here?" she asks, returning her attention back to her sister. "I'd love to see her before I have to head out."

"I think she's out on the lake right now with some friends. I'll get her." Kori opens the door wider. "Here, why don't you two come inside? You can just set your luggage down in the foyer for now, Selena."

I grab my suitcase and follow Mom inside, dropping my luggage on an Oriental rug in the foyer. Aunt Kori's heels click as she walks on the hardwood floor and into the living room, deliberately showing her house off to Mom. As I look around at the familiar surroundings, my mind floods with memories. The last time I was here I was only eight years old, saying goodbye to the family I had lived with almost six months.

It was miserable having to stay with my spoiled brat cousin even then, especially since we had just been kicked out of our home in Kentucky by my dad.

I sigh, wishing I didn't have to be here to relive my past. Or be reminded of my dad and the peaceful life we once knew.

"Didn't you used to collect china dishes, Jackie?" Aunt Kori asks as she leads Mom into her kitchen. "Let me show you the new china dinnerware that Ben's parents just brought from India. You're going to love it."

I glance at the stairs that spiral upward to the next floor. Every day in New York, I descended the dirty, crowded steps to the subway, or climbed the plain concrete steps to our apartment. I'd forgotten that stairs could actually be elegant.

I've also forgotten what it feels like to live in a real house, a place where I can listen to music without fearing my neighbors will bang on the door and start yelling at me in a different language.

A place to call home.

"No, thanks," Mom says as I enter the kitchen. "I have a few water bottles left in the car. I just want to see Whitney before I have to leave."

I walk over to the kitchen sink and pause as the scene out the window immediately grabs my attention. The sun rays beam down on the lake, almost as if they were welcoming me to North Carolina.

Okay, so maybe I have to agree with Mom just a little— I'd much rather stay here for the summer than stay alone in Brooklyn.

"Oh, yes. I'll go get her. What about you, Selena?"

I spin around. "Huh?"

"Are you hungry? Or would you like anything to drink?"

"Nah. I'm fine." We aren't a charity case, Aunt Kori.

"Alrighty, then." My aunt flips her dyed red hair. "Be right back. Let me go see if I can fetch Whitney."

Kori strides into the den and disappears through the sun porch's French doors. I run my hand across the black marbled counter-top that dust mites would never dare touch as Mom steps closer to me, her vinyl sneakers squeaking on the ceramic floor.

"Mind your manners while staying here, Selena," she says, lowering the level of her voice. "You need to say yes ma'am and no ma'am. We are very blessed to have a family that cares enough to let you stay with them while I get some help."

"Cares?" I can't help but laugh. "Kori made your life miserable when you were growing up. You said so yourself. And the only time you ever heard from her, other than when we used to live here, was when Grandpa died. She didn't even bother to go to his funeral! Now you're expecting me to actually be polite to this lady who has caused you so much pain for all these years?"

Mom's silver-blue eyes pierce right into my heart. "It's called forgiveness, Selena."

"Oh, really? Forgiveness?" I raise my eyebrows. "Okay, then tell me. If it were that simple, how come you haven't forgiven Dad? You know he's the one who has caused our lives to turn into such—"

My words stop as I hear the back door open. I follow hesitantly behind Mom as she walks into the den.

"Well, there you are, Whitney!" Mom says, her arms wide open. "Come here and give me a hug."

My cousin Whitney wears a bikini that I'm sure is made of dental floss. I must say, though, it's an amusing picture to see my short Mom standing next to her five-foot-eight blond niece.

"My, you're so grown up!" Mom says after their awkward hug. "You're Selena's age, correct?"

"I guess," she says, chomping on her gum. "Sixteen."

"Well, it's good to see you again. Selena is thrilled to be able to stay here for the summer and get to know you. Right, Selena?"

As Whitney looks at me, my fake smile turns into a scowl. The attitude in her eyes reminds me of the eight-year-old spoiled brat she used to be. I highly doubt that she's changed a bit since then.

The grandfather clock in the foyer seems to tick louder as the four of us stand around in the den, silence hanging over us like a heavy cloud before a storm. Mom still has a grin plastered on her face, but this one has switched back to the "perfect mother" smile.

A lump builds in my throat as I watch her eyes form pools of water. I've always hated to see her cry.

"Well, I guess I should be going. Gotta be in Greensboro by five."

Poor Mom. She probably wishes that she could relax and stay here with me for the summer instead of having to face her problems at rehab. A Christian addiction treatment center, nonetheless.

"It's great that you were able to stop by, Jackie."

Aunt Kori leads all of us into the foyer—well, everyone except Whitney. She stays behind in the den and turns on the television. Speaking of impoliteness.

"And I'm very glad that Selena is going to be staying with us this summer," says Kori. "She'll have so much fun. Don't worry about her."

Mom turns face-to-face with me now, wrapping her hands around mine. "Well, I shouldn't have to worry about you. Like I said, I trust you. Just be good, okay?" Her head bobs up and down. "Oh, and don't forget to take your anxiety medication."

She reaches over to give me a long, tight squeeze. I would love to cry on her shoulder and beg her not to leave, like I used to do when she dropped me off at daycare.

Mom hasn't shown this much affection to me since we lived in Kentucky with Dad and my older brother, Drake. Perhaps she's just doing this for the show. It surely would go along with the fake smiles she's been displaying since we arrived.

After giving Kori a goodbye hug, Mom opens the door, but then turns around to give me one last wave before stepping out onto the porch.

"Bye, Mom."

* * *

I stand at the entrance of my new bedroom, blinking to convince myself that this is not a dream. It looks as if a famous decorator has been in here since Mom stayed in this bedroom eight years ago. The first thing I notice is the window seat in the corner overlooking the lake. It's painted with a zebra print that reaches down to the floor, and the black satin overstuffed cushion complements the deep pink walls.

After dropping my bags onto my new queen-sized bed, I collapse into the window seat and look out at the sun's reflection glistening on the lake's ripples, surrounded by the Blue Ridge Mountains.

This is the perfect place for me to spend long hours sketching while I'm here.

I could definitely get used to this.

I continue scanning every detail of the room. The painted zebra-print dresser next to my bed. The odd-shaped lamp standing next to the door—

I jerk as my gaze lands on Whitney standing in the doorway, arms folded across her chest. The hot-pink bathing suit cover-up she wears makes her appear part of the décor.

"Mom wants to know if you're hungry."

Haven't I already answered this question for Aunt Kori? "I'm fine." I stand. "I think I'm going to go down to the lake, actually. After I unpack a few things first."

She glares at me as if she is judging my every detail to see if I fit her criteria. I've always hated being judged. Especially on my appearance. My dad's mom was full-blooded Mexican, so I have a bit of Hispanic heritage in me. Sure, I've been complimented on my eyes and cheekbones before, but I highly doubt I could ever match up to someone like Whitney.

"Let me get something straight, Selena." She closes the door behind her and takes slow, steady steps toward me. She reminds me of a mother, scolding her child as a warning to behave. "For some reason, my mom expects me to be—well—basically your babysitter for the summer. She wants me to introduce you to some of my friends and make you feel welcomed. I'm even being forced to invite you to go with me to a friend's party tonight. But you're sixteen. You're not going to come in and steal my friends and ruin my summer, alright?"

I laugh. "If it makes you feel any better, Whitney, I don't want to be here just as much as you don't want me here."

She straightens her posture and narrows her eyes at me. "I know you might think you're all-that and everything since you've been living in New York for the past couple years, but I can see straight through you. And if you think for a second that you're better than me and my friends, well, just remember the reason you're here."

"What's that supposed to mean?"

"You know exactly what it means." Her voice is even more snarky than I remember as a kid. She goes back to the door, but then turns around again before opening it. "The party starts at seven-thirty. Oh, and you might want to consider a shower before going. That is, if you're planning on making any friends this summer."

"Actually, I'd rather just stay—"

"Seven-thirty." Her glare is a threat. "Be ready."

I swallow, having a strange feeling that she's not just referring to tonight.

Chapter 2

"Whitney, do we have to go sixty in a forty-five mile zone?" I grab the armrest of my cousin's Mustang convertible and hold on as if my life depends on it.

Because it probably does.

"Oh, don't worry." She reaches over to turn down the radio playing Katy Perry for all the other drivers to hear. "Police are rarely on this road."

My body jerks as the car screeches to a halt at a stoplight. "Do you really think I'm more concerned about your getting a ticket than the possibility of me losing my life?"

"How are you going to ever have fun in life if you're so worried about following all the rules?" She glances at her reflection in the rearview mirror and adjusts her Chanel sunglasses.

"It's not that I'm worried about following all the rules, Whitney. I'd just rather not spend my first day in Lake Lure at the hospital."

"Well you do know what kind of party we're going to, right?"

To show the amount of interest I have in this conversation, I turn my head and watch the evening sun hover over the lake—only to be distracted by two guys in the car next to Whitney's, staring at us.

Then I notice: they're not looking at me. They're looking at Whitney. Of course.

"Did you hear me?"

"Yes ma'am." I look back at Whitney as she guns the engine, not even flinching at my remark. She probably thinks that she deserves that kind of respect.

"Let's just say that we won't be drinking punch at this party." I've never had someone's laugh make me want to gag—until now. "But I bet you're already familiar with strong drinks. You know, with your mom and all."

My eyes glare at this stranger whom I'm told is my cousin. "Don't talk about my mom like that. If you and your friends continue drinking, I'm sure you'll end up at the same place she is right now." I say this, although I know that I'm only trying to convince myself.

"Whatever. Look, if you're going to embarrass me by acting like Miss Goody-Goody, go ahead and tell me now so I can take you back home."

Although tempted, I remind myself that, to make any friends this summer, I'm going to have to go to a few social events. No matter how much I can't stand Whitney.

"No. I'm fine."

My mind changes the instant we arrive, walking into a house even bigger than Whitney's. The pounding music reminds me that this kind of party is probably not the best place for me to be right now. One of the reasons I had agreed to come to Lake Lure was so that I could get away from the temptation to drink—not to have it greet me at the front door on my first night here.

The various cliques huddled throughout the den remind me of animals separated into their own kind, not daring to join a group that isn't their species. Dancing. Drinking. Smoking. Reminding me of why I need to quit this lifestyle, but luring me to return.

I push my way through the clusters of teenagers, feeling all eyes on me as I awkwardly try to blend in with the crowd. Why is it that everyone seems to sense who is the new kid in town?

My mouth waters as I spot a snack bar stretched across the kitchen and covered with a variety of catered food. There are croissant sandwiches, chicken fingers, boiled shrimp with cocktail sauce, a cheese tray with assorted crackers, mini cheesecakes, and even a chocolate fountain surrounded by fruit. I feel like I'm at a wedding reception instead of a teenager's birthday party.

"Patrick, you've had enough cheese cubes for today," says a girl dressed in black from head to toe. She takes a white cheese cube out of a guy's hand and pops it into her mouth instead, revealing a piercing on her tongue. "You're not going to be able to go to the bathroom for a month if you eat any more."

I can't help but stare at this Goth couple who look as if they just stepped out of an ad for Hot Topic. I reach over them to grab a plate. "Excuse me."

"Sorry," the girl says. "Apparently my boyfriend here thinks he's a mouse and can eat all the cheese he wants."

I laugh. "It's fine."

I fill my plate with almost every food choice available and turn around, wishing there were actually some place I could eat my food in private. Instead I choose the next best thing—the empty wicker chair next to the couple.

I head over to them, hoping they won't reject me since I'm not wearing black.

"Is this seat taken?"

The girl looks up from her food and stares at me for a second—as if she isn't quite sure I am talking to her, or maybe she's wondering if I'm serious. "Nah, go ahead."

I feel her watching me as I sit down.

"You go to Lake Lure High?"

"I don't live here." I peel one of my boiled shrimp, trying not to cringe at her eyebrow piercing. "I'm staying with my cousin Whitney. You probably don't know her, though. She goes to some art school."

"Art school?" She crinkles her nose, looking as if she's about to regurgitate the cheese cubes. "You're not talking about Whitney Huiet, are you?"

I nod.

"Hayden isn't too fond of that girl." Her boyfriend flips his red-streaked black hair over to one side, enabling me to actually see both of his eyes. "She's like—like a walking Barbie doll. Very. Hot. Barb—"

Hayden elbows him. "Shut up and eat your cheese cubes, Patrick."

"But you took them away from me."

"Then just shut up."

"Well, quit treating me like a little kid, and I might."

Hayden turns her attention back to me as her boyfriend continues to mumble under his breath. "Sorry. It's not that I don't like Whitney. It's just that, well—"

"No, it's okay. I don't care for her that much either." At all, really.

She seems pleased with this response. "So, what's your name?"

"I'm Selena."

"Nice name. I'm Hayden." She places her hand on her boyfriend's shoulder. "And this is my soon-to-be-ex-boyfriend, Patrick. We've been dating on and off since sixth grade."

I dab my shrimp in cocktail sauce. "Sixth grade? Wow."

She giggles, and for the first time I notice that she's a little drunk. And, trust me, I know a drunk when I see one.

"But we love each other." Her monotone voice turns flirty, and she drapes Patrick's arm around her neck.

As Hayden leans in to give her boyfriend a kiss, I have no other choice but to sit here and watch a couple who was just arguing a second ago now climb all over each other. Seriously.

I stand up—almost out of instinct—and set my plate down on my chair. "I'm going to, um, get some pie."

Patrick immediately pulls away. "While you're up, can you get me some more cheese cu—"

"We'd both like another beer, actually. If that's okay with you."

I nod. "Coming right up." Since when have I been assigned to be their barmaid?

As I make my way back to the sofa—juggling a slice of key lime pie on my plate, and two beers—a most-likely-drunk girl dances into the kitchen. Before I can step out of her path, she stumbles right in front of me, taking me down with her.

Pie lands face-down on the stone tile floor, but somehow I'm able to maintain a firm grip on the beer.

"Oops, sorry!" She sits up and looks at me lying on the ground, her hand covering her mouth. There is absolutely no sympathy in her voice. Nothing but giggles.

I stand up and run my hand through my hair. Whatever. I am not going back to the snack bar. Forget it.

"Here you go." I stand in front of Patrick and Hayden, who apparently have yet to come up for air since I've been gone. I clear my throat to get their attention.

"Oh, thanks." Hayden grabs both of them and hands one to her boyfriend.

"Do you know where the bathroom is?"

"Up the stairs," she says, opening her can. "You'll see it on the left."

"Thanks."

Stepping into the den, I notice that the drinking and dancing have become far more intense since I first arrived. I feel bad for the owners of this Animal House. They're probably out of town and have no idea what's going on.

After shoving my way through the sweaty teenagers, I head upstairs—but my pace slows when I hear a door slam. Grabbing the railing, I reach the top and see a girl run out of a bedroom, tears streaming down her face. Behind her is a football-player type with a determined face, yanking her arm from behind.

"Baby, please," his deep voice pleads. "I'm sorry."

"Stop it, Ryan." She faces him, doing her best to pull away. "Let me go!"

I glance down, placing a thumb over the scar on my right wrist. Before flashbacks overwhelm me, I turn around and head back downstairs, refusing to stop until I've reached the kitchen.

Heart pounding, I collapse back into the wicker seat.

"You okay?"

I turn toward Hayden. "Mmm-hmm." I reinforce the lie with a smile. "I'm fine."

"You don't drink?" Patrick asks, watching as I take a sip of Diet Coke.

"No, I do—I mean, I did." I let out a sigh, wishing I didn't make such a rash decision about this commitment with Mom. "I quit drinking this summer."

"What? Are you serious?" he laughs, looking at my face to make sure that I am not joking. "Why now? Summer's the best time to party."

"My mom's an alcoholic. She decided that the only way she would go to rehab is if I also agreed to quit drinking." My finger traces along the rim of the Coke can. "Besides, I don't want to end up like her."

Hayden shakes her head in sympathy—"I'm so sorry. That must be really hard for you"—as if I had just told her that someone really close to me had passed away. "Oh, I have an idea." She reaches into her purse and pulls out a pack of cigarettes. "Come on." She waves a cigarette in front of my face. "My boyfriend here may not be the brightest on the planet, but he is right about this being the best time to party. You have to loosen up a little bit. It's summer."

Why is she doing this to me? It's like waving a piece of candy in front of a kid after his mom just forbade him from eating any sweets. "No, thanks. I quit smoking."

"I thought you quit smoking, too, Hayden."

I'm surprised Patrick was actually listening to our conversation. He appears to be in his own little world, playing air guitar to the song that blares through the house speakers.

"I did." She holds the cigarette to her mouth as she lights it. "But I allow myself to splurge every now and then."

I cringe, but inhale as she blows the cool menthol.

Right in my direction.

I may be able to withstand the smell of beer, but there is something way more addicting about a cigarette that makes me feel so—relaxed. It takes me back to the times in Brooklyn when I escape to the roof of our apartment, light a cigarette, and allow the smoke to drift on the cool night breezes. Almost as if my troubles are drifting along with it.

"I better go." I quickly stand to my feet before I lose all self-control.

"Already?" Hayden looks disappointed. "Hold on, let me give you my number."

She pulls a pen out of her purse and scribbles on a napkin. I just hope she's sober enough to get it right. I don't want to find out later that I called the wrong number and asked an old lady to hang out with me on the lake.

"Where are you going?" Patrick takes a swig of his Bud Light. "The party hasn't even started yet, Cindy!"

"Selena. My name is Selena. Not Cindy."

He kicks his legs up on an end table. "Psssh, whatever. You and Hayden are so much alike. You're both just rude. Hey, you should be the rude twins! Get it?"

He cracks up laughing at his own pathetic joke. Oh, the humor caused by alcohol.

"Here you go." Hayden hands me the napkin. "Feel free to call me if you ever need an emergency escape from Whitney. I feel for you. I really do."

If only I had enough courage to say same to you and point

to her immature boyfriend. "I definitely will. Bye, guys. Don't get too drunk."

* * *

A thirty-minute walk in the humid night air brings me safely back to my new home for the summer. With help of the GPS on my phone, of course. And an extra anxiety pill.

"Whitney? Back so soon?" Aunt Kori's voice trails from the direction of the den. She sits on the couch, leaning over the coffee table with a cigarette in her mouth and painting her fingernails an odd shade of lime green.

"Oh, it's you," she says, smashing her cigarette into an ashtray. "Sorry, I don't normally smoke inside. Did you come back all by yourself?"

"Yeah. I just wanted to finish unpacking before I go to bed. It's been a long day."

"Well, did you eat? Ben made a pot of stew last night, if you want some leftovers."

I shake my head. "I ate already. Not hungry."

"Well, alright then." She screws the lid back on to her nail polish. "Hope you have a good night's rest. I'm going to try to get some beauty sleep myself. I have an early shift at my tanning salon tomorrow morning." She pats my head, flashing me a Crest Whitening Strip smile before heading to her bedroom. "Glad you're here, hon."

After replacing my beer-stained clothes with a clean outfit, I grab my sketch pad, and dig through my purse in search of a pencil and a book light. Instead, my hands discover a pack of Virginia Slim Lights that wasn't there a couple hours ago.

How could Hayden have snuck this into my purse without me noticing?

Clenching the pack in my hand, I look across the room at the trash can sitting next to the dresser. I know I should throw the pack away. Hayden would never know if I did, and I wouldn't be tempted to give in and have a few.

Besides, how will I ever be able to sketch again if I keep going back to smoking? My therapist said that the reason it's hard for me to stop is because I rely on smoking to calm my nerves when I feel an anxiety attack coming on. She recommended that I replace this bad habit with sketching.

And I did. For a while.

Until the incident with my ex-boyfriend. Ever since then, all inspiration was sucked out of me and I began smoking again.

A cigarette or two shouldn't hurt anything. Not to mention, these were a gift. And I know how much cigarettes cost.

I gather all of my sketching supplies—along with Aunt Kori's lighter that she left on the coffee table—and open the back door, smiling as my bare feet step off the steps and through the damp grass.

In Brooklyn, when I want to go off by myself, I usually escape to the roof of my apartment—although the street noises never quite give me the feeling of being by myself.

It's much more peaceful here in Lake Lure. The chirping of crickets, croaking of toads, and occasional buzzing of a distant motorboat engine fill my ears as I sit down on the edge of the wooden dock. I stick my feet into the chilling water below, taking in the almost perfect reflection that the moon casts on the lake.

I lean back on my hands and gaze upward, very much appreciating the stars that peek through the thick darkness in the sky—especially after living in New York for years where the only lights I see at night are from buildings, street lights, circling planes, flood lights, and advertising neon.

Second thoughts begin crowding my mind as I look down at the cigarette pack in my hand. Is it really worth this? Am I really so weak that I have to sneak a cigarette the first night of my own rehabilitation?

I push the thoughts away and pull out a cigarette. This is my last one. Period. No, it isn't going to be easy laying off of them, but neither is it going to be easy for my mom to stop drinking.

I open the sketchbook and look across the stillness of the water, trying to figure out how to transform the scene onto the blank page in my lap. Looking back down at my sketchbook, I grab my pencil and draw a horizontal line that stretches across the page. A door slams behind me just as I almost reach the end of the line, causing it to become a curve instead.

I look over my shoulder, hoping it's not Whitney or Ben. How horrible would it be for them to see me out here, smoking on their dock? Mom would be unhappy to find out that I've broken my side of the agreement already.

I continue staring behind me before I am confident enough that no one is there. Still, it takes a while before my attention returns to the drawing.

I'm alone. No one is out here except me. So why can't I get over this feeling of being watched?

After straightening the horizontal line and forcing a few mountain curves onto the paper, I cringe. The sketch in my lap looks as if a toddler took over.

It's been fifteen minutes already, and the only thing I have to show is a horizontal line and a few curves. What is it with me?

"Wow," a male voice yells from the lake, breaking the silence.

My left hand reflexively swings the cigarette behind me as I look up.

Chapter 3

"Are you talking to me?" I ask the silhouette of a guy in a rowboat, my voice trembling with each word.

"I am." He rows closer to me before continuing. "I said you must be very multi-talented. Smoking and sketching at the same time."

"Excuse me?"

"Only someone with a lot of experience can pull that off."

What a jerk. At least he's not some old man wanting me to hop on that boat with him and row away somewhere. I don't *think* he is, anyway. His voice is deep—yet not too deep—which tells me he must be a teenager.

"I'm sorry, but who are you?" I close the sketchbook. It might be a better idea to finish this drawing tomorrow when the sun is out. When I'm not being spied on by creepy strangers.

The guy rows into the moonlight, confirming that he is only a teenager, with dark curly hair. "You're on the Huiets' dock. Are you one of Whitney's friends?"

"*Friends*?" I laugh. "Not exactly. I'm her cousin." I put the cigarette to my mouth and take a puff. "My name is Selena."

"Selena? Wait a second—Selena *Taylor*?"

All right, so maybe he *is* a perverted stalker dude. "Yes? And you are?"

"Austin Brewer, Whitney's next door neighbor. Didn't you used to live here for a while with Whitney years ago?"

I stare at the moon, searching my memory until the name Austin Brewer rings a bell. "Oh, yeah! You were the little annoying neighbor that Whitney and I always picked on. Where'd your glasses go?"

His lips hint at a smile. "There's a cool invention now called contacts. Thanks."

I laugh. "I can't believe you remember me. Sorry for any emotional damage that Whitney and I might've done to you as a kid. I never hated you—she just ordered me to bully you around. And I was pretty much terrified of her back then."

"You certainly weren't the only one." He stops rowing now. "Is this your first time being back since then?"

"Yep. And I'm not surprised that Whitney hasn't exactly changed so much."

He chuckles. "That's true. So where've you been hiding?"

I take a final puff of my cigarette before throwing it into the lake. "Well, my mom and I moved to New York once she finally earned enough money from working at Aunt Kori's salon. She rented us an apartment in Brooklyn."

"And what brings you back to Lake Lure?" he asks, leaning back on his elbows and propping his feet on the seat in front of him.

I pause before responding, debating whether or not to trust this half-stranger. "My mom's forcing me to stay here while she's at some Christian rehab place. Hopefully it won't be longer than a few months."

"Christian rehab?" He sounds interested rather than judgmental. "That's pretty cool."

I raise my eyebrows at his response. That's like someone saying it's "cool" that your mom—an ex-pastor's wife—is in jail.

Well, maybe not that intense. But close.

"You wanna go for a boat ride?" Austin asks. "But you'd have to leave your cigarettes up there. I don't care to be around smoke."

A rowboat trip sounds relaxing, especially on a night like tonight. Still, the awkwardness of the situation would just make it way too uncomfortable. I hardly know the kid.

"Nah, I should probably start heading back. I'm pretty exhausted." I stand, gathering my sketchbook and cigarettes. "It was nice seeing you again though, Four-Eyed-Brewer."

"Same to you, Selly." He laughs at the familiar nickname as I step off the deck into the yard. "Sleep well."

* * *

Sleeping in a bedroom three times the size of mine, and waking up to the sound of honking geese outside my window instead of honking taxis and buses—as much as I hate to admit it, maybe being in Lake Lure for the summer won't be as bad as I thought.

I pull off my sleeping mask and unplug my phone from the charger to find two things: one, that it's ten o'clock, way later than I usually sleep—and two, that I don't have any texts or missed calls on my phone from any of my few friends in Brooklyn.

I feel so loved.

Lured by the aroma of brewing coffee, I go downstairs

and find Uncle Ben standing in the kitchen, flipping pancakes at the stove. The corners of his lips rise only a little as he greets me.

"Morning," I respond, pulling myself away from his side hug. He looks the same as I remember—tall, muscular, and the same blond, spiked hair that points in all different directions. No new tattoos or piercings. Or implants.

None that are visible, anyway.

"You hungry?"

Why is that the only question the Huiets ever have for me? I'm starting to get the hint that they're not very happy I'm staying here. Did Mom bribe them to—as Whitney says— *babysit* me for the summer?

"I'll stick to coffee."

After opening several cabinets, I finally find the mugs. *Thanks, Uncle Ben, for your tremendous help. Or lack thereof.*

After pouring the coffee, I take a cautious sip, trying to decide whether I should add cream and sugar.

"Hi, Mr. Huiet," a deep voice says, causing me to jerk in mid-sip.

I cringe as a splash of hot coffee lands right on my green tank top. *Awesome.*

"Is Whitney up yet?"

"Sorry, Richard. She's still asleep."

I yank a paper towel from beside the sink and dab at the ugly brown stain.

"Who's this?" the voice asks.

Glancing up, I stop dabbing and nearly drool at the sight of a blond college-looking guy leaning against the refrigerator.

"Are you one of Whitney's friends?"

It takes awhile for words to find their way to my tongue. "Uh, um, no. I mean, I'm her cousin."

"Richard, this is Selena. Selena, this is Richard."

I give a shy smile. If I had known that this Channing Tatum look-a-like would be here this morning, I would've definitely taken a shower—or at least put on a little bit of make-up. "Nice to meet—"

"Richard?" Whitney yells, running all the way down the stairs until she reaches the kitchen, interrupting the cute stranger dude's romantic introduction. "I thought I heard you!"

He takes his hypnotic gaze off me and envelops Whitney in a tight squeeze. "Hey, baby."

Baby. Of course, Whitney's boyfriend. Should've known.

Uncle Ben stuffs his mouth with a forkful of syrup-saturated pancakes. "I've got to leave for work in five minutes. Why don't you kids go out on the lake? It's a beautiful morning."

"Actually, Mr. Huiet, I was thinking about taking your daughter out to Starbucks. If that's okay with you."

"Go ahead. Whit, don't stay too long now. Don't forget you have company." He points his fork towards me.

She laughs. "Of course I won't. How could I forget about *Selena*?"

Whitney wraps her arm around her boyfriend and gives me an evil grin. Almost as if she knows how hard it is for me to see her with this guy that I've been crushing on hard for the past two minutes.

I watch as the happy couple glides out of the kitchen and through the front door.

* * *

A sixteen-year-old should be spending an early June afternoon out on the lake with her friends or by a pool soaking up some sun—not rocking in a hammock all alone, *attempting* to sketch a pretty picture of the lake. I would call Hayden and see if she'd like to do something, but she and Patrick are probably still in bed right now with hangovers. The same bed, probably.

In fact, I doubt they even remember who I am.

A pop-country song plays on my iPod as two hands suddenly grab me from behind and give me a shake.

I look over my shoulder and see Austin Brewer doubled over with laughter.

"Do you enjoy sneaking up on people when they're in deep thought?" I yank out the earbuds.

He reaches down to pick up my pencil. "I don't really have any other talents."

I flip my sketchbook over so he can't see my current work in progress.

"You don't look like you're having much fun." He holds his hand out as if expecting to pull me up.

I hesitate. The afternoon sun beats down now, allowing me to see his features clearly for the first time in eight years.

He looks almost the same as he did when we were kids. Except no glasses. Taller, of course. Still pretty skinny. And the same brown, curly hair. The SpongeBob tee he used to always wear has now been replaced by an Aeropostale shirt.

Definitely not as bad as he seemed to look last night.

"So," I say, after I realize that we have been standing face-to-face without a word. "What is this?" I point to the strap around his neck.

"It's a camera," he says, laughing at my dumb question.

"You're, like, a photographer?" By the looks of the case, I'm guessing this is no ordinary camera.

Austin shrugs his shoulders. "Just love taking pictures. Especially of the lake. Here, I'll show you." He unzips his digital camera from its canvas case then holds it up. "That was the sunrise this morning. Beautiful, isn't it? God is such an amazing artist, don't you think?"

I bite my lip and nod. "But I thought you said you didn't have any talents."

His grin shows off his dimples—the same ones I remember from when we were kids.

"Richard, put me down! I am serious, if you—"

I turn my head, just in time to watch a shirtless Richard throwing Whitney into the lake.

Jealousy sweeps over me. I'm not sure which one of them I would rather be right now—Whitney, so I could be in Richard's arms. Or Richard, so I could throw her into the lake.

Although it would be more satisfying to throw her into hot lava instead.

Austin grunts as I turn my attention back to him.

"What?"

"That guy, Richard—Whitney's boyfriend."

"What's wrong with him?"

"Nothing, it's just—he's such a show-off. Thinks he's so cool because he's been blessed with good looks and decent athletic skills." He zips his camera in its case. "Everyone on our school football team is cocky, though."

I glance over at Richard as he cannonballs into the lake.

❯ Tessa Emily Hall

"Wait, he's just in high school? And you go to the same school as Whitney?"

"Yes and yes." Austin takes off his shirt and throws it onto the hammock, along with his camera. "He's going to be a senior. Guys like him are way too obsessed with themselves. But guys like me are—"

"Nerdy and geeky?" I ask, trying to catch up with him as he walks over to the dock.

He pauses, looking at me now with that same boyish grin. "You want me to throw you in too?"

"I thought Christians weren't supposed to judge."

He crinkles his eyebrows. "How was that judging?"

"I'm referring to the way you were talking about Richard." I cross my arms.

"Oh, right. Sorry."

"Sure you are."

He smiles at me. Then, without any warning, he kicks off his flip-flops and jumps into the lake, making a loud splash. I hold my hands in front of my face to block the water.

"Thanks, Austin," I say when he comes up. "You almost completely soaked me."

"Why don't you come in then? That way you don't have to worry about getting *almost* completely soaked."

I laugh. "Yeah, right. I'm not going swimming in my clothes."

"Why not? I do it all the time."

I'd rather not contribute to my already ruined reputation by hanging out with Austin. Whitney would have more reasons to make fun of me. But would she see me if I *did* go swimming?

I watch as she and Richard ride past us on a jet ski. I don't think she's even noticed that I'm out here with Austin.

"Just because I don't have bulging muscles doesn't mean I can't throw you in here,"Austin says, looking in the direction of my gaze.

"Okay, okay." I take my time letting down my hair then step up to the edge of the dock. "Here I go." With my eyes closed, I plunge into the water. Who needs a bathing suit?

Austin swims in front of me as I shoot up to the surface. "So, you like to draw?"

"Where did that come from?" I laugh, wishing I could somehow avoid answering that question. My passion for art is supposed to be private—I've always been afraid of someone making fun of my drawings. My best friend and my mom are the only ones who know that I keep a book filled with pencil sketches and watercolor landscapes, castles, horses and princesses. "You think that just because we knew each other when we were in third grade means you have the right to know everything about me?"

"That's not a personal question. Are you saying you're embarrassed by it?" He rests his elbow on the dock. "No offense, but I'd be more embarrassed at the fact that I smoke than the fact that I can draw."

Did he seriously just say that? "You know what, I think I'll just continue my drawing inside the house. I remember you being the geeky neighbor, not the judgmental freak."

His hand brushes my shoulder just as I'm about to jump up onto the dock. "Wait, Selena. I'm sorry for coming across as rude. I'm—I'm just trying to get to know you."

Most people would never continue hanging out with someone like this guy. But he looks so innocent. Maybe he really is telling the truth and just doesn't have much experience talking with girls.

"You really need to learn how to get to know someone better."

"Do you want to play Marco Polo?"

"What?"

He shoots a finger to his nose. "Not it."

"Oh, so that means I'm it?"

"You can't look," he says, putting his hand over my eyes.

I laugh. "Fine."

We play a few rounds of Marco Polo before Austin somehow talks me into going fishing with him on the dock. Since it's been several years since the last time I went fishing, it takes a while for him to instruct me on how to attach the bait, spool the line out, and reel it back in.

An hour passes, and we still sit on the edge of the dock, holding fishing poles above the water. Although it feels silly just sitting here doing nothing—especially since neither of us have caught anything yet—it's not too awkward, actually. Every time there's an uncomfortable silence between us, Austin always fills it in by asking a question about me and my life in Brooklyn.

I watch as he attaches an artificial worm onto his pole and casts the line out into the water. "So is there anything you're planning on doing this summer with the Huiets?"

"Nah." My fishing pole tugs a bit. Probably another fish taking the bait from my pole without getting hooked. "Playing random games of Marco Polo with an almost-stranger seems to be the only thing on my agenda so far. Why do you ask?"

He rubs the back of his neck. "Next week, my youth group

is having a summer camp called SummerThirst. I thought it'd be cool if you could come, you know. Get to know some of my friends and everything."

"A camp?" I try not to show my lack of interest in this invitation, but I think the tone of my voice gives it away.

"Only for three days. Not overnight or anything, but it costs thirty-five dollars." He ruffles his damp curls, still a little wet. "You don't want to stay here with Barbie and Ken, do you?"

Why can't you just do normal stuff like the rest of the kids here in Lake Lure? "To be honest, Austin, I haven't been to church since I lived in Kentucky. I'm just not sure if now is the right time, you know?" Not to mention I haven't had an anxiety attack in seven weeks. I'd rather not break my record so soon.

His gaze sweeps across the water. "Well, just know that you're still invited if you change your mind."

"Thanks." I smile. "I really appreciate it."

"No prob—"

"Whoa! Help, Austin!" I jump to my feet, pulling the pole as hard as I can so it doesn't go into the water. Or worse— take me with it.

"You caught a fish!"

"No, I think I caught a shark!" I let out a shriek. "What do I do? It's tugging!"

He laughs. "You reel it in!"

"What? You didn't tell me how to do that!"

Austin's laughter continues as he wraps his hands around mine, and we slowly reel in the unlucky fish.

"What is that thing?" I shudder. "It's huge!"

"This—" Austin holds the line as the determined fish, at least a foot long, fights to escape—"is a catfish. Look at him, he's so cute!"

I squirm as he shoves the whiskered beast right in my face. How can he touch that thing with his bare hands?

"That's just gross," a voice says behind Austin and me.

I turn to see Whitney standing on the other end of the dock, looking as if she's afraid she'll catch a disease if she steps any closer. "You two smell like fish and lake water."

"Hmm, that *might* be because we've been swimming in the lake and fishing." Austin smirks, tossing the catfish back into the lake. I can't help but giggle at his sarcasm.

"Very funny, Brewer." She shoots her glare at me. "Selena, you might want to take a shower. And hurry."

"Um, why?" I refuse to go to another party tonight.

"You're coming with me in, like, thirty minutes, to go out to eat with Richard and Erica. My mom is making me invite you—*again*." She puts her hands on her hips and narrows her eyes at Austin. "And no, you can't bring this kid with you. If you aren't all washed up by then, you can't come. And there won't be any supper for you." With a flip of her hair, my cousin spins around and stomps off the dock in her stiletto heels.

"Aww, she's so sweet," Austin says.

I shake my head. "I couldn't agree more."

Chapter 4

"**Y**ou're wearing *that*?" Whitney asks, giving me a disapproving look as she opens the front door.

I look down at my outfit. It was my third attempt at finding one that would win Whitney and her friends' approval.

I try to act unaffected by her criticism. "Is there something wrong with it?"

"Besides the fact that you're wearing jeans, combat boots, and a scarf in *June*?" Her car beeps as she clicks the unlock button on her keys.

Settled in Whitney's Mustang convertible, I give my seatbelt an extra tug. "First of all, this is a summer scarf. And I'm not wearing jeans. These are *jeggings*. Much thinner than jeans."

She shakes her head.

"I'm not accustomed to this humidity, Whitney." I have to practically yell over the rap music playing as soon as she starts the car.

"Not accustomed to the humidity, or not accustomed to fashion?"

I laugh. "You know, it really is crazy how you know nothing about me, yet you act as if you already can't stand me."

"You could've at least told me that you were leaving last night. I had no idea where you disappeared."

"So that's what this is about?"

"I thought I told you last night." Her hair flies back in the wind as she accelerates, guiding the car through the neighborhood. "My mom and stepfather may force me to babysit the less-fortunate, but I personally find it ridiculous. For starters, you are perfectly capable of taking care of yourself. Well, other than your little disability, of course."

"*Disability*?" I shoot the word back at her, knowing it won't do the same damage to her as it did to me.

"You know. Your anxiety attacks and everything."

I cringe. And not because Whitney just sped through a stop sign.

"You're just inexperienced, Selena. For starters, look at what you're wearing." She laughs as if telling a hilarious joke. "A half hour ago, you were hanging out with Austin Brewer. And those little pictures in your sketchbook are *so cheesy*!"

My throat tightens. "Who gave you permission to go through my sketches?" I wish I still had my hot coffee from this morning to pour over her head.

"You left it on the hammock. And since we are currently sharing the same house, I have the right to make sure you aren't sketching up a plan to murder us or something."

"Yeah, because I look like *such* a criminal." Jerk.

"You just need to get out more. You know, loosen up. Live life to the fullest."

"Yeah." My head leans back against the seat as I cross my arms. "Live life to the fullest and end up like my mother."

Neither of us speak another word the rest of the car ride

to the restaurant. Perhaps the smart thing to do is not speak another word to her all summer.

Once we arrive, I can understand why she made fun of my outfit. How was I supposed to know this would be a candlelit dinner outside next to the lake?

I especially wish that I had dressed up a little more when I see Richard waiting for us at a table. His gaze meets mine, and I can't help but feel all giddy inside.

The giddiness immediately goes away, though, when Whitney plants a kiss on his lips. "Hey, boyfriend. Is Erica not here yet?"

"Guess not." His greenish-blue eyes shift to me. "Hey, Selena."

I'm about to say hey back, until a short girl interrupts my drooling and sits in the empty chair at our table. "Sorry I'm late. There was an old lady driving in front of me the *entire* way here."

Whitney ignores her friend's tardy excuse. "Erica, this is my cousin, Selena. Selena, this is my best friend, Erica."

"Hey. Wow, I love your hair! It's gorgeous." She takes a strand of my long hair and twirls it around in her fingers. "It's so wavy. Who does it? You live in New York, right? Do you go to one of those expensive salons there?"

My self-esteem rises a few notches. This friend of Whitney's is actually complimenting my hair. Any girl would *kill* to have her thick hair and green eyes.

I shake my head. "Well, not one of the expensive ones. Every now and then I go to this barber shop that my mom's friend owns."

"Oh," Erica says, the excitement in her eyes fading.

Just then a clean-cut young guy dressed in a tux appears

at the end of our table. "Welcome to Silver Spoon. My name is Dave, and I will be your waiter for this evening."

Erica lets out a flirty giggle. "Well, hello, *David*."

He flips open his book. "May I take your drink orders?"

"I'll have a Tom Collins," Richard says, then points to Whitney. "And so will she." They both flash fake IDs, and Dave only glances at them.

I quickly scan over the drink menu. The prices make it easy for me to resist ordering, until I remember that Aunt Kori insisted I pay for my dinner with the fifty dollars she gave me.

Erica leans on her elbows, hovering over the menu. "Well, David, I am in the mood for a margarita today, if you don't mind," she says—very adult-like—and flashes her driver's license.

The waiter seems unaffected by Erica's flirting as he lowers his head to get a better look. "Would you mind handing it to me, miss?"

"You trust them, but not me?"

Richard laughs as Erica obeys the waiter's order and places her license in his hand.

He doesn't look too convinced, but scribbles down her drink order anyway. "And for you?" he asks, looking at me.

Now is my perfect chance to prove to Whitney that I am *not* inexperienced. Besides, I had my final cigarette last night, so why not just go ahead and have my final drink as well?

I place an order for a strawberry daiquiri and pull my fake ID out of my wallet, enjoying the sudden look of shock on Whitney's face.

After Dave brings us the drinks, Erica turns her attention to me. "So where do you like to hang out in New York? Uh, you're so lucky."

"Well, I live in Brooklyn," I say, stirring my drink with the straw. "But I'm not really much of a city girl. I was raised in Kentucky."

"Oh." She takes an unusually long sip of her drink.

I am not giving the kind of answers this girl wants to hear. *Think, Selena.* "There're a few clubs in the city that my friends and I occasionally go to, and we really like concerts. Oh, and I love going up to the roof of my apartment and painting. The view from there is breathtaking."

"You paint?" Richard asks, using his hand to block the light from the sun setting over the lake. "What kind of painting do you do?"

"Well, my favorite is watercolor. But I mostly like to sketch." The look of interest in Richard's eyes makes me feel more at ease to discuss this.

"Really? I love watercolor, too." His half-grin invites my giddiness to return. "That's awesome."

Whitney straightens her posture, sending me a dirty glare that forces me not to respond. So I smile at him instead.

"Richie," Whitney whines after slurping the rest of her drink. "I want a refill."

"Okay. But only because I love you so, so, so, so much." He leans over and plunges into a make-out session with his girlfriend.

Erica taps keys on her iPhone. "Just so you know, these two probably won't pull away from each other until the food gets here. Trust me."

I can't help but stare, imagining myself in Whitney's shoes.

Minus the five-inch heels.

* * *

My plan to wake up early and make it to the hammock in order to stay clear of Whitney's path is ruined, I realize, as I slip out the back door and find her stretched across her lounge chair on the patio. I hide the sketchpad behind my back.

She looks up only briefly from her magazine to give me a weak "Hi".

"Figured you'd be in bed right now with a hangover."

"Couldn't sleep," she says, adjusting her sun hat. "Tanning makes my hangovers go away."

Yeah. Whatever. "Can I ask you something?"

"Make it fast." She flips a page in her magazine.

"Where are your parents?" I take a seat on the lounge chair next to her. "They weren't home last night when we got back, and they're still not here. I mean, unless they're sleeping."

"They have *jobs*, you know. And it's not like there are little kids running all over the house that they have to keep an eye on."

"So they don't mind you coming home drunk at night?" Did I really just ask that?

She looks up at me now, and I get the feeling that she's becoming a bit annoyed with my questions. "I have a curfew on school nights. But they don't really bother during the summer. And of course they would care if I'm drunk—I just happen to be really good at hiding it." She reaches for her drink on the table between us and takes a sip. "Wanna try this? It's really good. Made it myself."

I take the glass of orange liquid from her hand and sniff. I don't have to ask if there's vodka in it. The strong smell gives it away.

I take a sip anyway. "Hmm, that's not too bad."

She crosses one of her greased legs over the other, and leans back in her chair. "Vodka is good in just about anything, really."

I nod, feeling slightly guilty for agreeing. Mom would be so disappointed in me right now if she knew that I haven't stayed away from drinking and smoking like I had promised.

Maybe it's *not* such a bad idea to go to the ridiculous youth camp with Austin.

Whitney's phone buzzes on the glass table, and starts playing a Jason Mraz song. I can't help but feel a tinge of jealousy as she goes inside to talk to her boyfriend.

I pull my sketchbook out from behind me and open it, slowly flipping through the pictures I've sketched and painted ever since my fourteenth birthday.

Some people keep diaries to record their feelings, daydreams, places they've visited, and memories, but I have my sketchpad. Well, *had* my sketchpad. Unfortunately, my relationship with Jeremy left me without the ability to see any beauty in anything anymore.

I flip to the sketch I've been attempting since arriving in Lake Lure, and just shake my head. How is it that I used to be able to compose an entire picture in five minutes, but now I can't even draw a simple picture of the lake and the mountains?

I grab the eraser to get rid of the crescent moon in the corner. I'm tempted to erase the entire picture and start from the beginning. Or perhaps give up all together.

The sun shines in my eyes as I look at the lake for inspiration, but instead end up watching as Austin parks his jet ski. An uninvited smile tingles my lips.

I know that Whitney disapproves of him, and I also know that hanging out with him will most likely ruin my reputation for the summer. Besides, he is sort of annoying.

Tessa Emily Hall

So why am I walking toward him right now?

"Guess who?" My hands cover Austin's eyes as if we are still in third grade.

He spins around. "Wow, you surprised me."

"Learned from the best."

He laughs. "So did you have a good time last night with your cousin and her boyfriend?"

I force myself to look away from his adorable freckles and smirk. "Don't ask. Whitney's friends are—" I struggle to come up with the most accurate adjective. Then I remember mine and Richard's flirty looks toward each other.

At least, that's what I thought they were.

The sound of a ringtone once again interrupts conversation. Austin reaches into his pocket and glances at the screen. "Sorry, I need to get this," he says, then holds the phone up to his ear. "Hello? Okay. No, that's fine, Mom. Yes ma'am. We'll be right there. Alright. Love you too. Bye."

"What?" I ask. I do not want Austin to leave me here at the Huiets' all by myself. I don't want to go anywhere again with Whitney, but I did not come all the way to Lake Lure just to be left home alone all day.

I get enough of that in Brooklyn.

Austin drapes his camera strap around his neck. "That was my mom. Audrey and I have to go help out at the coffee shop. It's busy there today."

"Coffee shop?"

"Mom owns it. Audrey and I work there sometimes." Water splatters on my face as he runs a hand through his wet curls. "Maybe you would like to come?" He shrugs. "Free coffee."

It takes a lot of effort to try not to show how excited I am over this invitation.

Or how curious I am to find out who Audrey is.

"Sure, I don't have anything else to do. Besides, I love coffee. I wouldn't mind helping out, actually. If that's okay. Don't worry about paying me, though."

After exchanging numbers, Austin and I go into our separate houses to get ready. I text him when I'm done, deciding to leave a note for Kori and Ben in case they happen to come home and actually wonder where I am.

Text from Austin: *We're waiting for you in my driveway.*

I grab my purse and head downstairs, wondering who the other person in "we're" is.

Then I see her when I step outside. A girl with dirty-blond hair sits next to Austin in the passenger seat of his car. It shouldn't bother me so much that he has a girlfriend. I hardly even know this guy, really.

I open the door to his olive green Jeep Wrangler, and Austin asks, "Selena, you remember my sister Audrey, don't you?"

As the girl turns around in the seat, I suddenly have a flashback of a little girl with big brown eyes who would always carry a blanket around with her and never said a word. "Oh, yeah! Sorry, I didn't recognize you. How old are you now?"

I can definitely tell she's Austin's sister when she smiles. "I'm going to be a sophomore in August. So you're going to be here for the whole summer?"

I nod, pulling on my seatbelt. The sun beats down on my shoulders as Austin lets down the top of his Jeep.

"I'm trying to talk her into going to SummerThirst with us next week," Austin says, steering us out of his driveway.

"Oh, you should!" She turns back around to buckle herself. "We had a great time last year."

"I've been thinking about it. What's it like?"

"We're going hiking and to a sliding rock this year," Austin says. "Should be pretty fun."

I continue to ask questions about SummerThirst for the rest of the five-minute drive to the coffee shop—only for the sake of small talk, of course—but by the time we reach Brewer's Coffee, I find myself giving this camp a little more consideration. It wouldn't be a bad idea to try making summer friends, and maybe some memories.

Preferably ones that *don't* involve my cousin.

Austin pulls his Jeep into a parking space as I look around. Brewer's Coffee Shop is a log cabin nestled at the edge of the lake, much more inviting than the Starbucks I go to in New York.

As Austin holds the door open for his sister and me, the smell of his cologne seems to almost overpower the sudden aroma of coffee.

The artwork covering the walls is the first thing I notice inside. I take a quick glance around the place, imagining what it would be like to sit at one of these tables, sip coffee, and take notes on the watercolor techniques used in some of these paintings.

"Mom, you remember Selena, don't you?" Austin asks a familiar lady who has curly hair similar to his own.

She looks up from wiping a table to give me a warm smile. "Yes, why, of course I do. My, you were tiny the last time I saw you. Austin was telling me that you're back in town for the summer, is that right?"

I nod. *Did he tell you the reason I'm here, though?*

"She wants to help out a little. Doesn't mind volunteering for a few hours without pay."

Mrs. Brewer runs a wet washcloth over another empty table. "Well, I'd feel bad for you working with nothing in return. But we really could use any bit of help we can get today. Austin, would you take her to the back room and show her where the aprons are?"

"Yes, ma'am."

I follow Austin and Audrey as they lead me to a small area where a tall girl stands in front of a sink, drying mugs.

"It's about time ya'll got here," the girl says, casting a glance over her shoulder at Austin. "Your mom is making me do all the dirty work."

"Selena, this is Brooke." Austin grabs an apron hanging on the wall and throws one to Audrey and me. "She goes to my youth group, and mine and Audrey's school. Brooke, this is my friend, Selena."

I struggle to tie the apron around my waist as Brooke spins around and looks at me as if I'm a misplaced customer. "Is this your first time working here?"

"Well, I—"

"She's just working for the day."

"Oh." She tucks her short brown hair behind her ear. "Nice to meet you." Brooke turns back around, and closes the dishwasher with her foot. "Sorry, tell me all the details later. We've got too many customers right now to chit chat."

Austin opens the closet in the corner and shows me where all of the cleaning supplies are, filling me in on everything I can do while I'm here. Clear and wipe the tables as soon as customers leave. Take the dirty mugs to the kitchen and place them in the sink. Sweep the floors every couple of hours.

He then takes someone's place behind the cash register

as I go over to an empty table where a mom and her daughter just left, and begin wiping it. I become distracted, though, looking around to take in this unique coffee shop atmosphere. The walls are brown with a soft blue trim, giving it a nice inspirational feel. Even the two chalkboards behind the counter with the menu on them are brown with blue writing.

The only thing that irritates me is a quote on the top of one of the chalkboards: *"I believe in Christianity as I believe that the sun has risen: not only because I see it, but because by it I see everything else."* - C.S. Lewis.

Other than that, this is the kind of place I can see myself working at someday.

For the next hour, I occasionally watch a couple in the back of the coffee shop. They appear in their late teens, but act more mature. Their conversation ranges from play productions they have attended recently to books they've read to their travel plans for the summer.

Maybe one day after I graduate high school, I can move here, meet my Prince Charming, and come to this coffee shop as often as I want. I can sketch the view from the window, pretending to listen as he goes on talking about something he recently read.

"Ready to go?" Austin taps my shoulder, startling me from my daydream.

"Already?" I take my gaze off the couple as he takes my broom. "Seems like we just got here. I really like this place, Austin."

He smiles, reaching for my apron after I've untied it. "Do you want coffee before we leave?"

"I can never turn down coffee, Austin. Just for future reference."

He laughs. I follow him into the back room where he hangs up our aprons and takes a piece of paper from the counter, handing it to me. "Here's the menu."

I can't help but lick my lips while scanning the list of lattes and iced coffee blends. I don't think I've ever been in a coffee shop that had this many variety of flavors: hazelnut, java chip, birthday cake, cookies 'n cream—the list continues, but I stop at peanut butter mocha.

Austin slips behind the counter to make my iced coffee, and I watch in amazement as he adds the espresso, milk, mocha flavoring, peanut butter flavoring, and whipped cream, then tops it off with chocolate and peanut butter syrup.

"Here you go," he says, reaching over the counter to hand me my drink. "Oh wait, I forgot one last thing." Grabbing the permanent marker on the counter, he scribbles "Selly" on the cup. "Here you go, ma'am."

I smile, taking the drink from his hands. I feel him stare at me as I take my first sip, shivering from the cold.

"So?" He keeps his gaze fixed on me while escaping from behind the counter. "How is it?"

"It's—bearable," I tease.

His mouth drops open. "Well, you better enjoy it, considering you will not be getting another one."

I laugh. "I'm just kidding. Honestly, I think it's safe to say that this even is better than a frappucino from Starbucks."

"Wow, that means a lot," Mrs. Brewer says. I didn't even realize that she was wiping a table right next to us. "You're definitely welcome to come back for another free drink anytime you please, Miss Selena. It was nice having you help out during crazy hour. Thank you so much." She sets the washcloth down on the table to give me a side hug. "Nice seeing you again. And please tell your mom that I said hello when you talk to her."

"I will. Nice seeing you again, too." I take another sip. "I can guarantee you'll be seeing me here a lot this summer. I'm obsessed with coffee."

"Well, let me know if you'll be looking for a summer job." She winks. "I might just be able to help you with that."

"Oh, I definitely will."

* * *

It's already evening by the time I get back to the Huiet's empty house.

Why do I feel I'll be spending more time with the Brewers this summer than with the Huiets?

After throwing away the note I had left for Kori and Ben on the kitchen counter, I desperately search their refrigerator for something to keep my stomach from growling. Since I don't have any other choice except fruits and vegetables, I grab a banana, run up to my bedroom, and collapse on the bed.

It's crazy how much more hopeful I feel about this summer than I did when I arrived. I'm not sure if it's because of Austin or the coffee shop.

Perhaps both.

Itching to share my excitement with someone, I dig my phone out of my purse and dial my best friend's number.

"Why haven't you called me yet, Hilarie?" I ask after she picks up.

"Sorry, I've been busy. How is everything?"

"Not too bad, actually." I give her a short summary of Whitney, the party, Austin, and the coffee shop.

When I finish, I pull the phone away from my ear and glance at the screen, wondering if she hung up on me due to her lack of response.

"That's great that you're having so much fun," she finally says. "I'm really happy for you."

I didn't even make my little summary sound as if I've been having fun. The fact that she apparently wasn't listening causes my curiosity to rise.

"You don't sound good, Hil. Are you okay?"

Sitting in the window seat, I look outside at a tree branch where a bird builds a nest.

The long pause hanging between us forces me to chew on my lip. Hilarie isn't one to be quiet, much less depressed about something.

But before I'm able to ask her what's wrong again, I hear crying. She is not like other teenagers who break down just because their week-long relationship came to an end. With Hilarie, if there are tears involved, then it must be something serious.

I lean forward, curiosity growing into concern. "What is it?"

My mind quickly starts going through the worst possible scenarios. Did her eighty-year-old grandmother pass away? Did her sister have an accident at college?

Is she moving?

"Hilarie?"

She sobs. "Selena—I'm pregnant."

Chapter 5

"Selena?"

I open my mouth, but nothing comes out. Say at least *something*, Selena! "Are—are you sure? I mean, how—how'd you find out?" My shaking hands brush a strand of hair from my face. "Those pregnancy tests aren't one hundred percent accurate, are they?"

"I know for sure that I'm pregnant." Even her saying it for the second time forms a knot in my stomach. "I've been scared I was for about a week. So I took two pregnancy tests yesterday. Both of them—" She pauses, her breath becoming heavier through the phone. "They *both* turned out to be positive. I'm pregnant. Pregnant with a baby whose father I caught cheating on me just last week."

Feeling lightheaded, I hurry down the stairs and through the back porch doors to get some fresh air.

Hilarie's been my best friend since sixth grade—we're even closer than Mom and I are—and I am not at *all* prepared to have this kind of conversation with her. Not until she's married.

"Who all knows about this?" I ask, leaning over the edge of the dock to scoop some water into my hand.

"Josh. He's the only one so far. Besides you." She lets out

a heavy sigh. "I went over to his place last night after work and told him."

"And what did he say?"

"He didn't believe I was telling the truth at first. He even had the guts to tell me he doubts the baby was his, as if *I* was the one who cheated on *him*! He knows he's the only guy I've ever slept with."

I shake my head, biting the inside of my cheek. Of course, Josh would say that. Of course, he would steal my best friend's virginity, cheat on her, then act as if none of that happened.

I sit cross-legged at the edge of the dock and just hang my head, remembering a time last summer after Jeremy and I had broken up, when I wanted to tell Hilarie that her relationship with Josh most likely wouldn't be worth it. And that, one way or another, it would probably end in heartbreak.

If only I had gained the courage to tell her. Not only *did* their relationship end in heartbreak, but Hilarie will have a baby to remind her of the pain it cost to give her heart and innocence away to someone who doesn't even care.

"Why do you have to be in Lake Lure during all of this?" My heart breaks at Hilarie's question, at the way her voice cracks while she's probably doing her best not to start bawling. "I wish so badly that you could be here. I can't tell my parents. I just can't."

"I'm so sorry, Hilarie," I say, hoping that my sympathetic tone will be enough to make up for my lack of words. "You'll get through this, though. I know you will."

Looking over my shoulder, I notice that Kori and Ben's cars are now in the driveway. They must finally be home.

After promising Hilarie that I'll call her back later, I go inside to find my aunt and uncle lounging on their couch, talking casually and sipping on wine.

) Tessa Emily Hall

"Um, sorry to interrupt." Not really. "Aunt Kori, can I talk to you?"

"Oh, well, of course." She glances at me, then at Uncle Ben, who gets up and goes into the other room, looking a bit annoyed. I take his seat on the couch.

She takes a sip of her wine then places it on the coffee table. "What's up?"

"You had Whitney when you were a teenager, right?" I blurt out, then quickly amend, "Oh, don't worry. This isn't about me. This is actually about my friend, Hilarie. And, well, she just found out that she's pregnant."

Why is my heart pounding so much? It's not like *I'm* the one that's in trouble.

Kori bows her head as if hiding the emotion on her face. "Selena, being a pregnant teen was the most difficult situation I've gone through. Ever." She looks at me now, her green eyes filled with tears. "All I can say is, be a friend to her. Support her in whatever decision she makes, girl. There is so much pressure on her right now, it'd *crush* her if her best friend criticized her mistake. I know."

I exhale slowly. "The thing is, she doesn't know how to break the news to her parents. What should I tell her?"

I've never seen Kori at a loss for words—her head hanging as if she is relating to Hilarie. Mom told me once that Kori took it really hard when she found out she was pregnant, but I had no idea that it would still be difficult for her to discuss.

"The best way to tell her parents is simply by telling them." Her voice comes out scratchy, and she reaches for her wine, taking a sip before continuing. "And the sooner the better. They may blow up at first, but when they realize that nothing they say can change what's already happened, they'll eventually learn to deal with it. They might even try to persuade her to get an abortion." Her red hair swishes as she shakes her head. "Selena, tell her she can't give in. One wrong cannot correct another wrong."

I nod. "I doubt that she'd ever make that decision, but I'll let her know. I just wish I could be there for her right now, you know?"

"Yes, I know. When I became pregnant, I lost many of my friends. For the first time, I felt what it was like to be truly lonely. I don't want your friend to feel that way." She smiles, almost contradictory to what she's saying. "What would you say if I booked you on a flight to Brooklyn tomorrow?"

I bite my lip, wishing I could please Kori by matching her level of enthusiasm, but I can't go back to Brooklyn now, especially by myself, without Mom's permission. It's just not a good idea.

Aunt Kori seems to notice the uncertainty on my face. "Look, now, I'm not sure how your mom would feel about me doing this, but she really doesn't know what it was like being pregnant as a teenager and feeling like you have no one. I, however, do. And I really think this would be for the best."

Mom's always told me that Kori was the adventurous one growing up, never thinking through her decisions. It seems like she would've grown out of that by now. "I don't know. I just—I couldn't do that behind Mom's back." I already feel bad enough about some other choices that I've made behind her back while I've been in Lake Lure. I don't want lying to be one of them.

I also tell Kori about the Brewer's invitation to go to SummerThirst. "So I just don't think it'd be a good time, you know?"

She takes another sip of her wine. "Well, I'll be glad to

book you a flight whenever you wish. Just let me know if you change your mind."

I put on my sympathetic smile before thanking my aunt for the advice. I had no idea there was actually a sensitive Kori underneath all this artificial stuff.

* * *

Aunt Kori decides the next day that it'd be a nice idea for me to go to the mall with Whitney and Erica to get my mind off everything.

After one hour of shopping, I realize that she was *definitely* wrong.

All I can think about is Hilarie, especially as I sit next to Erica and Whitney at a salon, feeling like a statue with a green mask plastered on my face and sliced cucumbers on my eyelids. "Remind me again why I agreed to come here. You said we were getting a manicure, but sort of forgot to mention this."

Erica laughs. "I still can't get over the fact that you've never gotten a face mask before. I get one at least each month since I was, like, in elementary school."

The girly genes must have skipped my generation. It's only a quarter 'til one, and I'm already wanting to go back to Whitney's house, relax in the hammock under my sleeping mask, or work on my latest sketch. It's stressful having to try on every single piece of clothing that these girls *swear* I'd look cute in.

Especially when all I can think about is Hilarie.

The green mud facial takes way longer than I thought it would. It's another hour before we can finally leave the spa and get some lunch—but as soon as we step into the food court, my appetite disappears. The smell of Chinese food, corn dogs, and pizza mixes together in an obnoxious miasma.

What makes me feel even more nauseous is the fact that every girl we pass in the food court seems to be staring at me. And not in a good way, either.

Overwhelmed, I excuse myself and go to the restroom as Whitney and Erica decide what they want to eat.

Just as I'm about to open the door to the bathroom, I think I hear someone calling my name. I turn around, assuming that it's probably meant for another Selena, but am proven wrong when I see Hayden and Patrick.

"Did you get the little gift I left in your purse?" Hayden asks. She looks a little less Gothic than she did at the party. Instead of wearing all black, today she has added a dark purple eyebrow ring and matching purple leggings.

I nod slowly. "Yes. Thanks, I guess. I used a few."

"I knew you'd come around to appreciating it eventually." She gives a sly smile. "So, you here by yourself?"

"I'm actually with Whitney and her friend," I say, pointing in their direction.

Patrick looks over his shoulder and laughs. "Whitney chooses the worst friends."

"Erica? She's not that bad, is she?"

"Uh, yeah." Hayden raises her eyebrows at me. "She goes to our school, and was kicked off the cheerleading squad because she was high during one of their practices."

I can't help but laugh as I imagine little Erica falling from a stunt because she thinks she's flying in the sky. I've never been high, but I've been around enough strung-out people to imagine what it feels like.

Hayden twists a black strand of her hair around a finger. "It's really not that funny. She's a horrible person. No one likes her except for your slutty cousin."

"Come on, Hayden." Patrick tugs her arm as if he were a little boy wanting his mom to hurry up. "I'm starved. Haven't eaten in two whole hours."

"Why don't you ditch them and hang with us? Save you from your misery."

"I can't. Sorry. We should get together soon, though."

"Hey, you should come to the My Chemical Romance concert with us tomorrow," Patrick says, letting go of Hayden's arm but now focusing on every food tray that passes by. "I think there's still some tickets left."

"I can't do anything for the next three days." I regret those words the instant they escape my mouth. I love going to concerts—I really don't think this spiritual life is for me anyway—but I know how badly Austin and his sister want me to go to SummerThirst. "Why don't the three of us hang out on Thursday instead?"

Patrick barely gives me a chance to finish my sentence before blurting out, "Oh, I know! We should all go to the park!"

Just as he finishes his sentence, Erica and Whitney walk past us with their food, looking at me as if I am a traitor for making plans with these two.

"Sure, I guess." Why did he have to announce that right as they walked by? "I'll call. Gotta run. Nice seeing you guys again."

And with a smile I take off to the restroom before they stop me.

* * *

I was hoping that we might leave when we finish eating.

But apparently not.

As the three of us are dumping the trash from our food into the trash can, Whitney points across the food court. "Oh my gosh, Erica. They added a Sephora! Come on, we've gotta go."

I let out a groan, dragging my tired legs behind Erica and Whitney as we walk into a shop that resembles Bath & Body Works. A mixture of smells greets us before we even walk through the entrance: sweet girly smells, sophisticated romantic musks, and soothing florals. Tables are covered with a variety of lotions, perfumes, bath products, and other skin care products. Erica and Whitney are immediately drawn to the makeup aisle while I decide to test some of the sample hand lotions.

"Selena," Whitney says, taking the lotion I was in the middle of smelling and setting it back down. "Come here, we found a foundation color that is just perfect for your olive skin tone."

She drags me by the arm over to the makeup aisle, where she and Erica begin dabbing my face with makeup samples. Without asking my permission, of course.

"Um, I usually don't wear much foundation," I say as Whitney cakes mud under my eyes. "I don't get acne, really."

She laughs. "Foundation isn't worn just to cover up acne, silly."

I'm forced to stand completely still as these two Barbie dolls paint my face with blush, smoky eyeshadow, brown eyeliner, and lipstick.

"Oh. My. Gosh." Erica stands in front of me. "You look like a *totally* different person."

I laugh as Whitney hands me a mirror—but when I look at my reflection, I can't help but agree. Every little detail is perfect. The brown eyeliner brings out the color of my eyes, making them look larger. The gray smoky eyeshadow glistens on my eyelids. The blush they've added to my cheeks highlights my cheekbones even more so than when I put it on myself.

Erica smiles. "You like it, don't you?"

"Wow," is all I can say. Part of me wants to rebel against this new reflection—but the other part of me wishes this makeup were permanent.

Whitney takes the mirror from my hands. "Now, there are times when you should have more of a natural look. But when you go out—say, to a nice restaurant or to parties—this is exactly how you should do your makeup."

She then shows me which products they used along with which steps they took to create this new look for me. As if I'd actually be able to do this all by myself.

"Thanks, you guys," I say after paying for my new makeup with the money that Aunt Kori insisted on giving me. "I really love it." However, I do feel silly wasting so much money on such a useless thing as makeup.

Erica nudges me with her elbow. "Now all we've gotta do is find you a man."

I laugh. Doesn't sound too bad to me.

Chapter 6

Sweat trickles down my forehead as if I am running a race in the middle of the desert rather than through the woods. I continue to push my weak legs until I come to two paths.

Breathing heavily, I stop running for a moment to analyze my options. The dark shadows of trees hover along one path, making it impossible to see where it leads. My eyes scan the other path. Sun shines in the distance, highlighting the luscious fruit growing in the trees. Small, friendly wild animals scurry through the bushes.

My feet trip over each other as I pick up my pace, choosing the path most obvious. If I weren't carrying these heavy bags, maybe I wouldn't keep stumbling every few steps.

Fear and loneliness overtake me as I enter this path, which only adds to my confusion. It would've made more sense if I had felt this way from choosing the dark one.

I try to ignore the fact that my body is begging me for water and rest as I continue to push forward. I cannot possibly take a break until I have reached the finish line, even though I have no idea how to get there, or even how I ended up in this wooded area.

Since the beginning of this race, there have been people along the sidelines, advising me to go different directions.

Someone calls out my name softly.

I jerk back as a hand reaches down through the clouds and touches my face.

I awake in panic, but the hand belongs to Aunt Kori, and I am only in my bedroom.

"Good morning, Selena," she says with a yawn.

I notice two things. One, that Aunt Kori's voice was much deeper in my dreams—and two, that she looks way too perfect so early in the morning.

"You told me to wake you up at six for SummerThirst." She reaches down to pick up a tray from my nightstand. "I brought you breakfast."

"Oh, thank you so much." I force myself to sit up and take the tray from her hands. "I don't know if I've ever had someone bring me breakfast in bed."

"Your mom never wakes you up with coffee or anything?"

I begin to peel a banana. "It's usually the other way around. She gets in late."

She seems shocked. "Well, I hope you like the food. You better hurry if your friends are picking you up at seven-thirty. Don't forget to bring your money, or the papers Mrs. Brewer gave us yesterday to sign. I left them on the kitchen counter."

I thank her again as she exits the room.

Flashbacks of my dream continue to replay in my mind as I get ready for the first day of SummerThirst; but as soon as Austin pulls his Jeep into the church parking lot, I realize that I'd much rather return to the nightmare instead of living this reality. I walk with Austin and Audrey toward the church as distant rock music plays. As Austin opens the church door, I notice the music is actually coming from inside the building and not a nearby car.

This surprises me. I know that churches have changed a lot the past eight years, but I would've never guessed they'd play this style of music. My dad would have *never* accepted this in the church he preached at, which he called God's "holy temple".

I hand in my papers and money at the check-in table, and look around the lobby. "SummerThirst" posters cover the walls.

Why didn't Austin warn me that this little summer camp was basically the same thing as Vacation Bible School, but for teenagers?

Once we finish putting on our name tags, Austin takes me around the room and introduces me to several people. Grin plastered on my lips, I answer the same questions over and over: where I live; how I know the Brewers; how long I'm staying here, and for what reason.

I'm just thankful that no one has asked me yet if I go to church. Or, even worse, if I'm a Christian.

After finally making an escape from an awkward conversation with a girl who likes to talk a little too much about her vacations in New York, Austin asks if I've ever been hiking before. I shake my head.

"Well, I put you, Audrey, Brooke, and Cole—Brooke's brother—into a group, which means the five of us will be hiking and doing everything together this week."

He slips a plate into my hand. We have somehow drifted into the breakfast line.

"Oh, no, thanks. I ate already."

He doesn't look convinced. "It wouldn't hurt to gain a few extra pounds, Selena."

"But I'm not hungry," I say, then take the plate from

his hands anyway, knowing that I'm not going to win either way. Besides, I definitely wouldn't want my new little church buddies to assume that I'm anorexic. "If we're going hiking, then why are we at church?"

Why are we going hiking, anyway?

Austin spreads cream cheese onto his bagel. "We had to come here first to check-in and everything, then after we do praise and worship, the vans will take us to where we'll be going on the hike."

I drop a few grapes on my plate. I'm not hungry the least bit, but this extra energy will be useful for whatever I face on the hike today.

* * *

"Wanna piece of gum?"

"No, thanks," I say, taking my gaze off the trees passing by the van window to focus on the pack of gum that the girl who was washing the dishes at Brewer's Coffee holds in front of my face. "I don't care for Juicy Fruit."

"Oh, I have other kinds of gum." Brooke tucks the pack into one of the pockets of her gym shorts. "Do you like spearmint or cinnamon? I also have the kind of gum that changes flavors from berry to mint. Actually, I think I left that one at ho—"

Austin laughs next to me. "You don't even carry a purse, Brooke. Where do you keep all that gum?"

She pulls the packs of gum from her pockets. "Where do you think?"

"I'll have this one," I say, reaching for the spearmint pack. "Thanks."

After I unwrap a piece of gum, the driver announces that

we'll be arriving at the hiking trail within the next ten minutes. My knees quiver and I chew my gum hard, the dream last night replaying again in my mind. I've never had any of my dreams come true before—but I also hardly ever have a dream, so why is it that I just so happened to have one the night before going hiking?

When we arrive at the trail, the doors of the van swing open and teenagers pile out all at once. If only I was looking forward to this as much as everyone else is.

"Good morning, everyone," their youth pastor, Carson, says into his megaphone after the other van arrives. "I hope you all had a good breakfast this morning because you're definitely going to need it. Now, I need everyone to listen very carefully. There is a trail assigned to each group, and each group has been assigned to one of these beautiful team counselors beside me."

PC—as everyone calls him—goes on talking about all the rules and everything that will take place on the hike. I drown out his voice for a moment, forgetting all about the hike as I watch Austin already taking pictures. I don't blame him. The mountain we're on is gorgeous, the morning sun beaming through the trees above us making the perfect picture-capturing opportunity.

I can't help but smile when Austin shows me the photos. Perhaps I should start bringing my sketchbook around with me everywhere I go, like he does with his camera, to capture these kinds of breathtaking scenes.

That is, if I ever get past whatever it is that's holding me back from finding my inspiration.

After PC releases everyone, I follow Brooke as she pushes her way through the crowd until finally finding Audrey, who stands talking to the lead singer of the band that played for praise and worship.

...ere you guys are," Brooke says. "Selena, this is my brother, Cole. Unfortunately."

The lead singer and I exchange awkward hi's, then he turns to Brooke and asks, "Who's our team leader?"

As if on cue, Austin joins our little circle along with one of the counselors behind him. She smiles and hands each of us a bag.

"Hi, ya'll. For those of you who don't know me, I'm Miss Lexie, Pastor Carson's wife." Her southern accent and over-friendliness reminds me that I am no longer in New York. "In the backpack I'm passing out, you will find two protein bars, one brick, some real fruit along with some fake fruit, three water bottles, a notepad and a pencil. Now, before we begin, let's all go around the group and share our name and one thing about ourselves. I'll go first. You may call me Lexie. I'm twenty-six years old, and I love to write. What about you?"

She looks up from her clipboard, her gaze landing on me. Of course, I'd be the one to have to go first. I'm probably the only one in our group she's never met before. "My name is Selena, I'm sixteen. Um, I like to draw and watercolor. I like to act, too, I guess."

"That's great! Do you know about the SummerThirst skit?"

I shake my head.

"No? Well, every year during SummerThirst, each of you have the chance to audition for a skit that will be performed a few weeks after the camp. Our first meeting is tonight. I am actually the director for it this year."

"I think you should do it, Selena," Austin says. "Audrey and I are, too. It'll be our first time."

"Same with Cole and me. Anyway, hi." Brooke waves to our group as if we didn't already know her. "My name's

---

Brooke. I'm sixteen. One thing about me is that I love sports. I also do some modeling."

My eyebrows raise when she says she's a model. I hardly even know this girl, but the athletic clothes she wears today and the plain outfit she wore the other day—not to mention the fact that her face looks as if makeup has never dared to touch it before—had me assuming she was a tomboy. However, she is freakishly tall, skinny, and has high cheekbones. But still, I find this amusing.

Lexie seems almost as amazed as I am. "I didn't know you modeled. What kind do you do?"

She looks down at the ground and kicks a rock. "My agency is E-Modeling Productions, and I mostly do promotions, fashion shows, and just whatever else they get me to do."

"Yeah, yeah, yeah," Cole says, interrupting Brooke. Like his sister, he is tall, but unlike his sister, he has blond hair. Also unlike Brooke, there are piercings in both of his ears. "My name is Cole. I'm seventeen. Love music. I'm in a Christian band. Your turn, Austin."

Austin gives a small shrug. "There's not much interesting about me. I'm sixteen, I take pictures. Oh, and my name's Austin."

I swear Lexie's smile couldn't grow any wider.

She looks at Audrey now, who adjusts the straps to her backpack and blushes a bit. "Well, my name is Audrey and I'm fifteen. I just have small, random hobbies, such as cooking and singing."

"You're so shy about it," Cole says. "She's a great singer. That's why she got accepted into Lake Lure Academy of the Arts."

"Wow!" Lexie says. I didn't know it was possible for

be so interested in people who are, like, ten years ..yer than she is. "You go to school there?"

"Yes. But so does Austin, Cole, and Brooke. Selena doesn't live here."

"Well, then." Her ponytail flips as she finally starts walking along the trail. "I was assigned to a very talented group. This hike will take about an hour and a half. Once we finish the trail, there will be a clearing where all of the groups will meet and have lunch."

"Question." Brooke raises her hand as if this were school. "Why are the backpacks so heavy? And why is there a brick and fake fruit in it?"

"The food and the water in our backpacks are for us to eat along the hike, so we won't run out of energy. We'll discuss the rest when we meet the others at the end of this hike."

"You *do* know where we're going, right?" Austin stops walking a moment to snap a shot of a squirrel perched on a tree branch, nibbling on a large acorn.

She holds up a piece of paper. "I have a map. Do you guys see the markings on the trees? The blue and red ones are to fool us. We have to follow the yellow markings and not pay attention to the other ones, or we won't end up at the correct destination."

I hear crunching behind me, and turn around to see Cole already digging into one of the snacks in his backpack.

"What?" he asks, chomping on a granola bar. "I'm a growing boy. If food is available, I must eat."

"You might want to save the food for later, though, in case you get hungry." Lexie looks down at the map, her eyebrows pushed together as if she's reading a different language.

It's a good thing I remembered to take my anxiety pills this morning. The fact that we're in the mountains, in the woods, and with no cell phone service, could trigger an anxiety attack. And, of course, the fact I had that dream last night.

The sun beats down harder the closer it gets to noon. Even the shade created from the occasional canopy of trees along the path isn't enough to keep me cool.

You'd think the one who has lived in New York half of her life would be the fastest walker of the group, so why am I the only one dragging behind? Everyone else seems fine, not at all affected by walking up a mountain in June when there's not a cloud in the sky.

"Listen, Austin," I say as he slowly walks backwards to snap a shot of the trail behind us. "I'm not trying to be a baby or anything, but is it possible for us to, like, turn around and go back?"

He glances up at me before taking another picture. "You've come too far to turn around now, Selena. Don't worry. I'm sure we'll get there soon."

I let out a sigh, trying to take my mind off unspoken complaints and instead focus on the beauty of nature around me.

But I can't help it. I can't remember the last time I've sweated this much.

Maybe if this backpack weren't so heavy, then I wouldn't feel so weak. Why did they put a brick in it, anyway? Are they trying to kill us or something? I knew I should've told them about my anxiety attacks.

I pull my hair up into a tight ponytail. The way I look is the least of my concerns right now.

I'm exhausted.

And I want to go home.

"You alright?" Austin asks, pausing for me to catch up.

"I'm not much of an outdoor kind of girl." *As if you haven't realized that already.*

"I can hear the others in the distance," Lexie calls out. "We'll be there soon."

"Soon" doesn't come soon enough for me. It feels like another hour before we finally reach the clearing, although it's only twenty minutes. Everyone else is at the picnic tables, enjoying the meal.

After our group is seated at one of the wooden picnic tables, Lexie places a notebook before her and says, "Before we begin to eat, we have to have a little discussion about the activity. You may take notes on your notepad if you'd like." She waits as all of us dig around in our backpacks. "So, would anyone like to share what they learned from this hike?"

I flip open my sorry excuse for a notepad. "Never go hiking in ninety-degree weather again."

She laughs. "What do you think the spiritual significance of this hike is, though?"

Austin taps his pen against the table. "The hike was sort of like our walk with God. We have to follow His Word so we will know where to go and what traps to steer clear of. If we do, we'll eventually reach Heaven."

Lexie praises Austin's response, but I'm not exactly sure why she's so proud of him. His little speech seemed corny to me.

Brooke pours the last bit of her water bottle over her head. "I still don't get the whole fake fruit and brick thing, though. It made our backpacks way heavier than they needed to be."

"I think I understand," Audrey says. "The food was so that we wouldn't run out of energy, which is the same with

God's Word. I think the fake fruit is like the food that we keep feeding ourselves to fill our emptiness, but it doesn't satisfy like real food does. And the brick—I guess that is just useless weight we're carrying around."

My chin rests on my hand as I doodle hearts and cartoon faces. Everything Audrey is saying goes completely over my head.

"I guess there's no need for me to explain anything since you already did a perfect job of it! Shall we eat now? Cole, would you mind saying the blessing for us?"

Cole takes off his hat, bows his head, and prays. I look down at the drawings I've scribbled as Austin and Audrey's words about the hike replay in my mind.

Then another flashback of my dream hits me.

And my mouth slightly drops open.

Chapter 7

"Why don't you come to our place for dinner?" Austin asks, pulling into his neighborhood. "It's the least we could do for you helping us out at the coffee shop the other day."

"Sure," I say, surprising myself by the amount of excitement in my voice. "I mean, if your mom doesn't mind, of course. I might have to take a shower first though. I'm so sweaty."

"Oh, don't worry about that," Audrey says from the passenger seat. "We're all kind of gross right now."

The inside of the Brewer house is very similar to how I remember it. Definitely not as large and spacey as the Huiets', but the stone fireplace in the den, warm hues and soft brown interior adds a touch of comfort that reminds me of how the inside of a mountain home *should* be.

Austin drops his bag and camera beneath the coat rack and calls for his mom. "We have company."

Mrs. Brewer appears from the hallway, her face without any makeup and hair wet, as if she's just gotten out of the shower. I would feel bad for being here without her permission, but her polite grin tells me that she doesn't mind.

"Well, hello again, Miss Selena. Will you be eating with us tonight?"

"Yes ma'am. If that's okay with you. Austin invited me."

"Well, of course it's okay with me!" She walks into her small kitchen. "I hope you don't mind a little bit of southern cooking. We're having chicken fried steak that Audrey cooked last night."

Austin comes from the kitchen and holds two glasses out in front of me. "Water or tea, madam?"

I laugh at his fake accent. "I'll take water. Thanks."

As I help the Brewers set the table in the dining room, I can't help but notice that this is probably the first time since living in Kentucky that I've eaten a real home-cooked meal at the dinner table. With an actual family.

Sure, I've had supper at my friends' houses before, but most of them don't have both parents living at home. We usually sit on the couch and eat on TV trays. And it's never southern cooking.

While setting the table, I notice how different the atmosphere feels here than at my friends' homes. Or my own, for that matter.

After Austin's mom says grace over the food, she asks questions about what we thought about our first day of SummerThirst.

Audrey stabs a green bean with her fork. "I can already tell that it's going to be even better than last year."

"Isn't Cole's band leading the praise and worship this year?"

Audrey nods. "They're really good, too."

I want to laugh. Sure, the music wasn't bad. Neither was Cole's singing voice.

But the so-called "praise and worship" was a bit awkward

---

for me, having to stand in the midst of all those Christians as they jumped around and praised their mystical God.

I stuff my mouth with mashed potatoes as Austin gives his mom details about the hike and the lesson that we were supposed to learn.

"And did you enjoy the hike as well?" Mrs. Brewer asks, looking at me.

I nod. Why are people always forcing me to lie? "It was fun. I love your church's atmosphere, too. Very—laid back. Different than what I'm used to."

"That's what first attracted, um, Matthew and me to Lake Lure Fellowship." Her smiling eyes become somber at the mention of her husband's name.

"Where is Mr. Brewer, by the way? Is he at work?"

When Austin's mom doesn't respond, I plunge my fork into the mashed potatoes, afraid I said something wrong.

Austin catches me looking at him, then glances over to his mom with an expression that's difficult to read. "My parents aren't together anymore."

I forget to chew before swallowing a piece of steak. "Oh— I'm sorry. I know how that kind of thing feels." *Well done, Selena.* I seem to have a real talent for ruining such cheerful atmospheres.

Ms. Brewer gives me an appreciative smile back. "It's alright," she says, then begins talking a hundred miles an hour about everything she loves about the church and their pastor. She doesn't stop until after we've eaten and put all of our dishes in the sink.

After thanking her for having me, and thanking Audrey for the food, I tell Austin that I should probably start heading back.

"Wait." His hand on my elbow keeps me from moving toward the door. "It's still early. Come outside with me so we can play. I mean—not play." A corner of his mouth rises slowly. "I have a surprise."

I laugh. "Play? Sounds very mature."

The urge for Austin's hand to remain on my elbow surprises me.

"It's because I remember us as kids playing games outside during the summertime. Follow me, I'll show you."

Since I seem to have no choice, I follow as he leads me through the familiar trees in his backyard and into a more wooded area along the lake. My legs weaken with each step. "Didn't we already go on a hike today?"

I focus on the ground and carefully decide where to step, just in case there's a snake hiding in the leaves. Something stops me from moving forward. I look down at my shirt: it's snagged on a tree branch.

Fabulous.

"We're here," Austin says as I detach the shirt from the branch.

He stands between two trees a few yards from the lake. Hanging from both trees are wooden swings.

I take a few steps closer, struggling to figure out why they look so familiar. It seems as if I've dreamed about them before, because I remember being afraid of falling into the water as I would swing over the lake.

"Don't you remember?" Austin asks, anticipating a surprised reaction.

The sound of a croaking toad seems magnified in the silence.

"My dad built these for Audrey and me when I was six," he finally says at my lack of response.

"Oh, yeah!" A door to my childhood opens as several images of my past reel through my mind. I grab the ropes of one of the swings, carefully sitting onto the wooden seat. "How could I forget? Whitney and I used to make you push us."

"Not funny," he says, crouching down to snap a picture of the empty swing with the lake in the background. "That was torture, getting a tiny kid like me to push two spoiled brats like you girls."

My feet kick the dirt as I push off. "Hey, I wasn't the spoiled brat. I was just the spoiled brat's servant."

The fact that these swings probably haven't been swung on in years doesn't scare me a bit. I allow the sudden rush of wind to take me all the way back to childhood as the swing flies over the edge of the lake.

Austin showed these to me when I was eight. Back then, being away from Daddy was new to me. The swings reminded me of him, and I started crying, thinking back to when he would push me on the swing set in our backyard. I had been so confused, not able to comprehend why Daddy wouldn't want me when we had been best friends. Austin had been concerned, seeing my tears—but Whitney made fun of me, telling me that I was a baby and only crying because I was homesick.

A bright light flashes in the corner of my eyes.

"Did you just take a picture of me?" I ask, turning my head toward Austin.

He ignores my question and looks down at his camera screen, laughing at his cleverness.

"Austin! Take pictures of the sunset, not of me. It's much more picture-worthy than I am."

"Don't say that," he says, his laughter fading into concern as he wraps the camera strap around his neck and takes a seat on the other swing. "Why are you always so down on yourself?"

My feet skid across the dirt to slow my pace. "I don't know what you're talking about."

"Yeah, you do."

My ponytail flies in my face as I turn away from his stare.

"You don't like it when I take pictures of you."

"That was only one time!"

"You keep complaining about the way you look. You hardly ate any breakfast this morning. Or supper, for that matter."

Defensive words stir up inside of me, ready to explode like a volcano. "I told you that I had already eaten breakfast this morning. Why are you so nosey and judgmental, Austin?"

I regret the outburst as soon as the words escape my mouth. The softness of his eyes reminds me that he's only trying to help.

He shakes his head. "Never mind."

I kick hard off the ground to begin swinging again, not enjoying it as much as I did before Austin's little comment.

Before we entered into this thick silence.

I let out a huff. "It's not that I'm so down on myself. It's just that—girls like Whitney are the attention-getters." As my swing comes to a complete halt, my mind goes back to the guys staring at Whitney in the car next to us the other day.

I glance at Austin now, a bit ashamed at the confession. "I'm so pitiful. Sorry, I don't know why I—"

"No, it's good that you got that off your chest." Golden sunlight bounces off his curls, showing off his auburn sun-bleached highlights. "And you are beautiful, Selena. All of that material junk doesn't define true beauty."

My heart warms over Austin's compliment. "Well, thank you." I bite my lip, trying to think of a way to insert humor to lighten the situation. Nothing comes.

As I swing, I feel as if I'm flying, rising above the edge of the lake and watching the sun begin to hide behind the mountains.

"Can I ask you something personal?" I ask, wiping a strand of hair stuck on my lips.

Austin spins around. "Sure."

"What happened to your dad? I mean—if you don't mind telling me. I feel horrible for mentioning it at the dinner table, and—"

He glances at the ground before responding. "My parents seemed to be the perfect couple. When I was thirteen, though, Mom supposedly found out that my dad had been seeing another woman. I never really got to hear his side of the story, though."

He lets go of his camera to reach out and catch a lightning bug that glows between us.

"He's not the type that would cheat on my mom. She just blew up and told him that she couldn't live with someone she couldn't trust. She has some big trust issues." Austin opens his hands to release the firefly. "I think that's the main deal."

It takes a while for me to find the right words. "I'm so sorry. I know that must be hard for you. But at least you get to visit him."

"Visit him?" He laughs. "I wish! I've only gotten to see him a few times since the divorce. Mom won't let us. We still keep in touch and all, but—" He shakes his head. "We were best friends."

I kick my feet really hard to get the feeling of soaring over the lake again. "Life is just too complicated."

"No. I mean, yes, life is complicated. But it's not *too* complicated." Austin reaches down, putting his camera strap around his neck again.

He stands, and takes a few more photos of the sunset morphing into night. I shut my eyes and lean further back in the swing, trying to figure out what Austin meant.

Click.

"Austin!" My eyes open to see him aiming his camera upward.

He laughs. "No, that was a good picture! I promise."

I jump off the swing, sliding onto the grass. "Let me see."

He hands it to me, and I take a quick glance of the picture before holding it up towards his face. "Hmm, that's—"

Click.

"You did *not* just take a picture of me."

"See what it feels like? And don't worry, Austin. That was a good picture—"

My laughter dwindles as he looks up from his camera, catching my gaze with his.

"—I promise."

The distance between us grows smaller, until the only thing that separates us is his camera.

Austin's chocolate-brown eyes reflect the orange shades of the fading sunset. This captivates me and I become numb, unable to pull away as his hand gently brushes against my forehead.

I close my eyes.

Chapter 8

"Lightning bug," Austin's breath tingles my lips, but he doesn't touch them.

I open my eyes to see him cupping his hands together over a firefly. He looks up at me and says, "This little guy was on your forehead."

"Oh," I say, releasing the breath I had been holding. I walk back to the swing, grab the ropes, and sit back down. Why did I want him to kiss me? Does he realize what was on my mind?

Click.

"Okay, Austin." I jump up from the swing and attempt to steal the camera from his hands. "Your photo-taking session is officially over for this evening."

"Oh, it is, is it?"

I nod. "Yep. So give me your camera."

"That depends."

"Depends on what?"

"If you're still as good at chasing me as you used to be."

My stomach feels all warm and tingly inside every time Austin's smile reveals those dimples of his. But before I can comprehend what he just said, Austin takes off running.

I laugh, then hurry to try and catch up with him. We run through the woods until the trees clear, and we've returned to his backyard.

Catching my breath, I look up into the sky now turning dark blue. Another lightning bug glows in front of me, so I reach out to catch it, observing this strange little creature as I walk over to the Brewers' dock. I say goodbye to my new friend, releasing it, and it flies off my hand and above the lake.

"Beautiful, isn't it?" Austin's voice says behind me.

I nod, and sit down on the edge of the dock, staring up into the night sky. "Have you ever wished that you could transport yourself to the moon?" I really wish my mouth would wait for my brain before it speaks out.

His leg brushes against mine as he sits down Indian-style next to me. "Can't say that I have."

"I know this seems crazy, but what if we could paint the moon a different color? Like—purple?"

"I think you're getting a little sleepy, Selena," Austin laughs.

"It's just that—" The crescent moon shines down on us, reflecting off the water that ripples as it fades into the distance. "The night sky has always intrigued me," I say, taking off my shoes.

He laughs again, making me feel a little silly. "Why?"

I dip my feet into the cool water below, preparing to share with Austin one of my favorite—yet painful—childhood memories. "One time when I was six, my parents, my brother, and I were spending all day outside, riding our horses and playing all sorts of outdoor games. At twilight, we started catching fireflies and putting them into empty jars. My dad always came up with great ideas. He had interesting lessons for almost everything, especially nature." I pause to cup my hands around a lightning bug that flies between Austin and me.

"That night, my dad had been talking to my brother and me about how Christians are supposed to be the light of the world. He used the fireflies we had in the jars as an example. And as he was telling this, I looked up at the sky. The faded sunset had left an intense red glow in the deep blue sky. Then I looked at the crescent moon. It was purple. A purple moon. The red and blue colors from the sunset had reflected onto the moon, mixing together to create the most beautiful purple I've ever seen. It was a perfect, magical night." I let out a deep sigh, wishing the story could end there.

"About a year later, though, just about everything had changed. My dad's church was growing faster than he could handle, and the stress was unbearable. He no longer told me fairy tales like he always used to, and my parents fought almost every night. One night as they were arguing, I slipped outside to catch fireflies in a jar like he had shown me. Except this time, I decided not to release them. Instead, I took them inside and put the jar on my nightstand. I wanted to hold on to the fireflies forever. Thought it would keep the memories alive. The next morning, though, their lights had gone out. They were dead.

"I cried for hours. It was as if all of my hopes, dreams, and happy endings were also dead." I lower my head and stare at my blurred reflection in the water below. "And, just like the fireflies, my dad's light had also burned out. He was no longer the imaginative, nature-loving Daddy he used to be."

The rays from the moon shine down on my face as I lean back, resting on my elbows.

"Now, every time I look up at the moon, I remember that

night. Even though the times have changed, the moon is always the same." I inhale deeply, pulling my wet feet back up onto the deck. "That's what gives me hope, knowing that the moon that glowed in the sky on that magical night is the same one above us now."

At least one part of that night hasn't left me.

"Just like God," Austin says. "Even when our circumstances change, He's always the same."

My eyes look away from him at the mention of God.

"What is it?"

I have seriously got to learn how to keep my face from reflecting what I'm feeling.

"Nothing. Just—I really don't consider myself a Christian. If there is a God, and if He really loves me, then why did all that stuff have to happen? None of it makes sense."

"Trust me." Austin lets out a sigh. "I know what you mean."

I shiver. Are these sudden chills brought on by the sincerity in Austin's voice, or by the light breeze coming off the lake?

"But you know," he continues, "without the dark, we'd never see the stars. There also would be no use for the moon if there was never a night."

I pause, taken aback at Austin's beautiful words—although I'm not so sure how true they actually are. The chirping of crickets fills the silence between us, but not in an awkward way.

"Oh, that reminds me—do you know what your name means?" he asks.

"My *name*?" I look up at Austin. "Am I supposed to?"

"It means moon." He holds his camera in front of his face, aiming it upwards to the sky. "Ironic, isn't it?"

"Wow." I smile as this new information sinks in. "Wait a second, you looked it up?"

The moonlight helps me see the dimples on each side of Austin's shy grin. "When I was eight."

I giggle. "Okay, that's creepy. Please explain."

He sets his camera down in his lap, his curly hair swooshing as a boat passes by a little too close. "In school one day, my teacher passed around a name definition book for an assignment, and I decided to look up yours. I don't know why, honestly. I guess because you were sort of my only half-friend back then."

"Wow. Interesting." What's even more interesting is that he still remembers that.

"And what was the meaning of your name?"

"Honestly, I can't remember. Don't think I was a stalker or anything, please." He laughs. "I was such a weird kid back then."

Actually, that's sort of cute, in its own creepy way.

"You still are a weird kid, Four-Eyed-Brewer."

* * *

"Stop it!"

Richard hovers over Whitney on the couch, tickling her as I open the back porch door. He stops when he sees me, and Whitney's smile turns into a scowl.

"Where've you been?"

It takes a little too long for me to focus on her question rather than on how good Richard looks in his tight-fitted tank. "I've been with—I mean, I've been at the Brewers'. Hey, Richard."

❯ Tessa Emily Hall

A corner of his mouth raises as he gives me a wave. His girlfriend speaks instead. "Ew, what is that smell?"

Oh, great. I have completely forgotten about my desperate need to take a shower. "Probably me. I went on a hike today."

"A hike?" She wrinkles her nose. "Why on *earth* were you hiking?"

I force myself not to giggle at her unintended pun.

"Austin's church." Why must she ask me these questions when Richard is sitting *right there*?

But more importantly, why does it bother me so much that she is?

"Of course they would make you do something that lame." Apparently, flipping her long, blond hair behind her shoulder makes her feel as if she's better than I am.

"Don't act like a snob, Whitney," Richard says. "Not all churches are lame."

I raise my eyebrows. Is he taking up for me?

"Right. Like you would know."

"And you *would*?" I ask, feeling defensive over my cousin's comments, even though I'm not a Christian myself. "Have you ever been to church before?"

"Actually, yes, I have been," she shoots back, intimidating me with her evil glare. "But I think we stopped going once we heard what your hypocritical dad did."

I narrow my eyes at her.

"Please leave now. You interrupted us."

I struggle to swallow my anger and stomp past the two of them without retaliating.

Whitney's strange ability to act so nice toward me one

day, but the next satanically evil, makes me wonder if there really is something seriously wrong with her.

As I shower, I attempt to take my mind off of Whitney and her multiple personalities, and instead think about my dream the other night. And my dad. And the moon. Even fireflies.

A smile creeps onto my lips as my mind floats to the moment when I thought Austin was going to kiss me.

And then, as I brush my teeth, I think about Richard. How he took up for me. The way he looked at me as Whitney tore me apart right in front of him.

Or tried to, anyway.

I hear a tap on my door as I change into my pajamas, followed by Aunt Kori's voice. "Selena?"

I quickly slide my arms through a T-shirt. "Come in."

"You received this letter in the mail," she says, opening the door. "It's from your mom."

As Kori hands the envelope to me, the smell of cigarette smoke on her clothes reminds me of the unfinished pack of cigarettes in my purse.

"How was the camp thing?"

"Not too bad," I say, studying the envelope in my hands. "It's been a very long day, though."

"Then I'll let you get your rest. Don't forget that tomorrow y'all are going to Sliding Rock bright and early. Be sure to wear a bathing suit underneath your clothes."

"I will. Thanks, Aunt Kori." I collapse on the window seat. "Goodnight."

She shuts the door, and my fingers rip apart the envelope. I didn't think I'd miss Mom as much as I do.

Selena,

These few days have been a whirlwind of meetings, making new friends, and getting used to a new environment. But, as busy as I am, you are always in my heart and prayers. I would love to be spending this summer with you—healthy and whole—but please understand that I cannot be the mother you so deserve until I first work on myself. Although I miss you, I know I'm where I'm supposed to be.

As I write, I am sitting by a lovely reflection pond here. This is a place where we can go for quiet time after our counseling and group sessions—a place to reflect, study, write in our journals. I sit here, wondering how I can tell you all the things I wish to say—some things I am only just now realizing. What really impresses me now is how selfish I have been most of your life, and for that I truly apologize. Since your father kicked us out, I have struggled with deep emotional and financial issues. I dealt with my problems by self-medicating with alcohol, partying, and even taking my frustrations out on you—the one person I love more than anyone in the world. I cannot even imagine, sweetie, what you must have been going through. You are the best daughter anyone could ask for. If only I could relive those eight years, I would be the one reaching out to you, caring for your every need, taking you out to breakfast. I would discuss things with you rather than lash out or argue. I would pray with you rather than curse.

I pause, wiping the tears from my face. My throat tightens as I try to gain enough strength to continue reading.

> *I want you to know, Selena, how proud I am of you. You were strong when I was weak. You mothered me when I should have been mothering you. But, somehow, you always managed to maintain your high grades. Selena, you are blessed with artistic ability that is a true gift from God! I know you've made your share of mistakes, but you are a real trooper, an overcomer, and I admire you. I hope that you will stick up for what you know is right, and not run from your problems as I have all these years.*
>
> *I love you more than anything, sweetie. I hope you're having a wonderful summer. I'm praying for you every day. We'll both be okay, Selena, I know it.*
>
> *Love,*
>
> *Mom*

I grab the pillow from behind me and bury my head under it, letting go of all the tears I've held back for so long.

Mom has never been this open with me before.

She has *never once* apologized.

I sit up to reread the letter a few more times. The more I read it, the more emotional I become.

A part of me thinks that she only made up those words because she feels guilty about making me stay with her sister for the summer—yet the other part of me wants to believe that every word she wrote came straight from her heart.

❯ Tessa Emily Hall

This is not a typical thing for her to do: write a letter to me. Apologize. Say that she admires me and is praying for me.

I fold the letter into fourths and stick it into my purse, deciding to write back another time when tears aren't blurring my vision.

Lying in bed with the sleeping mask covering my eyes, I try to ignore the overwhelming flood of emotions and sleep.

But it's useless. Even when I try to focus on something else, like how much I am *not* looking forward to the church camp again tomorrow, I end up thinking about the letter. About my mom. About the past eight years.

Giving up on any possible sleep tonight, I yank off the mask, switch on the lamp, and grab my sketchpad from underneath the bed. I sketch everything. Lightning bugs in jars. Castles. Horses. Cigarettes, even.

And, for the first time in what feels like forever, I allow myself to make mistakes. I'm not trying to create a pretty picture—I'm allowing everything inside me to get out. It feels good to finally be able to express myself on paper again.

Time passes as my pencil dances along the pages.

I feel hopeful. And not just because I think here I might finally be able to find inspiration to begin creating again—but hopeful for my mom and our relationship.

She's said the words "new beginning" to me far too many times to count.

But, for some reason, I have a feeling Mom might actually be right this time.

Chapter 9

The moment I see Austin waiting for me in his Jeep with the top down, my heart does a little leap, and I completely forget I only slept five hours last night.

"Morning," he calls out, even though it's still dark outside. The way he grins at me causes butterflies to dance in my stomach. "You get the passenger seat today."

"Oh, I do?" It's a struggle for me to open the door and sit down in a graceful manner.

I'm not exactly sure what happened between Austin and me last night, but whatever it was, it makes me want to over-analyze every movement I make in front of him now.

I turn around and say hey to Audrey before Austin puts his hand on the side of my seat, looking behind him as he backs out of their driveway. "Lexie asked if we could drive separately to Sliding Rock, since we'll need to leave early for the skit meeting tonight. Brooke and Cole will be riding with us."

"Fine with me," I say, not showing exactly how fine it is with me that we're going to leave early.

My sleepiness returns as soon as Austin pulls up to the church. Fortunately he only stops to talk to one person in the lobby before going in the sanctuary—but, *unfortunately,* rather than having praise and worship today, Pastor Carson welcomes a preacher from a different church to the stage to give a little "mini-sermon" before heading out.

I sit in between Austin and Brooke, looking at my phone every five minutes during the sermon to check the time. My ability to remain awake surprises me as this old man preaches about some Bible story I remember Daddy teaching me when I was little. Twenty minutes pass before this overly dramatic preacher finally wraps up his sermon in a prayer.

After dragging Cole away from the breakfast prepared for us in the fellowship hall, my group piles into Austin's Jeep, all awake and hyper. Except me, of course.

"Nice shades, Austin," Brooke says as he's setting up the GPS. "I thought we were going to Sliding Rock, not to the beach."

"Shut up, Brooke," Cole says. "I happen to think blue tinted shades are awesome."

"Thanks, Cole. So, the GPS says we'll get there in about an hour. That is, if I don't stop to drop Brooke off back at her house. Or on the side of the road. Either will do."

Brooke starts to say something to defend herself, but Austin ignores her by reaching for his iPod underneath his stereo and saying, "Why don't you choose some music for us, Selena?"

I take the iPod and scroll through his artists: Adele, Coldplay, Michael Buble, Rascal Flatts, Sleeping With Sirens, and artists I've never even heard of before.

"Nice taste in music. I don't think there's a genre here that you left out."

He gives me a sideways glance, along with that half smile of his. "Creative people need to have a broad perspective of things. You should know that. There has to be a variety of inspiration for us to choose from."

"That's interesting." I shake his iPod so it'll go on the shuffle setting, and am surprised at the first song to start playing.

"Really, Brewer?" Brooke says. "Taylor Swift?"

Audrey laughs. "You're such a girl."

"Shush, you two." He reaches over to turn up the volume. "I happen to like this song."

I laugh as Cole belts out the chorus in a high-pitched girl voice until Brooke finally puts her hand over his mouth, muffling the screeching of his voice.

Austin brakes at a stop sign. "Quick, I need my camera." He points to the floorboard underneath me. "Can you get it for me?"

"Austin, please." Audrey leans up in her seat. "Focus on driving. I'm sure you have close to a thousand sunrise pictures already."

He puts the car into park before taking the camera out of my hand. "No two of them are exactly the same, though, Audrey. I can't miss this one." He stands on his seat and snaps a picture of the morning sun rays reaching down through several clouds just above the lake.

I shake my head. He is so unlike any other guy I have ever met, treating a beautiful scene like a sunrise over the lake as if it is a present—as if it doesn't happen every morning.

When a car comes up from behind us, Austin is forced to sit back down and put the car into drive. I look through the pictures on his camera until we finally arrive, and as we trudge up the steep hill that leads to Sliding Rock, I wonder why I decided to go to bed so late last night. Everyone else seems to be bursting with energy and eager to slide down the rock as soon as PC announces the rules.

When Audrey and I reach the top of the massive rock, I dip my toes into the water flowing down the rock and test the temperature, then immediately pull my foot back.

"That's freezing!" Audrey squeals before I have the chance.

I shake my head at the ridiculousness of this. "There is no way I'm sliding down that rock and being dumped into a pool of icy water."

Brooke comes up behind Audrey. "Why haven't you two gone down the rock yet? And why did you even bother to wear makeup?"

"Well, not everyone is a model like you are, Brooke," I say.

She laughs, pointing to her hair. "Uh, do you see the way I look?" Strands of her short hair stick up in all different directions, framing her pale face and not exactly making her look like too much of a model right now. "You're the only one who actually cares about appearance. You girls need to at least go down the rock once. You did pay for this, you know. There's not much time, since we have to leave early for the skit audition tonight."

My feet stay planted on the ground as she reaches for my hand and Audrey's. "Come on!" she says, tugging until we finally start moving forward and reach the starting point.

Audrey and I both let out squeals as our feet step through the stinging layer of water covering the rock.

Brooke finally lets us go, and crosses her arms. "You girls are so high maintenance."

"I think I'll just sit here for a while until I can get used to it." I squat down, biting my tongue to hold back complaints as the water races over my legs.

"See, Brooke?" Audrey says, joining me. "This isn't so bad. We're halfway in the water, halfway out. Sort of."

"Fine." She sits down next to us at the summit, and begins to gradually push herself off the rock. "But you know what the Bible says about that. It's either all or nothing."

At the end of her sentence, she takes off—sailing over bumps and gaining momentum, bumping into other people— until she's emptied into the pool of water with everyone else.

I shake my head. "She's crazy."

"There is no way anyone can get me to do that."

I jump as two cold hands rest on my back. "You girls sure about that?"

Before I have the chance to turn around, the hands give me a shove, and Audrey and I are pushed down the rock and into the icy water. I glance over my shoulder. Cole and Austin stand right where we were, doubled over in laughter.

It's too late to turn back now. We both zip down the rocks, bouncing and probably bruising the entire way down.

My body numb, I am emptied into the pool of deep water at the bottom of the sliding rock. I gasp for air, fighting the water to stay up. Audrey laughs in front of me, also struggling to use her limbs to keep her head above the water. Unlike her, I find no humor in this situation.

"We've got to think of a way to get the guys back," Audrey says, shivering from the cold.

"Oh, don't worry. We will."

The sun's warmth thawing us, we walk back up to the top of the rock.

❯ Tessa Emily Hall

"I have an idea," I say once we've joined everyone else. I bend down and scoop up a pile of black ooze from the wet ground.

Audrey grins. "Perfect. Where are they?"

I scan the scattered group of young people standing at the top of the rock until I spot a guy with brown curly hair, talking to Cole.

I can't help but feel like a little kid again as mud oozes between my fingers. Audrey and I take slow steps toward the guys, sly grins plastered on our faces.

"On the count of three," Audrey whispers. "One, two—"

Before she can get to three, the guys start walking. We take a few quick steps then reach around them from behind, shoving the mud right into their faces.

They spin around, faces completely covered with the brown goo.

"Oh, that hurt." Cole wipes his eyes.

Too bad guys don't gross out as easily as girls do.

Austin looks at me with a smirk. "Revenge?"

I nod. "Sweet, sweet revenge."

"I see," he says, then leans over to whisper something to Cole.

They grin at each other before facing Audrey and me again. We back away in fear as they step closer to us, but it's too late. The guys splatter the mud on both of us—fortunately, though, none of it gets on my face or in my hair.

Austin crosses one arm over the other. "Revenge is pretty sweet, isn't it, Cole?"

Cole laughs and is about to say something, but seems

distracted as he looks off into the distance. "Oh! Where's Brooke? I have an idea."

"I'm right here," she says from behind the boys. "So you girls finally decided to slide down the rock?"

"We didn't exactly have a choice," I reply. Audrey and I narrow our eyes at Austin and Cole.

"You guys are geniuses." Brooke holds her hand up for a high-five with Cole, then looks at her hand in disgust. "Um, may I ask why ya'll were rolling around in the mud?"

"Revenge," Audrey says.

Brooke drops open her mouth. "Ugh! You could've at least invited me."

I laugh. "So, Cole, what was your idea?"

We follow him over to the top of the slippery rock where he instructs all of us to sit train-style, connected by wrapping our legs around the person in front of us. Audrey and I finally give in—we don't have much of a choice.

The five of us scoot forward until the water picks us up and we zoom down the rock. I scream. Why did I let myself get talked into this? Eventually, the water doesn't seem quite as cold anymore, although it's probably because my body has lost all feeling. Each time I reach the pool below, I want to do it all over again.

Once the announcement is made that it's time for lunch, everyone rushes over to the picnic tables. I feel kind of upset that I have to leave for the skit instead of staying here and continuing to slide down the rock. I don't think that I ever actually agreed to audition for it, anyway.

"Oh, no." Cole takes the top piece of bread from his sandwich. "What? I didn't order turkey!" He spits his chewed-up food into a napkin as if it's poisoned.

I have the sudden urge to gag. "Um, what's wrong with turkey?"

"He doesn't eat meat," Brooke says, not even closing her mouth as she chomps on a carrot.

Cole stares down at his food in horror. "I don't know what to do!"

"Dude, you'll be fine. You only had maybe two bites."

"Yeah, Austin, but what if my stomach starts having convulsions? I haven't had meat in, like, three years!"

"Why can't you eat meat?" Audrey asks, pulling away the crust from her bread.

"Why would you *want* to eat meat, Audrey? It's an animal. Animals are living and breathing, just like us. And people kill them just so we can eat them. God gave us vegetables and fruits to eat, not animals."

Austin laughs, and I join him, releasing the laughter I was struggling to hold back. Cole does not seem like the type to be a vegetarian. Brooke, maybe. But not Cole.

"You guys! It's not funny." He reaches over to steal a potato chip from Brooke's plate. "What if my stomach starts to hurt? What if—what if I start to feel nauseous from eating turkey guts?"

"Cole!" Brooke almost shouts. "It's not the end of the world, okay? You'll be fine! Gah, you're such a little girl sometimes. It's not even guts; it's *meat*!"

"Look at his face," Audrey says to me quietly.

Cole shoots a glare at both of us—which, of course, only makes us giggle more.

"This isn't funny, girls." Cole takes a bite of his now meatless sandwich. "You'll both be sorry if I end up in the hospital later on."

I almost choke on my Sprite. Austin just shakes his head, giving up on trying to convince his friend that he's not going to die.

As I finish eating the rest of my sandwich, I tune out the conversation Brooke begins about something church-related, and watch the people at the other picnic tables laugh over their own conversations, not even pausing long enough to take a bite of their food.

No matter what has happened in their lives, everyone here seems genuinely happy, which is a pretty big contrast from the friends I hang out with in New York. Not just the amusement that comes from acting stupid and making a fool of myself, nor the type of counterfeit happiness I get from being drunk, this happiness is fresher. More natural.

I want that.

* * *

"No way." Brooke stands frozen in motion as I swing open the Huiets' front door. "Why didn't you tell me you came from a wealthy family, Selena?"

I laugh. "Because I don't. Trust me, it's only my aunt and uncle who have the money."

Audrey seems a little less shocked than Brooke. "They've made a lot of changes since the last time I've been here. What is it that your aunt and uncle do again?"

"Kori owns Lake Lure Tanning Salon & Spa, and Ben owns an engineering firm, whatever that is." I kick my muddy tennis shoes into the shoe closet. "They're hardly ever home."

Brooke lags behind Audrey and me as we go upstairs. When she finally catches up with us, she once again stands frozen at the doorway, observing my room in awe. "Seriously, Selena?"

She walks over to my bed and sits down on the edge. I try not to cringe, remembering that she's wearing a damp bathing suit under her dirty clothes.

"It is pretty nice, isn't it?" I say, realizing that I have a missed call from Hilarie.

To Hilarie: *Sorry, I've been gone all day. I'll call you this evening.*

"What's this?" Audrey asks, sitting down at my window seat.

"It's a window seat."

"I know *that*, Brooke." She holds up my sketchpad. "I'm talking about this."

I nearly drop my phone back on the dresser, and hurry over to the window seat. "Um, that's just—"

"You drew these?" Her innocent doll-like eyes widen as she looks up at me. "Selena, this is insane."

Brooke rolls over to the other side of the bed. "Jeez, you said that you liked art, but you didn't tell us you were this good!"

I almost feel as if they're sneaking a peek into my private diary—yet, even though this makes me feel nervous, I'd rather not take it from them. A little self-confidence boost might be nice for a change.

Audrey shakes her head at the random doodles I drew last night. "How long have you taken lessons?"

"I haven't."

Brooke's jaw drops even lower. "You're kidding?"

"No." I laugh at their expressions. "I mean, I took basic art class in school. But I'm mostly self-taught."

"You should see my drawings," Brooke says. "They're the most attractive stick figures ever drawn."

Audrey still studies my doodles. "If only you could move here and go to Lake Lure Academy of the Arts with us. That'd be the perfect place *ever* for you."

I grab the zebra-print pillow from behind me, and put it on my stomach to cover up any rolls of fat that my tight tank top might reveal as I'm sitting. "I wish I could. I mean, living in New York is all right, but I'm much more of a small town kinda girl. What is your school like? I can't even imagine going some place other than public school."

"Oh my goodness, you would *love* our school." Brooke sits up straighter, pulls a pack of gum from her pocket, and hands Audrey and me a piece. "They have classes for acting, modeling, visual arts, music, creative writing, dance, photography"—she pauses to catch her breath—"and the list goes on. It's actually a pretty small school, too, since they're really strict about who is accepted. And it's *way* different from public school. Honestly, I don't care for public school very much. No offense, by the way."

I laugh. "It's okay. I don't really like it, either."

She hops up from the bed. "Well, I'm gonna go jump in the shower, since it doesn't look like Audrey will be finished looking through your sketches any time soon. Plus we really need to hurry so we won't be late for the auditions." She walks out of my room and into the hall. Three seconds later, she reappears at the door. "Um, it might help to know where the bathroom is?"

We both laugh as I direct her to the hall bathroom and then show her how to turn on the shower. She is astonished at how much the bathroom resembles a spa.

"Have you shown these to Austin?" Audrey asks when I come back into my room. She's still going through my sketchpad.

"Not really."

"Why not? He's huge into art, you know, with his photography and everything."

I sit down beside her on the window seat and shrug, wondering myself why I haven't shared with him.

Then, as Audrey flips to a picture I drew of the charm bracelet my dad gave me—the last sketch I drew before I quit art and went back to smoking—I remember.

And place my thumb over the scar on my wrist.

If people really got to know me—my weaknesses, my pain, my "bad habits"—they'd reject me in a heartbeat. That's what I fear. But whether or not it's true, it's just safer not giving them the chance. Easier for me just to allow people to only know what I reveal to them about myself. Nothing deeper.

That's how I've felt ever since I made the mistake of opening up my heart to Jeremy, giving him permission to completely stomp on it when he didn't like what he saw.

And it's how I have decided to remain. Once I begin to trust people enough to give them the key to my heart, they have access to knowing all about me—and permission to make fun of my flaws. That's when I get hurt.

Then I'm scarred forever.

Chapter 10

The youth building at Lake Lure Fellowship is probably half the size of my dad's entire church, the way I remember it when I was a little kid. As I walk through the front door, I notice a row of video games along the back wall that leads to a small kitchen in the corner. I sit with Austin and Audrey on one of the couches at the front of the room—yes, a *couch*—and listen as Lexie begins to tell us about the skit we'll be performing.

"This year we will be acting out a skit to the song 'Everything' by Lifehouse, so you will not have any lines to memorize for this." She goes around the room and asks for everyone's names, jotting them down on a clipboard. "Have any of you seen this skit before on YouTube? It's pretty popular, actually."

"Oh, yeah!" A girl named Tara throws her hand in the air. "That's the first skit I've seen that actually made me cry."

Lexie bobs her head. "The message is truly powerful. In fact, you may find yourself doing a little soul-searching of your own as we rehearse. I actually have the video on my laptop, for those of you who haven't seen it yet. Cole, would you mind pressing play for us now?"

Everyone turns their attention to the screen above the platform as Cole hits play on the video.

I sink further into my seat as it begins, and decide to check Facebook on my phone. I don't want to be at all affected by whatever "powerful" message Lexie was talking about. Why did I think this would be a happy-Sunday-school type of skit?

As soon as the video is over, Brooke is eager to share what she thought about the skit and its message. A couple of other people—including Austin—throw in their comments as well, which makes me start to wonder if I'm the only one in this room who actually *isn't* a Christian. Hopefully it's not obvious. How embarrassing would it be for them to find out that one of the people performing in this life-touching skit isn't even "saved" herself?

Just one of the many reasons it's best to keep to myself sometimes: so that I won't be judged.

"Now," Lexie says, returning to her seat on the platform. "I don't see the point in auditioning each one of you for the skit, so I'll just have to trust that all of you have decent acting skills. I'll go around the room, and you tell me two parts you would like to have."

A guy sitting in a recliner next to Cole shares his preferences first. "I wouldn't mind going for Jesus or, you know, the other guy that's like Satan or whatever."

Lexie scribbles something on her clipboard then moves on to Austin.

He shrugs. "Either of those would be fine for me, too."

"All right." She looks up at me after writing down Austin's preference. "And what about you?"

Everyone stares at me, waiting for my answer. But all I can come up with is, "Um—"

"I think you should go for the main girl," Austin says, nudging me with his elbow.

I feel my cheeks flush as Brooke and Tara also agree that my "innocent look" would fit the main character perfectly.

My teeth clench down on the inside of my cheek. Do I really look so innocent?

Lexie gives me a wink. "I think you might fit that part. I'll decide later tonight, and let all of you know at the next practice which role you will be playing."

My hand runs through my hair as I let out a long sigh, sinking deeper into my seat.

Great.

I'm probably going to be the main girl in a silly skit that I don't even want to be involved in. Isn't acting about passion? I have no clue what it feels like to be a Christian. Other than, of course, the time when I was supposedly one as a kid, but even then it was just fake. All of it's fake.

Good thing this is called acting.

* * *

"Hey, Selena," Uncle Ben says as I arrive home around eight o'clock. It disgusts me how arrogant he and Aunt Kori appear, sitting at the kitchen table as they sip wine and use chopsticks to eat sushi from a crystal platter. It makes me wonder why they don't just eat in their fancy formal dining room rather than the small table in their kitchen.

I show no teeth—or friendliness, for that matter—as I smile back at my uncle and go through their refrigerator in search of a water bottle.

"I hear you've been involved this week in a church event with the Brewers. Is that right?"

Cold water chills my empty stomach as I take a quick drink. "Yes."

"That's pretty cool."

For the sake of conversation rather than awkward eye contact, I ask, "Just curious. Do you guys go to church?"

"Oh, we used to," Aunt Kori responds, her bright red lipstick somehow unaffected by the small sip of wine that she takes. "But you know, hon, we just can't seem to fit it into our busy schedules. And Sunday mornings are the only time Ben can squeeze in golfing with his buddies, and he really needs his down time. But we do occasionally watch preachers on cable. That's almost the same."

I nod as if agreeing, although that's the first time I've ever heard about preachers being on cable. But why do I care, anyway?

"It's nice," is all Ben says before stuffing another roll of fish into his mouth. No more comments, or even eye contact for that matter. Apparently I'm just a bother to him, considering the fact that he has probably spoken a total of ten words to me since I've been here.

"Whitney's been with her friends today," Aunt Kori tells me, as if I am actually interested in what her daughter is doing. "She should be home within an hour. Oh, if you're hungry, we ordered sushi. It's in the fridge."

"Okay." I bite my tongue to prevent myself from saying "thanks" out of habit.

It bothers me that they don't even think to ask me what I like to eat, just assumed that I like everything. Guess it looks like I'll be skipping supper tonight. Again.

After finally escaping to the solitude of my bedroom, I change into pajamas then relax against the window seat. The quietness of this house is really nice—different from the apartment in New York.

I turn on my phone. No missed calls or text messages. Remembering that I had told Hilarie I would call her back, I select her speed dial and hit send.

"Hello?" she answers, her scratchy voice sounding a bit rough.

"Hey, Hilarie." I twist my hair with my finger. "How've you been? Have you talked to your parents yet?"

"Yeah," she sighs. "I told them. My dad was upset, of course, but he actually took it better than my mom did. I guess it's not as hard on him, since he lives miles away and won't have to deal with it anyway. But Mom—she freaked out. She thinks it'd be easier just to cover everything up by getting an abortion."

I shake my head. "Hil, no—"

"I told her what your aunt said. She's been calming down a little. Both of them are furious with Josh, though. But everything's alright." She pauses, her last words not the least bit convincing. "How is your new summer life, by the way? I've been so involved with my problems, I've totally forgotten about your transition. Any hot guys?"

I smile, and give her the latest update on Whitney and her friends, Austin, my mom's letter, and even SummerThirst. Hilarie's not a Christian, but she isn't an atheist, either. Sort of like me, I guess. So I know I can tell her all this without fearing that she'll judge me.

"Sounds adventurous. Guys and God. Funny, I never thought of you much as the adventurous type. Or the religious type."

"Trust me, it's weird for me, too." I peer through the window. Half-covered by a cloud, the moon hovers between trees, a sight I can't see from my window in the city. "Hil,

I have to go. Oh, please tell Sarah and Mickey that I said thanks for keeping in touch with me."

She laughs. "I will. Love you, girl."

"You too. Bye."

After gathering Mom's letter, a pen, and paper, I sit back down at my window seat, keeping the door to my emotions locked up to prevent more tears as I reread the letter and write a reply.

I tell Mom almost the same details that I just shared with Hilarie about my new friends and the church. And about how much I am already in love with Lake Lure.

Mom and I don't ever really share many details of our personal lives, but I feel as though she deserves to at least know how my summer's going so far, especially since she poured her heart out to me in her letter.

My fingers ache as I continue to write with no concept of time. I tell her how much I forgive her and love her. I apologize for some of the words I've said to her in the past, and for not being the best daughter that I could be.

> *I never asked for a perfect mom. I just need a mom who is genuine, and will never stop loving me through all the pain in our lives. You've been that to me.*
>
> *I love and miss you!*
>
> *Your daughter,*
>
> *Selena Joy Taylor*

* * *

The morning sun greets SummerThirst as we gather in a woodland clearing next to Lake Lure Beach. I don't blame

Austin for taking so many snapshots of the beautiful scenery. It's all breathtaking, nothing like the endless clusters of buildings I'm accustomed to seeing every day when I go outside.

There's such a peace here—a peace I haven't felt since living in Kentucky with all of my family.

In front of the glistening lake, Cole and his band set up their instruments for praise and worship while Austin—as if reading my mind—stands up to take a picture of the sunlight shining through the morning mist just above the mountaintops.

"This is going to be a great day," he says after snapping a picture. He raises his head and looks out into the distance, breathing in the morning air with its accompanying peace, the same sense of peace that is warming my heart right now. "I can feel it."

I cross my legs on the grass, trying to hide the smile on my face. I wonder if only artists can feel peace like this—such a gentle, inconspicuous peace that an ordinary person might not even notice. It's nice to have someone like Austin who can relate to how I feel.

"I can't believe it's the last day." Audrey walks up from behind me and sits down. "It's gone by too quickly."

Brooke finally looks up from the notepad that she's been studying, her eyes lighting up. "I have an idea! Why don't we all hang out on your boat tomorrow, Austin?"

It seems as if I keep having to ruin the plans for everyone. "I can't. Already promised some friends I'd hang out with them."

Audrey lifts a hand to shade her eyes as a passing cloud overhead reveals the sun it had been hiding. "What about Saturday? Why don't you two spend the night with me Friday, then we could go out on the lake the next day?"

) Tessa Emily Hall

"Or, how about the girls sleep over at my—I mean, the Huiets' house," I say. "And Cole at your house with Austin. I'm sure Kori and Ben wouldn't mind if you spent the night."

Brooke clasps her hands together. "Perfect. Friday it is, then."

Audrey smiles. "Can't wait!"

"Everyone, listen up," Pastor Carson says into a microphone on the platform. He pauses for everyone to hush as we fix our attention on him. "In case you were wondering, we decided not to plan any activities for today in order to focus only on God, since it is the final day of SummerThirst. A few of our camp counselors are passing out pens and paper, so while the band plays, separate yourselves from your friends— yes, you can for five minutes, it won't be that hard—and write a letter to God. We aren't making you do anything with this letter, just keep it with you. But before you do that, let's pray."

This time as PC prays, I close my eyes and imagine what it would be like if I were one of the Christians, convinced that God hears every word we say. That He actually cares.

After the prayer, everyone stands up to find a place by themselves. It takes me a while before I finally find the perfect tree to sit under right next to the water. I watch as little kids play at the edge of the lake just a few feet away from us, splashing in the water.

Cole's band plays a soft melody, one that is familiar to me but I haven't heard in a while. It's a hymn we used to sing at Dad's church.

The one Dad used to sing to me when he'd rock me in the rocking chair at night.

I recognize it as soon as the first word is sung, but the band sings the hymn with a modern twist.

Closing my eyes, I allow the hymn to sink in as I rest my head against the tree behind me.

When I open my eyes, I notice a bird soaring above the lake with its wings spread wide. He flies toward me and lands on a tree branch just across from where I am sitting.

This song has definitely hit a soft spot for me, but I refuse to allow myself to get emotional. Not here.

Cole's band continues to play the hymn as I try to somehow convert my thoughts into words on paper—but I decide that, rather than writing a letter to God, I'll write a journal entry, perhaps place it in my abandoned diary when I get back to Brooklyn.

Ever since we moved to New York, I have carried such a weight of depression—that, for some reason, I haven't felt here in Lake Lure—I've gone through the past several years wondering if God exists at all. I can't believe I'm actually saying this, but now I think He does.

I reread what I just wrote, and shake my head. I wasn't even planning on writing that. I didn't even realize I felt that way until it was written down on paper.

I look across the stillness of water in front of me and listen to the chorus of the hymn before continuing to write the journal entry.

So, God, I haven't talked to You in forever, but I really need some intervention in my life. I'm afraid to trust You completely. It just seems like You've been so far away from my family. I want to know for sure that You are real, and that You are with me.

If You love me as much as everyone says You do, then prove it.

* * *

The letters of my initials are shaped onto my notebook from the blades of grass I've been pulling up during Pastor Carson's sermon. If I dare to look up at him, my hypersensitivity will kick in, and cause me to give in to his potential myths.

Many of my friends have called me gullible, and I know it's true. So why am I allowing myself to be swayed into wondering if what PC is proclaiming right now is the truth?

He closes in prayer as Cole's band comes to the stage and plays their acoustic set.

"If any one of you feels like you need a new start—if you would like to accept God's love—come up to the front of the platform. Find your group leader so they can pray with you."

I force myself to stay glued on this patch of grass. What are they trying to do? Embarrass us by letting these Christian kids know which of us are the bad ones?

My eyes widen as I look around. Two people have stood up, and are now heading down to the platform. One of them is in tears.

Pastor Carson repeats the invitation. "You can't be afraid, guys! If you need God, or if you feel you should recommit your life to Him, come down now."

A butterfly flutters in front of me. My hands tremble.

This is not something I would normally do—stand up in front of people, practically announcing that I'm a "sinner"—but I know that if I don't, then I'll regret it tomorrow.

I need a new start. This is why I came to Lake Lure, isn't it? Now is the perfect opportunity.

It's hard to get up and take the first step, but not as hard as what Mom is doing.

I'll do this for her.

My knees feel weak as I take one step at a time to where Lexie stands. Her teary eyes glisten, and she lays her hands on my shoulders. "Repeat after me."

We bow our heads together, and I repeat the prayer of salvation. Lexie then asks God to bless me and give me a new direction in life.

She looks up after finishing the powerful prayer that made me feel no different. It seems as if the prayer had more of an effect on her than on me, based on the water in her eyes.

Maybe she's just more experienced.

"Selena, I'm so proud of you." Her hands still lay flat on my shoulders. "Now, go begin your new life. I'll give you my number before we leave today, so you can call me any time you need a sister-to-sister chat."

I smile, hopefully convincing enough to make up for my lack of words. "Thanks."

She pats me on the shoulder before moving to pray for another teenager who stands beside me, bawling.

The band fades into another song. I turn around, coming face to face with Austin. He holds his arms out, offering me a hug that I fall right into. It's nice, inhaling his cologne, his arms wrapped around me. I smile, realizing that this is the first time we've hugged.

"Congratulations," he whispers, his breath tingling my cheek.

Perhaps the only reason I feel slightly emotional now is because of the atmosphere, but I know that I did the right thing. For Mom, for myself, and for my friends. "It's all thanks to you, Four-Eyed Brewer."

More teenagers join the mob up front, almost everyone raising their hands and singing along to the worship song.

God, I'm trying this out. I admit, I'm afraid—afraid to trust You, to become a true believer. Just please help things to get better in my life. That way I can trust You more, and know for sure that You exist. Amen.

Mom said that when I know what's right, then I should do it. If this actually works, I will know for a fact that it was what I was meant to do.

Besides, Austin will like me better if I'm a Christian like he is. Right?

Chapter 11

"Are your eyes open?"

I turn my head toward Austin. "Do they look like they're open? You tied this sweater way too tight around my eyes."

He chuckles. "That was the point."

I hold firmly onto the armrest of the car door as Austin's Jeep swerves then slows to a stop. "Are we there yet?"

"Maybe." The radio stops playing as he turns off the car ignition.

"How do I know you're not kidnapping me?" I feel around to unbuckle myself.

Austin slams his car door at the end of my sentence. I would usually never allow a guy to take me someplace in his car with a sweater tied around my eyes, especially not at nine o'clock at night, but this is Austin. He wanted to surprise me because, according to him, every new believer should have some sort of celebration in honor of beginning new life as a Christian.

The passenger door opens, and Austin takes my hand, guiding me out of the Jeep.

"Can I take this off now?" What if other people are watching me right now?

Austin places his hands on the back of my shoulders, steering me through what I assume is a parking lot. "Hold your nose."

"What?"

"I can hold it for you, if you'd like."

I let out a frustrated sigh and pinch my nose. A door opens, and my shoes click on tile floor. Austin continues to steer me a few more steps, then spins me around and unties the sweater that's obscuring my vision.

I release my nose as the blindfold falls from my eyes. The scent of strong coffee fills my nostrils before I can even see clearly again. We are standing behind the counter at Brewer's Coffee. A thrill rushes through me as I realize that no one else is here. I've never been in an empty coffee shop before, with access to the all of the coffee-making machines.

I turn to Austin, who is leaning back against the counter, arms folded across his chest. "You know, most guys don't surprise a girl by taking them to a coffee shop."

Dimples sink into his cheeks as he smiles. "And most girls wouldn't look as happy as you do over such a simple surprise as this."

I grin. "I guess that's true."

He turns his back to me and grabs a to-go cup from the stack. "So, if you had a choice to create any coffee or tea blend, what ingredients would you use?"

My fingers tap on the counter. "Well, mocha's my favorite. If I had to make my own drink, though, I'd probably want a latte with dark chocolate, peanut butter—a tad bit of caramel, maybe."

Austin places the cup in my hands, then begins to give me instructions on how to operate the espresso machine. He explains in detail how to steam milk and add flavored syrups and espresso to make my dream drink.

"Think you're ready?" he asks.

I didn't realize I was supposed to be memorizing everything. I bite my lip and turn back toward the complicated coffee-making robots, not able to recall anything Austin just taught me.

I raise my eyebrows. "You're going to help me, aren't you?"

"I'll help you steam the milk just this time, since that can be a little tricky. The rest is up to you. I explained the steps— now let's see if you can make your own."

I try to act as if I understand as Austin takes a stainless steel pitcher, partially filled with half-and-half, and inserts a steaming wand that makes weird noises as it heats the milk. He then tells me to go ahead and add the flavorings and espresso to my cup. I have to guess how much dark chocolate, caramel, and peanut butter syrup to use, along with how many shots of espresso. Then I carefully pour the steamed half-and-half into my new mixture, and add only a very thin layer of froth on top.

"Looks like I'm not that bad of a barista," I say, topping it off by adding a squirt of whipped cream, a swirl of chocolate, then quickly grabbing a small handful of mini chocolate chips before he can tell me that I'm adding too much.

Austin studies me as I put the lid on my coffee. "You still haven't tasted it yet," he says with a know-it-all smirk on his face.

My hands wrap around the warm drink as I raise the cup to my lips to take a careful sip. I wrinkle my nose as the bitter latte breaks through the whipped cream and meets my tongue.

"Just what I thought," Austin says, grabbing another cup from the stack. "You added way too much espresso and not enough syrup."

"Why can't I just fix this one instead of starting all over?"

"It has to be *perfect*."

I watch in horror as he takes the drink I just made and empties all of it down the drain. He guides me a little more closely this time as I make the drink, showing me exactly how much espresso to add, as well as just the right proportions of the syrup and steamed milk. But, after spilling the caramel syrup all over the counter, I begin to reconsider my dreams of owning a coffee shop.

"This better be good," I say when drink number two is complete.

I blow on the latte a bit before placing the lid onto the cup, then take a careful sip.

All of my friends know what a coffeeholic I am. I treat every coffee like it's the best I've ever had.

But this coffee is seriously—as Austin suggested—my *dream drink*. Not too sweet, not too bitter. And the rich taste of the coffee isn't overshadowed by the sweetness, either.

I close my eyes briefly to take another sip before giving the report. "Okay, Austin. If you don't think this one is perfect, then something is *seriously* messed up with your taste buds."

"Let me try it." He takes the cup from my hands and takes a sip, then looks as if he's actually having to think about whether or not it's good. "Not bad. Actually, that's pretty good. If only you lived here. My mom would hire you in a heartbeat after tasting this."

I grin at the thought.

We spend the next few minutes wiping off the mess we made on the counters. I catch myself tuning out Austin's voice and daydreaming what it would be like to work here with him, Audrey, and Brooke.

My latte has finally cooled down enough to drink as he drives us home. It's dark outside, peaceful. The thin sliver of a crescent moon is poised just above the lake.

"Do you know what the Spanish name for beautiful is?" Austin asks over the soft music coming from his stereo.

"I'm pretty sure it's bonita. Why?"

He slows the car while going up a curvy road. "The coffee you're drinking is officially named Luna Bonita Latte. Well, officially after I tell my mom."

"Wait—what?"

"You chose the drink's ingredients, so I get to make up the name."

I laugh. Luna Bonita Latte doesn't sound too bad, actually. "And why, exactly, are you naming it?" I have to take a careful sip as he comes to a halt at a stop sign.

"My mom adds one new drink to the menu every couple of months and takes one off. Luna Bonita Latte is going to be the new drink on the menu. And it'll stay there, permanently. I'll make sure of it. And you make sure not to lose the napkin that I gave you. I wrote a note for you on the inside of it. Don't read it until you get home. Sorry, I didn't have any paper."

"Austin—" I stare down at the cup in my hands. "I really don't deserve this."

"Of course you do, Selena."

I look back up at him again as he pulls into his driveway.

"Don't feel bad about it," he says, his dark brown eyes

capturing me as he takes the keys out of the ignition. "You always seem to feel guilty over the smallest things."

I start to open my mouth to defend myself, but decide to just keep it shut.

If only he knew the real reason I feel so bad about this. All I did was repeat a prayer.

Anyone can do that, can't they?

* * *

Three teenagers sitting on a blanket at the park with PB&J sandwiches, teddy grahams, and juice boxes is probably an interesting sight for the parents of the little kids playing around us. This doesn't seem to bother Hayden and Patrick, though. Patrick especially acts like he belongs here.

"What's a Farkle?" I ask after Hayden gives a five-minute speech on her plans for us today.

Patrick looks totally offended, his grape jelly-circled lips creating a perfect O. "You've never played Farkle before?" His words are muffled by a mouth filled with teddy grahams that crumble out as he speaks.

I laugh. "Can't say that I have."

"Patrick, that may be because we're the ones who invented the game."

He crinkles his eyebrows together as if he's confused at his girlfriend's response, then something finally seems to click in that tiny little brain of his. "Oh—"

She throws a teddy graham at him. "We actually stole the name from a dice game. But anyway, it's a dare game. You first choose a dare, then the group forms a circle and holds up either one or two fingers. The minority is out, and then they repeat the process of elimination. The last two people left in the circle have to play rock-paper-scissors. Whoever loses must do the dare. Got it?"

I nod slowly.

"Here." She takes Patrick's sandwich out of his mouth and drops it on the blanket. "We'll show you."

Hayden and her boyfriend do a demonstration of "Farkle" by holding up either one or two fingers, then playing rock-paper-scissors. I'm not sure why they couldn't just skip the beginning and go straight into the rock-paper-scissors to determine who does the dare, but I decide not to ask.

"More people usually want to join in playing as the game goes on."

Patrick folds his legs so he's sitting Indian-style. "We should make the first dare something, like, dangerous. Since no little kids are playing with us right now. How about—" He squeezes his empty juice box while trying to think up a dare. "Oh! I got one. Smoke a cigarette on the playground, then blow the smoke in a little kid's face."

I pop a teddy graham into my mouth. "I don't really think that'd be appropriate, Patrick."

"Why not?" Hayden asks, her dark outlined eyes looking at me as if I'm crazy. "It's not that genius, but I think it'll be fun. You have to do it to a kid in view, though."

"I don't know." I'll only look like a wimp if I don't play this silly little game with them. "Okay, fine."

The three of us create a circle—a triangle, rather—and begin the game. Hayden is the first one to go out, which means that Patrick and I have to do rock-paper-scissors to determine who will be the one to do the dare.

Patrick laughs before I can comprehend that his "scissors" have cut my "paper".

❭ Tessa Emily Hall

"Get out a cigarette, girl!"

I let out a groan while searching my purse for the pack of cigarettes Hayden loaned me. I don't think that this should count as breaking my promise to Mom again, since it's not really my idea. "I don't have a lighter."

Hayden tosses hers. "Here."

"Thanks." Not really.

I'm sure that God would not approve of this.

Trying to convince myself it's only a game, I take a practice drag and blow it right in Patrick's face. He coughs.

"That's what you get for coming up with this disgusting dare." I jump up from the picnic blanket and head toward the playground.

Why me? Smoking on playgrounds has to be illegal.

My pace slows as I approach the playground area. Innocent little kids' laughter fills the air, not making this dare any easier. *God, please forgive me for this sin I'm about to commit.*

After finding my victim near the swings, I squat down on his level and smile at him. "Hi, what's your name?"

He pushes up his glasses. "Noah."

My shaking fingers put the cigarette to my mouth, and I inhale. "And how old are you, Noah?" As I talk, the smoke goes directly into the poor little boy's face.

He starts coughing, shooing away the smoke with his hand. "You're not supposed to smoke at the park, lady."

"Oh, right. I'm sorry. Don't ever smoke, okay?"

I pat his head, throw the cigarette down in the grass, then smash it into the ground with my foot. Noah looks at me curiously before running back to the playground.

"You guys are sick," I tell Hayden and Patrick, rejoining them on the picnic blanket.

Patrick puts his hands together in a clap. "No, dude. That was awesome."

Fortunately, the new dares we choose are much more innocent than the first one. Even some of the kids from the playground join us, including Noah. Later, though, the game dwindles down as the kids begin to leave.

"Okay," Hayden says to the last two kids left in our Farkle game. "This is the last round."

"Oh!" A chubby boy standing next to Patrick raises his hand as if Hayden is his teacher. "This dare should be to take a picture of that old lady over there after telling her that she's beautiful." He points to the elderly couple sitting on a bench near the pond.

Hayden smiles. "Perfect."

All of us hold our hands up for the final round of Farkle, and watch as the chubby boy's paper covers Patrick's rock.

"Are you serious?" Patrick groans as the rest of us laugh. "I've lost the last three dares! Fine. Give me your camera." He snatches it from Hayden's hands as if it were all her fault that he lost the dare, then puts on a fake smile and skips away toward the couple. His black hair, streaked with red highlights, swishes with each skip.

We watch as Patrick talks briefly to the old woman, takes a picture with her, then shakes her hand before skipping back over to us with a wide grin.

"Her husband looked at me like, 'Dude, why are you flirting with my wife?'" He holds up the camera for all of us to see the picture. "It was hilarious."

I think what's hilarious is the way we're able to find humor in such ridiculous dares.

) Tessa Emily Hall

After the three of us say goodbye to our new Farkle buddies, we take out the kites Hayden brought and find a large field nearby where a young couple is throwing a Frisbee. We fly our kites with no concept of time—running, giggling, gazing in awe as our kites soar, dive, then fly even higher on the evening breezes.

It feels free, enjoying life with only an occasional knot or tangle that is quickly fixed. How I long to be that kite.

It's not until Patrick suggests that we stop and feed the ducks our leftover sandwich bread that the magical moment disappears, suddenly forced into the past with my childhood memories.

It's hard for me to relent as Hayden takes the purple kite from my hands and packs it into her picnic basket—but once we reach the pond, I notice the perfect reflection in the water of the sun setting behind the mountains. Although I've seen this sight several times since arriving in Lake Lure, I don't think I could ever take it for granted.

"So this is what you guys usually do for fun?" I throw half a piece of bread into the pond, and watch as the entire flock swims over to it. "Play at the park on a summer day?"

She laughs. "I haven't been on that playground since I was a kid. But when Patrick and I aren't at a party, or when I'm not at work, we usually do random things like this. Life is too short, you know? You have to make the best of it." She brushes a black strand of hair from her face before dropping a whole piece of bread into the water. "Do things most teenagers wouldn't do."

I don't think I've ever met a Goth girl who is so adventurous and enthusiastic about life.

Patrick sits on the dirt, a piece of bread hanging from his mouth rather than from a duck's beak. "You haven't played on the playground since we were little, Hayden? Why don't we go now? There aren't many kids over there anymore."

"Actually, I should probably head back." I drop the last of my bread into the water. "I'm not sure what time the Huiets want me to come home, but it's already starting to get dark."

Now breadless, Patrick jumps up and runs toward a group of ducks, causing them to scurry into the water for safety.

"Well, the next time we hang out, we should definitely play on the playground." Hayden closes the plastic bag containing the loaf of bread. "Apparently that's where my boyfriend belongs."

He spins around. "Why do you have to say that, Hayden? You know, we've had a great day of no arguing. Why do you have to start something now?"

She shoves the picnic blanket at him. "I'm not starting anything, Patrick. You're the one that said you wanted to play on the playground, not me. Now something has started. And it's your fault."

"Yeah, just like everything else. Always my fault."

It's a struggle for me to keep from laughing as they argue over nothing. When we reach Hayden's car, the sky is completely dark, and I start feeling sorry that I told them I had to leave. It's not like Uncle Ben and Aunt Kori would even notice if I stayed out late.

Hayden rolls down her window, allowing her cigarette smoke to blow into the evening air as we exit the park. I roll down my window as well, hoping to inhale fresh air and trying hard not to think about how relaxing a smoke would be right now.

Cigarette smoke. Screamo music—the same kind Jeremy used to listen to.

I place a hand over my right wrist to cover up the scar, as well as the memories.

* * *

The back door slams shut as soon as I open the front door.

Stepping inside the den, I see Whitney, hands covering her face. Crying.

"What's wrong?"

"Why do you care?" All sympathy I had towards her vanishes as she looks up at me. "Where have you been these past couple of days, anyway? I thought you and I were becoming friends. But no, you would rather hang out with freaks than be with your own cousin."

The scent from her strong perfume lingers in my nostrils as she stomps past me and runs up the stairs. I stand frozen, unable to figure out what I could have done to cause her to become so upset.

I swing open the back door. A summer night breeze greets me, sending shivers up my spine. Pitiful doubts flood my mind, the kind that demand attention, no matter how badly I want them to leave me alone. It's as if someone is standing next to me, whispering over and over, *"What were you thinking? There will never be a new beginning. This is reality, Selena. Temptation. Rejection. Horrible memories that won't fade away. Scars are permanent. None of this will ever go away."*

The letter.

My body almost jerks as I remember that I have yet to read the letter Austin wrote to me. Perhaps this will help to give me some hope. I take the napkin from inside my purse, and run down the porch steps and into the Huiets' back lawn.

My eyes squint, trying their best to make out the handwritten words on the napkin, but it's useless. The only light available comes from the moon and a few boats on the lake in the distance.

I look down at the grass and walk back toward the house, but before I reach the steps, I sense a nearby presence and slowly raise my head. A bulky figure stands just a few feet in front of me, right next to the porch steps.

I back away.

And let out a scream.

Chapter 12

The dark figure jumps toward me and blocks my scream by pressing his large hand on my mouth. "Shhh, it's just me."

He removes his hand, enabling me to see him more clearly.

I let out a deep breath. Those bluish-green eyes could only belong to one person. "What are you doing here, Richard?"

"Jeez, girl. What are you so jumpy for?"

"Sorry. I've lived in Brooklyn too long."

My heart thuds, even though I'm not in danger.

At least, I don't think I am.

"Why are you out here?" I ask, cramming Austin's letter back into my purse.

"Well, I *was* with Whitney."

"Wait, are you the reason she was crying?" I have to look almost straight up in order to make eye contact with this guy.

He looks out at the lake behind me, and scratches his head. "It's a long story," he says, his piercing gaze now landing right on me. This doesn't exactly make it any easier for me to calm my racing heart. "Follow me, and I'll explain it to you."

"*Follow* you?"

He nods, and walks backward, but somehow manages to keep those gorgeous eyes focused on me. "I need someone to talk to. Whitney—well, she just dumped me. And there isn't exactly anyone else I can—" He stops, and lets out a sigh. "Look. I know that you and I hardly even know each other. And I probably sound so ridiculous to you right now. But, I mean—Whitney breaks up with me. I go outside to leave, and hear someone walking down the steps. Thinking it's her, I come back over here, but see that it's you."

I blink.

"In other words, you seem like the perfect person to talk to about this. And since I don't know you very well, I know that you won't judge me."

Although what he said makes little sense, I continue following him. "So you're saying that you want me to walk with you?"

"Just around the neighborhood." He turns around and heads toward the driveway.

I give in, and walk fast to catch up with him. "So tell me. Why did she break up with you?"

"That's just it. I have no clue. All she said was that she was tired of dating me. Well, not in those exact words, but we've dated all through high school, and I just think she's ready for a break. I can take a hint. She even started her fake crying to make me think she really cares." He shakes his head. "But I know she doesn't."

"I'm sorry." I try to make my voice sound sympathetic rather than enthusiastic. It's not that easy.

"Shouldn't surprise me, though. I've never been good enough for anyone."

Yeah. I doubt that's true. "I don't see why she would want

to break up with you. I barely know you, and I can already tell that you're a really great guy."

He looks down at me. "You think so?"

I nod, crossing my arms as he steps a little closer, which makes the moment even more awkward.

"You know, Selena, you're a pretty cool girl yourself."

I want to say thanks, but I'm afraid my voice will shake.

He slows his pace to a stop for a moment, and reaches into his pocket. I take this time to look behind us, at how far we've walked.

I have to admit, it's kind of creepy how there are trees everywhere in Lake Lure. I don't really feel comfortable with Richard like I am with Austin.

"Want one?"

I face him, watching as he lights a cigarette. Why must everyone smoke in this town? "Um, no, thanks."

"Smoking is comforting on nights like this. Just sayin'."

I dig my teeth into my bottom lip, but the pain becomes unbearable. "Fine. I'll take you up on that offer."

"You sure?" he raises his eyebrows at me, and reaches into his pocket.

No, I want to say, but I nod, ignoring the voice in my head that tells me to refuse. "Guess I could use at least one."

He grins, handing me a cigarette and his lighter. "You know how to use that thing?"

I respond by placing the cigarette in between my lips and lighting it.

"No offense or anything, but, uh, you don't seem like the type of girl who would smoke."

I hate it when people say that. It only makes me want to prove them wrong. "You don't seem like the type of guy who would get his heart broken."

He takes the lighter from me, and puts it back into his pocket. "That's true."

We continue walking again without either of us saying anything, only listening to the chirping of crickets and the sound of a few cars in the distance. As the number of houses around us decreases, my nervousness increases. I try not to make it obvious that I do not want to get too close to Richard physically, but I'm sure he can tell by the way I drift away every time he steps nearer.

"Is it okay if I, sort of, you know, vent my feelings to you?" he asks, his voice sounding a bit deeper than before. Almost as if it is a struggle for him to ask me that.

I inhale the cigarette smoke deeply before responding. "Sure."

"Okay. See, I'm considered a jock at school."

"Really?" I look up at him, widening my eyes. "With muscles like those? I never would've guessed."

He laughs. "But, the thing is, I don't really even care about sports. My parents have always forced me to play them, ever since I was a kid, but—" He pauses, as if pondering whether or not he should admit all of this to me. "I really love art."

"You mean, more than football?"

"See, *that* would be the reaction if I told people. But, yes, I do. I love it. I had a big argument with my parents today about me not wanting to play football this year. I just need a break. But they wouldn't hear of it, especially since I'm a senior and all. The truth is, I don't want to play college football. Not sure if I even plan on going to college."

He takes a long drag from his cigarette. "So I came over here and asked Whitney what she thought about all of this. Told her how I really feel about art. I spilled my guts out, Selena." He shakes his head. "She started crying. Said that, since she's a cheerleader, she should have a boyfriend who's on the football team."

"I'm not surprised. She only cares about what other people think."

"I just wish someone could like me for who I am, you know?" His voice softens and seems to become more sincere. "Not because of my reputation or my muscles. Or even my position on the football team."

The closer the Huiets' lake house comes into view, the slower Richard's steps become.

"I understand that, Richard. You just want to be accepted."

"Exactly!"

My stomach churns as he places his hand on my shoulder. "You get it, don't you?"

I throw my cigarette butt on the road and nod, trying to convince myself that his hand on my shoulder is only a big-brother gesture type of thing. Nothing more.

We walk up to the front yard, and he now places both of his hands in mine, twirling me around to face him. "Where've you been, Selena? I've needed you for so long. You seem to understand me so much already."

My heart pounds. How can Austin not like him? Richard's so cute and innocent, way different from any other jock I've ever met.

Not to mention, one of the best-looking jocks I've ever met.

"Well, I should probably get going," I say, releasing my hands from his as I back away.

His smile falls. Before I can say goodbye, he steps closer, filling in the space between us. "There's something about you, Selena."

I swallow. "What do you mean?"

He brushes a strand of hair away from my face, then places his fingers underneath my chin.

"Richard, I—"

He leans down, placing his lips on mine.

He doesn't even give me a chance to resist.

Not that I'd have the strength to, anyway.

"We can't do this." I pull away before he has time to go any further. "I mean, you and Whitney *just* broke up. It's not right."

"But it feels right, doesn't it?" His shoulders give a light shrug. "So what's the point in waiting?"

I tilt my head, wishing he'd realize how wrong this is.

Or that I'd allow myself to appreciate that Richard just kissed me, rather than over-analyzing it so much.

"You're right," he says, shoving his hands in his pockets. "I'm such an idiot sometimes. See you later."

He glances at me only once more before heading over to his car in the driveway. I'm left frozen under the moonlight, lips still tingling from the kiss, wondering if this has all just been a dream.

"Wait!" I yell, chasing after him before he has the chance to open his car door.

He does not deserve to get rejected twice in one night.

) Tessa Emily Hall

He spins around. "Wha—"

I throw my arms around his neck, pulling his face to mine for another kiss that tastes like cigarette smoke.

"Wow," he says when I pull away. "You're a better kisser than Whitney."

"Same with you. I mean, I've never kissed Whitney, of course—"

He laughs. "So, I'll see you around?"

"Yes." I nod, perhaps a bit too eagerly.

After exchanging numbers with each other, we give one last goodbye wave—and peck on the cheek—before he gets in his car and drives away.

I can't help but smile as I walk back toward the Huiets' backyard. Just as I'm about to go back up the steps, I hear something shuffle several yards on my right. I look up, watching as something scurries behind a tree. A neighbor's pet, possibly?

Or maybe I'm only imagining things, still a little on edge from the scare with Richard.

Still, I hurry up the porch stairs until I reach the house and am safe.

* * *

I haven't had a sleepover in forever.

In New York, friends sleep over, or I spend the night at their apartments, but we usually don't consider it anything special, or even fun—just an escape from our own families for a night.

The last time I had a sleepover with more than one other girl, and at a *house*, I lived in Kentucky.

"No, Brooke, I said *two* eggs." Audrey lets out a frustrated sigh.

"Oh. Whoops." Brooke drops the egg shells into the trash. "Guess we're gonna have to eat very cakey brownies."

"It's okay," Audrey says, stirring the brownie mix over the Huiets' counter. "Sorry, I'm a perfectionist when it comes to cooking."

As I help pour the mix into a pan, the front door clicks open, and then Uncle Ben comes into the kitchen to set his briefcase down on the table. "Brownies?" he asks, looking at me.

"Yep. Uncle Ben, this is my friend Brooke. And you know Audrey."

"Yes. Nice to meet you, Brooke." He gives them each a small nod before heading into his bedroom.

Audrey puts the brownies into the oven as Brooke and I help ourselves to some leftover mix from the bowl. The front door slams shut again, and Whitney struts into the kitchen, blond hair flipping with each confident click of her heels. It's as if the kitchen is her runway, and we are her audience.

Without looking at any of us, she goes straight to a cabinet and pulls out a glass. "You know, eating after seven o'clock is really unhealthy." She sets the cup down to pour a drink. "You're actually eating the mix? That's just gross. You know you're eating raw eggs, right?"

"I would assume so," Brooke says, batter smeared across her lips, reminding me of Patrick yesterday at the park with the jelly all around his mouth. "Since, you know, we were the ones who cracked the eggs and emptied them into this bowl."

Whitney spins around and looks at Brooke as if she's *shocked* that someone would have the guts to talk to her that way. "Who are you?"

She hops off the counter. "Brooke James. You know, the girl who was in your chemistry, geometry, and theater classes this past year."

"Nope." Whitney pivots around to set her cup in the sink. "Don't remember. And, just so you know, our counter is *not* a chair."

"What? *Really?*" Brooke asks, gasping as if she just realized this. "I'm so sorry. Guess I just got confused, considering they look *so similar* to each other."

Whitney looks as if she's about to say something back, but instead shuts her mouth and gives Brooke a harsh glare before stomping off her make-believe runway.

Brooke raises her brows at me. "Whitney Huiet is your cousin?"

I nod. "Unfortunately."

"Ugh. That's just horrible," she says, licking the brownie mix off her fingers.

"Yes, I know. Thanks for the reminder."

* * *

I lie awake, unable to fall asleep—and not just because I'm sharing the bed with Brooke and Audrey, who keep tugging on the comforter. I mentally replay the truth-or-dare game the three of us just played. Well, more like *truth*. Many interesting questions were asked, but one in particular lingers in my head.

"No," I said after Brooke asked me if I had a boyfriend. "I broke up with my ex, Jeremy, last summer. Haven't had one since."

"Why did you break up with him?" she said, dropping crumbs all over my bed as she devoured probably her sixth brownie.

I blinked, wishing this game wasn't called *truth*. "I guess because the relationship was getting too—unhealthy. And it was hard to, like, trust him with certain areas of my life."

"Do you have a crush on anyone?" she then asked, catching me off guard.

I laughed, but only to cover up how uncomfortable I felt answering these questions. "I don't know. I mean, I haven't really given it much thought."

Yes, that was a lie. I had given it thought. Much thought, in fact. Especially these past few days. But why should I share every little detail of my love life with these two girls whom I barely even know?

Of course, Brooke didn't believe me. She just wiped the milk mustache from above her lips and gave me an unconvinced look. "But you're a girl, Selena. I mean, I'd understand it if I didn't think about these things, but come on. Almost all of those sketches you drew had to do with fairy tales. You're romantic. I can tell."

I shrugged. "I guess I just let whatever happens happen. Play it by ear." My thoughts went to Richard last night, when he kissed me.

But that's not what is to blame for my clouded mind tonight.

It's what Audrey said next.

"Selena." She looked down at me from the window seat. "I have to tell you something, but you have to promise not to say anything."

I nodded.

"My brother—he used to be crazy about you. Used to talk about you nonstop when you lived here before. I know that was, like, what, eight years ago? But from the way he looks at you, I can tell he still has feelings for you. It's strange. He's never had a girlfriend." Her dirty blond hair swishes back and forth as she shakes her head. "Ever."

I wanted to burst into a smile when she told me this. "Seriously?"

"Why do you look so shocked?" Brooke asked. "Of course he likes you! You don't see him constantly talking to *me*, do you?"

"I guess not. I mean, I thought he was just being polite." And trying to make me become a Christian. I wanted to say this, but I was afraid it might offend them.

"Well? Do you like him?" Brooke flopped down on her stomach, waiting for me to give her a response.

I looked around my room, trying to come up with something that would satisfy them. Instead, a stupid grin sneaked up my lips and decided not to leave.

"All right," I said, embarrassed by being put on the spot. "Enough about me. Audrey, is there anyone that you like?"

She bit her lip. "Ummm."

"Come on," Brooke said. "We won't tell anyone. Promise!"

One of those secret-revealing-smiles snuck up Audrey's lips also. "Yeah, but Brooke, you're the one person I wouldn't want to tell—"

Brooke's grin vanished as her jaw dropped. "No!"

"Please, please don't tell him, Brooke! Cole is just—"

"Wait a minute—*Cole*? As in, Brooke's brother?" I couldn't help but laugh. "Sorry, it's just that he's total opposite of you. I think you two would be cute together, though. But he's just all like—"

"Total music freak, weird, and disgusting?" Brooke completed my sentence.

"Yeah, sort of. And you're, like, all quiet and sweet and total opposite of weird and disgusting."

Audrey blushed. "I know. But I really can't help it, you guys! I've always liked him. He's the type of guy that has always intrigued me." She looks down at the pillow in her lap. "Great singer and musician, Godly, funny, outgoing, different from other guys. Not to mention really, really cute." She looks back up at us now, the corners of her mouth still turned up. "Opposites do attract, don't they?"

"Audrey," I said, "if you like him, then why don't you tell him? He probably likes you, too."

"Yeah, right. He's probably into girls with funky hair and nose piercings."

Brooke sets her plate full of brownie crumbs down on my nightstand. "Actually, he's always had a thing for shy, innocent-type girls, like you. Plus, he's more attracted to blondes. Although I'm totally and completely against the idea of you dating my brother for your own sake, I think you should talk to him if you like him that much."

"You really think so?" Audrey's voice sounds higher, more hopeful.

Brooke and I nod in unison.

"Okay," she laughed, her cheeks still pink from the confession. "It's your turn, Brooke. Do you have a crush on anyone?"

She adjusted her posture, then went on to explain how she doesn't believe in dating at this age, and how she has other things to focus on: God, school, sports, and modeling.

I couldn't help but shake my head. "You have strong opinions on just about everything, don't you?"

"Is that a bad thing?"

"No, it's just I admire you for that. I mean, for not wanting to get involved with anyone. I don't think that would be at all possible for me. Like you said, I'm too romantic." It's impossible for a girl like me to *not* fall for a guy.

"What time is it?" Audrey asked, yawning. "We should probably go to bed soon if we're going to the lake early tomorrow morning."

Brooke and I took Audrey's motherly advice and went to bed.

Since then, my mind has not been able to stop thinking about the fact that Austin might like me. Even hearing that he liked me when we were little gives me a rush of excitement.

I reach over to the nightstand and pull on my sleeping mask. After lying there for a few more minutes, I finally realize that the mask does not block out my thoughts.

It's useless trying to get any sleep.

I slip out of the bed quietly and sit at the window seat, looking out at what Dad used to call God's fingernail in the sky. Thoughts about Austin whirl inside of my head, almost making me feel bad about being with Richard last night. I shouldn't, though. I mean, it wasn't anything other than sympathy. There's no real connection between the two of us anyway.

Yet, even as I try to convince myself, I have a strange feeling there might be a little something between us.

And I don't know if I should feel hopeful about this—or terrified.

Chapter 13

Memories of living on the lake in the summer come back the next morning as I sit in the back of Austin's boat next to Brooke and Audrey, trying to keep my balance as we go over waves. The heat from the sun, the rush of the wind that blows my hair back, and cool drinks in the summer humidity remind me again why I love summertime at Lake Lure.

"How in the world did you make this fruit smoothie?" I ask Audrey after slurping the last sip through the straw, having to yell over the boat's engine and Jack Johnson's voice singing through the radio.

Brooke answers for her. "Audrey has some secret ingredients that you'd rather not know about."

"Well, it must be so secret that *I* don't even know about them, Brooke. To make a strawberry smoothie, Selena, you only need three ingredients." She holds up her fingers and lists them. "Those, my friend, are strawberries, yogurt, and lots of crushed ice."

"Creative," I tease.

My eyes shut as I lay my head back, allowing the rush of the wind to relax me. I'm just about to fall asleep when I hear a loud thump and look up to see Cole—who was sitting next to Austin—trying to step over us as he carries his fruit smoothie in one hand. A passing boat causes our boat to jump the wake, forcing him to fall. His drink leaps out of the cup and splashes all over Brooke.

She gasps and jumps up. "You jerk!"

Audrey and I look at each other and start laughing along with Cole. Which, of course, only makes Brooke even more upset.

She narrows her eyes at us. "This is not funny, you guys. You did this on purpose, Cole!"

"No, Brooke! I tripped. Promise."

Even though I witnessed the stumble myself, Cole doesn't sound very convincing through his heavy laughter.

"There are a few towels in the back," Austin yells. "Clean it up if it spilled on the seat."

Brooke shoots Cole a glare, then stomps over to Austin sitting behind the wheel. "All you care about is the seat? Stop the boat. I want to jump in the water and get all of this stickiness off of me."

Brooke and Cole dive into the water right when Austin stops the boat. I take off the tank top covering my swimsuit, and decide to get in the old-fashioned way—little by little. I lower myself down a ladder that hangs from the edge of the boat, and get chills as soon as my feet touch the top of the water.

Audrey sits next to me, her legs dangling just above the water. "Are you getting in?"

"I would, but I'm not sure if—"

Austin runs right in between Audrey and me, taking a jump into the water.

"Austin!" Audrey leaps to her feet. "I'm all wet now. And the water is freezing!"

"You wouldn't be as cold if you would actually *get in* the water." He backstrokes away from us, obviously unaffected by the water's temperature, or by his sister's annoyance.

I shake my head. "That's easier said than done."

"Can't be that hard. The three of us just did it." He flips to his stomach and swims away to break up the dunking fight between Brooke and Cole.

Audrey laughs. "Now I'm definitely not getting in."

"I don't think I will, either." I lean back, allowing the sun to soak up the water that was splashed on me.

"Selena, what are they up to?" Audrey asks.

I open my eyes. Austin, Cole, and Brooke are huddled together in the water, whispering to each other. Then they look at Audrey and me, and begin to swim in our direction.

I jump to my feet. "Oh, no."

We back away, but it's too late. Cole and Austin charge toward us and jump up onto the boat.

"No!" I yell as Austin scoops me up in his arms. If I weren't about to be thrown into the cold lake, I would appreciate this moment in Austin's arms.

Audrey and I scream right before we hit the water—me being thrown in by Austin, and she by Cole. I come up as fast as I can, trembling from the cold.

"That wasn't funny," I tell Austin through chattering teeth. He only smiles at me, as if he did me a favor.

"Who's ready for some tubing?" Brooke walks up next to Austin, holding one tube in each of her hands.

Audrey and I look at each other and groan.

Thirty minutes later, we lie across a tube in the water, waiting for Austin to start the boat's engine. I say a desperate prayer as I hold on for dear life and fly across waves.

"*Aaagghh!*" I squeeze my eyes shut so I don't freak out over the end of my life. My grip tightens around the tube's handles as it carries Audrey and me over the rough waves, almost bouncing us off the tube and into the lake.

Please, dear Lord. I really don't feel like dying today. Thanks.

The moment I open my eyes, I see Audrey's body flying into the air as she screams. A panic rushes through me. What am I supposed to do?

Just as she hits the water head first, my hands start slipping out of the handles. With all my strength, I force myself to grab tighter as more choppy waves approach.

But it's useless.

As soon as the tube hits the wave, I soar above the lake and take a not-so-graceful belly flop into the water.

I try my best to get out of the water as fast as possible, in desperate need of breathing. Audrey swims to catch up with me as we wait for Austin to turn around and pick us up.

"That was hilarious," he laughs, pulling us up onto the boat.

Cole throws us a towel. "Nicely done, girls."

"Thanks," I say, running the towel through my wet, tangled hair.

Brooke crunches on potato chips in the back of the boat, and holds up her free hand. "High fives for the most entertaining falls I've ever witnessed."

Audrey laughs. "Trust me, I've had way worse tube falls. Lake sports just aren't my thing."

My hair flies back in the wind as Cole takes the wheel of the boat. Instead of joining Brooke and Audrey's conversation, I take in this moment. It feels almost as if I'm on a rollercoaster, going up and down, feeling the wind tangle my hair.

The boat comes to a stop when Cole finds what he calls "his island". Brooke and Audrey decide to stay on the boat and eat while I join Austin and Cole on the island, only so I can check my phone for missed calls or text messages. To my surprise, I actually have service.

After seeing that Richard has tried calling me, I go over on the other side of the island, away from where Austin and Cole are throwing rocks into the water. Hopefully they'll be too involved with their games to realize I'm on the phone.

"Hey, beautiful," Richard's voice says after the second ring.

My heart soars with his new nickname for me. "Hey. Did you call?"

No answer.

"Richard? Hello? Hold on, I must not be able to hear you." I walk further away from Austin and Cole until the fuzziness on the other end has cleared. "Can you hear me now?"

"Be ready at seven."

"Seven?"

"I thought that you might want to go see a movie with me."

I smile. "Sounds good to me."

"Make sure you don't mention this to Whitney."

"I won't," I say, kicking a rock into the water. "See you later."

After hitting the "end" button, I turn around—my smile completely vanishing as my gaze meets Austin's.

"So, how's your new boyfriend?"

Chapter 14

Austin spits the word *boyfriend* out of his mouth as if it is the most nauseating word he has ever tasted.

It takes me a few seconds to figure out what to say. I cross my arms. "You know Richard isn't my boyfriend."

"Oh, so *that* would explain the kiss I saw a couple nights ago."

My jaw drops as I remember the figure I saw the other night that ran behind the bushes. "I cannot believe you were spying on me!"

He kicks a rock with his foot. "I was not spying. I heard a scream earlier, so I ran outside to see who it was. When I saw you with Richard, I decided to hang around at the lake for a little while 'til I knew for a fact you were okay."

I narrow my eyes at Austin, not the least convinced that his spying on me was innocent.

"Besides, I'm always outside at night," he continues. "It's the best time to talk to God—or catch some teenagers making out."

I feel the sun burning my shoulders, but that is the least of my concerns right now. "For your information, Richard and

I are *not* dating. Whitney had just broken up with him, and he needed some comfort. That's all."

"Right." He gives a bitter laugh. "Some sympathy comfort, or a sympathy *kiss*?"

I tense. What do *you* know about kissing, Four-Eyed-Brewer?

"I warned you already. That boy is nothing but trouble."

"And I assume that you know him personally to be qualified to make that sort of judgment." I lower my head, keeping my gaze on Austin. "Am I right?"

He opens his mouth, but I speak instead.

"Didn't think so. Not all football players are the same, you know." I lower my voice a notch, looking around in hope that none of the others hear us arguing. "Richard happens to be a sweet guy with a nice heart. It might lead to something more, it might not. That's why I agreed to go to the movies with him tonight. Just to find out."

"*Movies?*" From the tone of Austin's voice, I think he's got the role of playing my dad down pat.

I nod, actually enjoying the look of jealousy on his face.

"I was right." He shakes his head. "You must be *very* talented at doing two things at the same time, especially in your ability to be at both practice and the movies tonight."

Oh, great. I completely forgot about my stupid commitment to this skit thing. "Okay, I forgot. But I can't just call him back and cancel our plans just because you're trying to make me feel bad about this whole thing." Well, I could. But I'd rather not. "I'll try to make it up to you."

Austin takes a step closer to me. "Too bad *I'm* not the one you're going to have to make it up to." He glances over his shoulder toward the boat. "Tonight's practice is important. I can almost guarantee that Brooke is going to be furious with you."

Why can't Christians just mind their own business? "Well, you aren't going to tell her why I'm missing it, are you?"

"I will if she asks. I'm not going to lie, Selena."

Of course not. Because you're *way* too perfect for that.

He stares at me a little longer before finally backing away. "You can't have both lifestyles. It's either one or the other. Take your pick."

* * *

I take one last look in the mirror to make sure my makeup and hair are perfect. Richard's type is obviously perfection, based on his previous dating choice. I've decided to wear a brown designer top that I bought the other day at the mall, along with a pair of skinny jeans. Whitney was determined that I buy these jeans. They're so tight around my legs that I can barely even sit down—but if she's gotten guys with this look, then I'm sure it'll be worth it.

My phone rings on the dresser. I know who it is without even having to look at it.

"I'm here," Richard says after I answer. "Parked in front of the house across from theirs. Hurry, I don't want Whitney to know."

"Coming."

I throw my phone into my purse, and smile at my reflection in the mirror. I may not be making the right choice, but Richard isn't as bad as some of the guys out there. Besides, I can't let this whole religion thing make me judgmental, as Austin seems to be.

"You look great," he says when I open the passenger door, keeping his gaze locked on me as I pull down the seat belt.

"You don't look too bad yourself."

Buzzed blond hair, handsome jaw line, and bluish-green eyes that could make any girl fall in love with him. He gives one last smile of approval at me before pressing the gas, not going as fast as his ex does in this neighborhood.

We arrive at the theater ten minutes before seven, just the right amount of time for him to buy our tickets and the popcorn. There are barely any seats taken when we enter the theater, which makes me wonder why Richard leads me toward the row at the very top.

"I like being up here for special reasons," he says as we sit down.

I force a smile so he'll think I'm not nervous, but I'm only fooling myself. The way he said those words creeped me out a little bit. I know I'm probably just being paranoid, but how do I know for sure I can trust someone like him?

"Is your seat broken or something?" Richard hovers over my shoulder as I twist and struggle to get situated in the padded seat.

I lean back. "It's just a little unbalanced. It'll work, though."

"Why don't I just move down a seat?"

"No, it's all right. I'm fine." Grasping the popcorn bag in my hands, I scoot as far away from his face as I can without making it obvious.

My hands shake lightly as I throw the popcorn into my mouth. If I take my time eating this, then perhaps Richard will be so into the movie that he won't try making any moves on me.

My plan is almost as useless as this theater seat. Just as I lean over to take a sip of my Pepsi, Richard's arm sneaks through mine. I cringe as his hand glides down to meet mine.

My eyes meet his as I glance up, trying to convince myself that he's just the same, adorable Richard that I drooled over when he was with Whitney.

"Selena—" his breath warms my cheek.

I swallow at the intensity in his eyes, in his voice. "Yes?"

He draws his face closer, then presses his lips against mine. The salty, butter popcorn taste of the kiss creates an unsettling feeling in the pit of my stomach. I pull away, my heart pounding as if I am drowning. "What is it?"

He glances at the movie screen—which is now showing previews—then back at me. "Well, I wasn't planning on telling you here, but—"

I almost tell him never mind, that I'd rather not hear whatever it is. Especially not here, not now.

But he clasps my hand more firmly. "I can really find myself falling in love with you, Selena."

The beautiful way he said those words almost numbs the uneasiness that I feel, and I am shocked into silence.

"Did you hear me?" Although his voice is a whisper since the theater is now quiet, I can tell he's offended at my lack of response.

I swallow the dryness in my throat. "Uh huh."

He frowns, the intensity in his eyes now transformed into sadness. Richard stares at me for only a second longer before putting his attention back on the screen as the movie begins.

Since I seemed to have ruined Richard's mood, I grab his hand to show that I do care for him.

I have a hard time fully giving my attention to the movie. Instead, I'm enjoying how this feels, my hand in Richard's. Being on my first date since Jeremy.

Sure, he may be wanting things to go a bit too fast. But why is that so bad? It's only because he needs me right now. And he must really care for me. He needs someone to understand him. Someone who won't pressure him to be someone else, as my cousin apparently did.

Besides, Richard and Jeremy are completely different people. The reason I first connected with Jeremy was because his dad was a drunk—just like my mom. But what I *didn't* know was that his dad was physically abusive. I also didn't know that Jeremy had anger problems, or that he, too, could become a bit too aggressive when he was drunk.

Richard doesn't seem like that type. He seems like the sensitive guy, the kind that you would drool over in a chick-flick. The one who comes across as a tough ladies' man, but is actually a softie, an artist. Someone who doesn't have a huge ego like other jocks.

And he certainly isn't Jeremy.

Then why is it that I still cannot rationalize this discomfort? Perhaps it's just this chair.

When the credits start to roll, I grab my purse from the seat next to me and stand to my feet all in one motion, before Richard has the chance to make any more advances.

My legs feel achy from sitting too long. Keeping at least a foot away from Richard, I follow him out of the theater and into his car.

"So," he says on the drive home. This is the first thing he's spoken to me since I disappointed him in the theater.

It seems I've been disappointing people a lot recently.

"What'd you think?" His voice is low, as if trying to fill in the silence before arriving at the Huiets'.

"Well, I don't know about the movie, but the other stuff was romantic."

He appears slightly amused, but I can tell that hidden beneath that smile is leftover disappointment.

I squirm in my seat until I absolutely cannot take this harsh silence anymore. "Richard—"

He stops the car in front of a neighbor's house. "Yeah? Hurry, I don't want Whitney to notice—"

"I know I hardly know you and everything"—I stare into his eyes to show him that I mean what I'm saying—"but I really feel like I could fall in love with you, too. I think we have something." Sure, that *something* might seem a little frightening to me right now.

But since when has love ever *not* been scary?

"Took you long enough," he says with a grin. "I just want to put everything I had with Whitney aside—almost pretend like she never happened. You know, maybe she was part of my life so I could meet you. If so, then it was worth it." He squeezes my hand. "Definitely worth it."

This time, I don't try avoiding the kiss.

Until I remember Austin and quickly look out the window, hoping that he didn't just witness this again.

"Thanks for tonight, Richard," I say, grabbing my purse from the floorboard. "I really had a great time."

"Wait, I forgot to ask you." He stops me just as I'm about to stand up. "Are you going to Erica's party on Monday?"

I try to remember the dates for the skit practices, but Monday doesn't seem to ring a bell. "I'll be there if you are."

❯ Tessa Emily Hall

The corners of his mouth slowly turn up. "I'm so lucky to have found you, Selena."

I open the car door and jump out before he has a chance to give me one last goodbye kiss. "See you later."

* * *

It seems as though all of the creative inspiration I had the other night after reading Mom's letter is already gone.

I sit at the window seat and just stare at the drawing I've been attempting to sketch since arriving here. Perhaps this art thing just isn't for me anymore.

My phone vibrates in my lap. I look at the screen, relieved to find that it's not Richard.

"Selena," Brooke's voice spews out before I can even say hello. "Austin gave us your sorry excuse for being absent from the meeting tonight."

I run a hand through my hair. "So, I missed *one* practice. Not really that big of a deal."

"I'm not upset you missed practice. It's the *reason* that you missed it." Her tone sounds almost like my mom's when she's drunk.

"Brooke, look. I—"

"—am just a total fake just like everyone else in this town? I don't know why I didn't catch on to that sooner."

I draw my legs up to my chest, and inhale deeply through my nose. Every time I get into an argument—even a small one—I start to shake, feeling as if I'm going to hyperventilate.

"I can't believe you would do something as low as this," she says, her voice still shrill but becoming calmer now. "Not just because of the skit, but because of Austin. The next meeting is Tuesday. You better be there." She pauses. "Oh, and by the way, you landed the main character of the skit. *Congratulations.*" She makes no effort to hide the sarcasm.

"Brooke, look—" I stammer. "You're really over-dramatizing everything."

There's a short beep, and I pull the phone away from my ear. She hung up on me. Of course.

I throw the phone on the bed and slam my sketchbook shut. How dare Brooke say that I'm fake? She doesn't know a thing about me.

As I'm changing into pajamas, I catch a glimpse of myself in the mirror and stare intently before turning away. My reflection is just another reminder that I am not perfect, no matter how much makeup I wear.

Raindrops fall against the window as I crawl into bed and pull the sleep mask over my eyes. Perhaps this will block out my thoughts—and the rest of the world.

* * *

"You slept in, Selena. It's almost one." I hear Aunt Kori shut the dryer door in the laundry room before she steps into the kitchen. "You feelin' okay?"

"Didn't sleep well last night," I say, pouring myself some coffee.

"You don't look too good." She grabs her leopard print purse off the counter. "Can I do anything for you? I'm about to leave to go to work."

This is probably just one of her attempts at being a good host, considering that she's never home. "I'm fine, really. Just exhausted is all. Thanks anyway."

❭ Tessa Emily Hall

Aunt Kori's keys jingle as she sets them on the counter. "Is it the Hilarie thing?"

That's not the whole reason, but I nod before taking a sip of coffee.

"Look, Selena. I know you'd feel bad about going to New York behind your mom's back, but I really feel like it might be best—for you and for your friend—if you went up there for a few days."

I glance up at her to see how serious she is about this. "But what about my mom? And the money?"

She waves her hand as if it's not a problem. "I can take care of all that."

I shake my head. "Aunt Kori, I'm already staying here for the entire summer. I can't possibly make a sudden trip to Brooklyn for a few days, and expect for you and Uncle Ben to pay for it all. That's just too much." Although, for some reason, it sounds a lot more tempting than it did the first time she offered.

"It's really not a problem," she says. "Ben and I had already planned to go to Europe for a few weeks, but we had to cancel due to his business. We'll be able to afford a quick trip to Brooklyn for you. Money is really no biggie for us."

I want to laugh at her last sentence, but force myself to only smile. "I'd really appreciate that. I'm sure Hilarie will, too."

"It's no problem, girl," she says, picking her keys back off the counter. "I have to work until late tonight, so I'll look into the flights for tomorrow when I get back. Call me if you need anything."

"I will," I say as she disappears into the foyer.

As I get out a bowl for cereal, I hear Aunt Kori open the front door. "Selena, you have a visitor."

I place the cereal box back on the counter and walk to the foyer, curious.

But my hopes fall as I see Austin standing at the doorway, looking just about as rough as I feel right now.

　Tessa Emily Hall

Chapter 15

"Let me guess. You're here to lecture me on the sinfulness of my decision yesterday?"

"No, I'm not." Austin runs a hand through his hair and glances at the ground. Instead of the usual smile, today his mouth forms a complete straight line. "I actually just wanted to know if you'd like to go on a short walk."

I look down at my pajama pants and tank top. "Like this?"

"Does it matter? We'll just be walking along the lake."

I let out a sigh and cross my arms. Austin holds the door open wider, and I step onto the front porch. The grass is damp on my bare feet as we step past the driveway and into the backyard, and although the humidity today is high from the rain last night, it's not half as thick as the silence between Austin and me.

We walk in between several trees before reaching the edge of the lake. Austin bends down to pick up a rock next to the Huiets' dock and tosses it into the water, then stares expressionless as it skips across the lake before disappearing. When he leans down to pick up another one, I take a seat on the grass, not even worrying about how my pajama pants are probably going to be soaked when I stand up.

"I'm leaving for Brooklyn tomorrow," I mutter, crossing my legs.

Austin pauses in mid-throw and spins around. "Your mom's back from rehab already?"

I take a moment, enjoying the disappointment on his face. "I wish. She actually doesn't know I'm going. I'll only be up there for a couple days, though."

"For what?"

"My friend really needs me right now." I look past him and watch as an engine boat zips by on the water. "Aunt Kori thought it'd be a good idea for me to spend some time with her."

"Oh." He hefts the rock in his palm. "Will you be back for the rest of our skit rehearsals?"

I shoot my gaze back to Austin. "Of course. Wouldn't want to miss *that*."

Austin's expression drops, along with the rock in his hand, which makes me feel bad for saying that. The frown on his face reminds me of the little eight-year-old boy with glasses who would cry every time Whitney and I used to make fun of him.

"Austin, you know how much my life is screwed up," I say, my tone softer than before. "We live two completely different lives."

"What's your point?"

"Why do you even bother to talk to me?"

"*Why?*" He raises his eyebrows at me. "So, you're basically saying that I'm too good for you. Is that it?"

When I don't respond, Austin shakes his head and comes to sit next to me. "You really think I would reject you simply because you live a different life than I do?"

I can't tell if he's offended by my assumption, or just shocked by it.

☽ Tessa Emily Hall

Hearing it come from his mouth, I know that's not true. No matter how judgmental he seems—I know, deep down, that is not the kind of guy Austin is.

"Look—I know I should've handled the whole Richard thing differently." He lets out a heavy sigh. "And I'm sorry for getting angry with you. Just tell me—why him? I don't mean to sound jealous. I just—" he pauses, his eyes softening. "I don't want you to get hurt, Selena."

I nod, because I know that's true. Even though I haven't really known Austin for that long, I know he cares for me—in a way no other guy has before. Not even Jeremy.

So why is it that I want Richard instead of him?

I clear my throat, gathering the courage to speak. "When I was little, I used to dream of growing up, becoming an artist, and marrying my prince. Everything would be perfect and happy." I find a stick hiding in the grass, and stab it in the dirt. "But these past few years I've felt stuck, as if there will never be a new beginning in my life. Especially not the fairy tale I imagined."

Biting my lip, I ponder whether or not I should admit the next few details. I look back to Austin to watch his reaction. "I guess that's partly the reason why I got saved last Wednesday. To try it out. For a new beginning or something. I'm struggling with all this spiritual stuff. It doesn't make sense. It never has, and I doubt it ever will. I believe in God and everything, but how am I supposed to know for sure that He exists?"

Austin drops his head a little, probably trying to take in all that I just confessed to him. "It's like one of my favorite quotes by C.S. Lewis." The way the sun hits his face as he turns his head toward the sky is almost distracting—and I have to remind myself to pay attention as he speaks. "'I believe in Christianity as I believe the sun has risen: not only because I see it, but because by it I see everything else.'" He looks back at me now. "Just promise me that you won't give up, okay?"

I swallow. Give up—those words are so familiar. They're the reason I've been stuck in this hopelessness, searching for a fairy tale of my own.

"I'm not going to give up, Austin," I finally say, trying to ignore how the gray clouds are now covering the sun.

* * *

I would normally never do something like this—make such a rash decision behind my mom's back—especially if it includes boarding a plane or navigating the streets of Brooklyn all by myself.

But Hilarie needs me, and I could certainly use some best friend time of my own right now too.

Once I finish packing, I hurry downstairs and set my suitcase next to the front door. Kori comes out of her bedroom just as I'm pouring a bowl of Special K cereal.

"What did Hilarie say when you told her you were coming?" she asks.

"I actually only told her mom. I thought maybe it could be a surprise for Hilarie."

The corners of her lipstick-stained mouth rise. "Oh, I am certain she is going to be *very* pleased."

I fake a grin, then she fills me in on all of the transportation details. "You nervous about flying by yourself?"

I give only a light nod, not wanting her to know just how nervous I really am about this. Besides, I'm sixteen. I can handle it.

"It's not all that bad. I was only thirteen when I first flew by myself." She raises her coffee mug to her lips. "You'll be fine."

She was wrong. I realize this as soon as she gives me one last hug and walks away, leaving me standing awkwardly at the security check line in the airport. Alone. My hands shake like crazy as I place all of my electronics, my carry-on bag, and my shoes on a conveyer belt, trying to follow what everyone in line in front of me is doing so I won't do anything wrong and make a fool of myself, but the smallest details seem to confuse me and make me even more anxious than I already am.

I am definitely *not* the independent type.

After getting through security without causing a beep, passengers finally board the plane, and I breathe a sigh of relief as I settle into my seat. Although it was a struggle getting to this point almost by myself, I already feel as if I've accomplished something major.

The only bad thing about this plane ride is that I didn't get a window seat. And I'm sitting next to an old man, which means I won't be able to fall asleep, afraid my head will somehow end up on his shoulder.

My chest tightens as I feel the plane lift off the ground, and I hold my breath as it rises into the cloudy sky.

I'm actually riding on a plane. By myself. Without my mom even knowing. I could've at least gotten her permission first. What if it crashes, or I get kidnapped on the way to Hilarie's apartment?

In attempt to push away these anxious thoughts, I pull out my sleeping mask, as well as the earbuds to my iPod. I refuse to fall asleep, but as I listen to my music, I begin to relax.

That is, until the increased bumpiness of the ride wakes me. I yank off my sleeping mask, afraid we're crashing. But the clouds out the window tell me we're still safely in the sky.

I hope.

The second half of the plane ride is much smoother than the first, and once we land, I'm actually glad I didn't take a car. The plane ride really wasn't that bad—not to mention it's a much shorter ride than being in the car for several hours.

I feel all grown up as I go through baggage claim, catch the AirTrain to Brooklyn, then flag down a taxi without any difficulties. This is huge for me, considering I normally won't even ride the subway by myself. Especially since taxi drivers have always creeped me out a bit.

I peek through the window as the taxi drives through the Williamsburg area of Brooklyn where I used to hang out with my friends. Apprehensiveness fades into excitement. I'm going to see Hilarie in about fifteen minutes.

I know this trip will be worth it.

After the taxi driver helps me unload my suitcase onto the street, I hand him a ten-dollar bill, then start to feel a little nervous again as he drives away. The first noise to greet me—other than rap music in the distance—is the sound of a siren. A group of boys argue with a street vendor ahead of me, and I walk past a homeless lady pushing a cart filled with trash as she holds out a can for possible donations.

Home sweet home.

I flip my hair away from my face, and force my trembling legs to take a step of confidence. I've made it this far. Surely I can walk across the street to Hilarie's apartment building.

I reach in my pocket to check my phone. She should get home within the next ten minutes.

After walking up the steps, I let out a deep breath and push the buzzer. Almost immediately, her mom appears at the door, and whatever anxiety I've been experiencing today disappears as she reaches over to give me a tight squeeze.

"I'm so glad you could make it, Selena," she says into my ear.

"Me too." I smile as she pulls away.

I've always considered her to be my second mother, especially since she's never been a train wreck like my mom always seems to be—but from the looks of her now, perhaps I'm wrong about that. She gives me a polite grin back. However, under her gentle brown eyes are dark circles. Her unkempt hair looks as if she just hopped out of bed. And instead of the usual workout clothes she always seems to be wearing, today she wears a robe over her nightgown.

"Come in." She closes the door behind us, leading the way up to their second-floor apartment. "How'd your flight go?" she asks, her voice echoing in the stairwell.

"A lot better than I had anticipated, actually. I'm just glad it wasn't delayed."

She opens the door to the apartment, and I'm relieved to see that it looks about the same. The small den seems to be clean and all in place, just like it always has.

However, I have a feeling that this orderliness isn't a reflection of what they are going through right now.

I can't help but notice how Ms. Ross' smile reminds me of my mom's. The one she wore before going to rehab. "Why don't you wait in her bedroom 'til Hilarie comes? Should be here any minute now. And excuse the mess, please. She hasn't cleaned her room recently."

I give a light laugh as I take my belongings to her bedroom. "I doubt she would let it get too bad."

But when I open the door, I realize Ms. Ross isn't exaggerating. Dirty clothes scatter across the floor, empty cups are stacked on the dresser, as is a paper plate with leftover pizza crust, and even a few candy wrappers lay on the nightstand, waiting to be put into her trash can that sits only a few feet away.

Sitting on the crumpled sheets of her bed, I shake my head, not able to believe my own eyes. Hilarie is usually very OCD when it comes to her bedroom. She normally has to have *everything* in order.

A couple minutes later, I hear the front door open in the den, followed by Hilarie saying something to her mom. I sit up taller and glance in the mirror on the back of her door, making sure that my hair is in place before she comes to her room.

After she finally stops talking with her mom about her day at work, footsteps approach, and my anticipation grows. Hilarie opens her door—but her gaze doesn't meet mine. Instead, she turns around to look at herself in the mirror, not even noticing that I'm sitting on her bed.

Rather than speaking to let her know I'm in here, I move my head so that my reflection is seen in the mirror next to hers as she lets down her hair. She still doesn't see me, so I wave.

Hilarie spins around and lets out a scream, her mouth dropped open. "You about scared me to death!" She places a hand on her chest as I stand up to give her a much-needed hug. "Selena, what are you doing here? Your mom didn't drop out of rehab, did she?"

Pulling away, I notice Ms. Ross standing at the door. "She doesn't even know I'm here. Kori thought I should come and stay with you for a few days. Thought you could use some best friend time."

Tears fill her eyes. "You have no idea how badly." She turns to her mom. "Did you know about this?"

Ms. Ross nods.

"You could've at least told me to clean up a little!" Hilarie picks up a pair of jeans laying on the floor and throws them in her dirty clothes hamper. "Oh my gosh, I'm so embarrassed."

"Don't worry, I gave Selena a little warning." She gives me a wink. "Now, try to get her to go somewhere with you, Selena. She's hardly left this place at all this week. I'll be in the kitchen cleaning, if you girls need anything."

When her mom closes the door, I turn to Hilarie. "Why haven't you gone anywhere, Hil?"

She plops down on the bed. "Do you honestly think I'm going to show my face in public?"

"What? Are you afraid that you're going to run into someone from school?"

Hilarie drops her head as if this is true. As if she's ashamed of herself.

I push my suitcase underneath her bed, then sit down next to her. "Those chances are slim. And so what if you do?"

Her caramel blond hair swooshes as she shakes her head. "I have no one, Selena. Just you and Mickey, and she left yesterday to go to Miami."

I hate to see her like this—too embarrassed to even look me in the eyes. "You still have Sarah, don't you? So why can't you do something with her?"

"Don't even get me started."

"What?"

"She won't talk to me."

"What do you mean she won't talk to you?"

"I mean, she won't talk to me. At all." A cool breeze blows

in through Hilarie's half-open window. "She's, like, pretending to be all nice to me over text, but hasn't even called me. The two times that I've asked her to hang out with me, she didn't respond. Probably just doesn't wanna be seen with me, as if I'm some kind of disgrace or something." She sighs, finally looking me in the eyes now. "But whatever. I'm over it. Besides, she's too busy spending time with Jeremy to care about her pregnant best friend."

"Wait, what? As in, my *ex-boyfriend* Jeremy?" I laugh. "Why would she be hanging out with him?"

"Oh, you don't know? They started going out a week ago, right after she and Christopher broke up." She bites her lip, looking at me as if she's afraid the news will hurt me.

Of course it doesn't. Why should it?

"Well, that doesn't surprise me." I stand up, acting cool. "Their relationship will be dead by the end of summer, and she'll be happily dating another guy." Not that I care or anything. It's just sort of strange knowing that my ex-boyfriend is now dating one of my best friends.

I should've seen it coming, though.

After going through my purse for my makeup bag, I sit down at Hilarie's mirror to apply some powder to my face.

"I just think it's crazy that she's going with him when she knows how abusive he was to you."

"He wasn't abusive." I look over my shoulder. Hilarie seems surprised I'm taking up for Jeremy. "I mean—he had anger problems." I turn back around and twist open my mascara. "But that's only because of his dad."

"You don't still have feelings for him, do you?"

"Are you crazy?" I pause as I apply mascara, my laugh sounding fake even to my own ears. "Honestly—I don't know,

Hil. I mean, I don't miss him, but I miss us. Like, I miss the memories we made. You know, when it was you, me, Jeremy, and Josh. The times when the four of us could just hang out and have fun together."

"I know." She sighs. "Too bad they both ended up being jerks, though."

I zip my makeup bag before joining Hilarie back on the bed. She stares at the ground, as if her mind is racing through memories.

"Everything they said about how much we meant to them was fake," she says in a monotone voice. "They didn't love us, Selena. Only wanted someone to push around, someone to claim as their property." Her green eyes blink several times before looking away.

I place my hand on Hilarie's back. "You're making the right decision by keeping the baby. You know that, right? I'm proud of you. And I know that someday you'll meet someone who will treat you like you deserve to be treated."

A smile creeps onto her lips. "Thanks, girl."

"No problem. Now come on, your mom was right." I stand to my feet and reach for her hands. "You need to get out of the house."

She lets out a groan, allowing me to pull her up. "And where are you planning on taking me?"

"Oh, you'll see."

Chapter 16

I walk into my apartment, finding it just the way Mom and I left it. The loveseat in the corner of the den, with its peeling vinyl, and our small television set are the only furniture in our living room. Random boxes retrieved from storage a couple months ago still scatter the floor. It's a combination of being completely empty and a total wreck at the same time. This pretty much reflects the way I've been feeling recently.

"What a nice surprise," Hilarie says, stepping inside. "I never get to come here."

I laugh, glad to see that at least her sarcastic humor hasn't left. "I was planning on going to Central Park to have a picnic lunch until I remembered the creepy guys who stalked us the last time we went there alone in the evening. So"—I walk past several boxes in the den and step into the small kitchen—"I figured we could just make some Hot Pockets and sit out on the rooftop tonight. We haven't done that in a while."

She sits on one of the stools at the kitchen bar. "Hey, I'm not arguing. Summer isn't summer without eating Hot Pockets on the roof with your best friend."

I smile. How is it that she still has the same sense of humor—well, for the most part—even though she just found out that she's going to have a baby? Perhaps she's not really showing how she truly feels about this. I mean, it has to be bothering her. Right?

"Do you still have that stash of Little Debbie cakes in your room? I've been craving some recently."

"Isn't it a bit too early in your pregnancy for you to start having cravings?" I laugh, placing a Hot Pocket in the microwave. "Let me see if I have any left."

I step out of the kitchen and open my bedroom door, turning on the light. It's nice to be back in my room, although it can't even compare to my temporary home in Lake Lure. The walls are still painted gray from when we moved here a couple of years ago. I've tried to make it feel more like my room in Kentucky by buying purple decorations and even a purple bedspread, but it's never felt quite right. It's like forcing something that just isn't meant to be, but trying to make it work anyway. Which basically sums up my entire life in Brooklyn.

I open the drawer where I keep a stash of Little Debbie cakes and find that I have two Fudge Rounds left. Perfect. I take them and close the drawer—but just as I'm shutting the drawer, my gaze lands on the framed picture on top of the dresser. The only picture I have of Dad and me.

I take the picture from my dresser and observe it more closely. It was the last Christmas before Dad kicked Mom and me out, our very last beach trip as a family. While most people go to the beach in the summer, our family went each winter break—a trip to Florida to visit Mom's dad at his beach house. It was also just a few years before Grandpa passed away. The old beach house was eventually torn down, along with all of our memories.

I stare for a moment longer, wishing I could go back in time, wishing I could be the innocent little girl in the picture once again, sitting in Daddy's lap on Grandpa's back porch, the ocean in the background. My head rested against Daddy's chest, a blanket in my lap, and I wore Christmas pajamas. The sun was setting behind us, and we were having our annual Christmas Eve devotion as a family. On the glass table in front of us lay Daddy's Bible.

Mom never wanted me to have the picture framed; she said it only brought back bad memories. But not for me. It reminds me there were some good times in our family, times when I felt safe in Daddy's arms. It almost makes me forget about our goodbye—or lack thereof.

"Have you gotten lost?" Hilarie asks from the kitchen.

I laugh, setting the picture back on my dresser, along with daydreams. "I'm coming."

I show off all of my impressive cooking skills while making our Hot Pockets, then Hilarie and I climb up the ladder leading to the roof. The moon rays provide light for us as we pull ourselves up through the narrow opening that reveals my favorite getaway. If I lived in Lake Lure, this is probably what I would miss most about Brooklyn. Although the roof isn't very big, and certainly not as peaceful as Lake Lure, the lights from the city in the distance take my breath away.

"I love being up here," Hilarie says as we sit down in plastic lawn chairs.

I agree. There's something about coming up here—getting away from the rest of the world, being above the troubles below. To our left, we can see a panoramic view of the Brooklyn Bridge in the distance, always lit up and stunning at night.

Although the bridge is beautiful, I was hoping we could watch the sunset from the rooftop, but it's too late now. Instead, we're already surrounded by a blanket of darkness—

yet lights pierce through the night sky as if they're trying to offer little glimmers of hope in this dark city.

"You're eating your Fudge Round first?" I ask Hilarie as she removes the plastic wrap from her cake.

"The craving is just too powerful," she laughs, leaning back in her chair. "So tell me—what's the update on that guy in Lake Lure you were telling me about?"

I can't help but wonder if she's only asking these questions to avoid the topic of her pregnancy. She has never been one to open up and cry her heart out. Same with me, though, I guess.

"Who, Austin? Or are you talking about Richard?" Pepperoni burns my tongue as I take a bite of my Hot Pocket.

"There's two of them?" Her eyes light up as if she just heard some juicy gossip.

"Oh, no. Austin is Whitney's neighbor, the one I used to know when I lived there. Richard is Whitney's ex. He kinda has a thing for me now."

"Oh?" Hilarie's juicy-gossip-look returns. "So you're following Sarah's footsteps now?"

I feel my cheeks warm, wishing I would've worded that differently. "No, it's not like that."

"I'm just kidding, girl," she giggles. "So tell me about him. What's he like? How did this happen?"

While finishing the rest of my Hot Pocket, I tell Hilarie the entire story about Richard—starting from our *romantic* introduction the first morning in the kitchen when I spilled coffee on my shirt, until our movie date. "He's so—cute. The only thing is, though, I just feel like he's sorta pressuring me to be his girlfriend. You know?" I drop my gaze to my Fudge Round as I open it. "And I don't feel right about it, especially since he and Whitney just broke up."

"But you like him, right?"

I look back up to her and nod, my teeth clenching down on my bottom lip.

"Then what are you so afraid of?" she asks, wiping tomato sauce from her mouth. "That's just how guys are, Selena. It's their nature. They don't mean to pressure girls—they just can't exactly seem to comprehend the meaning of *taking it slow*. And why should you worry about Whitney? She's been a jerk to both of you. Besides, they're broken up now, and she should learn to move on."

I exhale a sigh of relief. "You're right. You know, you should seriously look into being a therapist one day, Hilarie."

She looks out at the buildings in the distance. "Yeah, right. I mean, that doesn't sound all that bad, but I can hardly even work out my own problems, much less the problems of others."

"Well, you've definitely helped me with mine plenty of times. Just saying."

"Right back atcha," she says, giving a slight smile. "So how are you doing with the whole cutting out smoking thing?"

I set my empty plate and Fudge Round wrapper on the ground. I was hoping she wouldn't ask. "Don't tell my mom, but I've already broken our agreement. This whole Christianity thing—it's, well, interesting."

A slight breeze lifts a wavy strand of hair away from Hilarie's face. "What do you mean?"

"I don't know, really." Why is eye contact always so difficult for me during deep conversations? "I'm just starting to wonder if I gave in to make myself feel better, you know? It all feels like a dream now, being so full of hope and everything. It's like—" I pause, trying to find the right words while looking

172   ◗ Tessa Emily Hall

out at the beautiful New York City lights in the distance. "It's like sketching something so beautiful and so peaceful"—my gaze shifts below to the dirty, run-down buildings surrounding us—"then looking away from the sketch, and seeing an ugly world that doesn't match the fantasy scene you just imagined. Sort of like false hope, I guess."

Horns on the street below us honk at one another, arguing over lanes. Almost as if they were trying to prove my point.

"Well, considering I'm not a Christian or anything, I don't know what to say about all of that religion stuff. But what I do know is that this world can't be all that bad. Sure, bad stuff happens"—she places a hand on her stomach—"but there's good hidden in every bad situation. You just have to find it. That's what Mom told me when we moved to Brooklyn while I was in middle school."

She crosses her legs in the chair, her eyes looking elsewhere, as if reliving the memory. "I was so mad at my parents for divorcing, mad at my mom for forcing me to move with her to Brooklyn, away from everything I knew in Chicago. I didn't think she was right when she told me that—I couldn't find anything good about moving here. But then on the first day of school I met you." She looks at me and grins. "And I discovered that you had gone through almost the same situation I had."

I smile back at her. How does she always know exactly what to say? "Hilarie, I came here to be a friend to you, so you could vent as much as you want to me. Not the other way around."

"Trust me, you being here is all the therapy I need. What you're going through is pretty rough also, Selena." She shakes her head. "You're stronger than you think you are, dealing with all this junk for so long."

I almost laugh. *Strong?* Why is it that both she and my mom have told me this? Where did they get the impression that I'm strong?

I feel so weak.

Every time I finally feel as if I'm headed in the right direction, I get pulled the opposite way.

When I decide to be done with drinking and smoking once and for all, I let my guard down and end up having "just one more" *again*. I am definitely my mother's daughter, and if there is anything I've learned about her these past eight years, it's that she is *not* strong.

I've realized more and more just how much I'm starting to take after her.

And that's what scares me the most.

* * *

"This is so unlike you," I tell Hilarie as I help clean her bedroom back at her apartment. "Why'd you let it get this messy?"

She shoves an empty paper plate into the trashcan. "When people become depressed, they stop doing the things they enjoy most. And I happen to like cleaning and organizing a lot."

Hair falls in front of my face as I glance down at her desk covered with magazines and loose paper. That can't be the reason why I suddenly stopped being inspired to sketch, can it?

I drop a pencil into a can on her desk then spot a scrapbook—the one I made for her sixteenth birthday—lying next to her computer, hidden underneath a notebook. Even though I've gone through the scrapbook several times before, I grab it and plop down on her bed.

The cover shows a picture of us hugging each other on the shore of Coney Island last summer. I flip to the first page that reveals random cut-and-pasted pictures of us—recent ones.

The pictures on the next page always frighten me just a little.

I laugh, pointing to a picture of the two of us making a peace sign for the camera. "Why did I always wear my hair like that in middle school?"

She places a folded t-shirt in her drawer then sits next to me. "Well I happen to think side braids are cute. At least you didn't have braces!"

"Hey, you got way more guys with those things than I did without them."

"I think you mean I was *dumped* by way more guys than I was without them," she says, flipping to the next page.

Pictures of our first dance and thirteenth birthdays cover the next two pages. I shake my head. It doesn't feel like it was that long ago, yet so much has changed since then.

"Don't you wish we could go back to the way things used to be?" Hilarie asks, stealing the words right out of my mouth. "You know, before high school happened and everything started to go downhill."

"I know what you mean." I can't stop staring at a picture of the two of us at our first dance, both dressed in matching sequined tops and gaucho pants. The troubles we had then are so small in comparison to the ones we have now. "Before all the drama started happening in our lives—before my mom went all crazy."

"Yep." She flips to the next page. "Then came the party years."

My eyes scan down the pictures of us with Josh and Jeremy, hanging out during ninth and tenth grades at each other's apartments, the mermaid parade in Coney Island, and dancing at a teen club in Brooklyn. "You have to admit, though, we did have some good times with those guys."

She nods, then places a finger to a picture of the four of us sitting on a blanket on my roof. That was the night we stayed up past midnight flirting with our boyfriends, playing cards, eating popcorn—making memories we thought we would cherish forever. It was in our early days, when the four of us used to spend time together and stay sober. Before we were brainwashed into believing that, in order to have a good time, there must be alcohol involved.

"I miss those times," I say, sinking into the memories the pictures held. "Not Jeremy, of course. Just having a boyfriend, you know?" The feeling of having someone to hold me, to whisper in my ear that he loves me. The security I felt when we were in a crowded club and I had a boyfriend's hand to hold on to. "Wasn't that around the time I tried my first cigarette?"

"I think so," she says, her gaze not leaving the picture. "You hated it at first. Couldn't stop coughing."

"If it wasn't for Jeremy always smoking around me, I would've never started." The feeling of remorse fades into anger now as I look at the other pictures of us, smiling at the camera, his arm around me. His dark eyes still make me shudder.

There's no doubt that we had some good times, but it doesn't take away the fact that he is to blame for my smoking habit, as well as my fear of getting close to a guy.

I turn the page. "If only I could go back in time and tell myself that smoking is just not worth it. At all." Because now,

I don't think I'll ever be able to quit. No matter how many times I say that I will. No matter how many times I try.

I'll be tempted again. I'm not strong enough; I'll give in. It's an endless cycle.

"I wish I could go back in time and tell myself not to lose my virginity to Josh," Hilarie mumbles, looking up at me, sadness in her eyes.

Who do those boys think they are, treating us as if we are their property, taking away our innocence?

"Yeah." I look up at my best friend and let out a sigh. "If only."

* * *

It doesn't take much to convince Hilarie to go shopping with me the next day. *I'm* the one who actually needs some convincing. And not only because shopping is not my favorite thing in the world, but just because I'd rather spend the day in my pajamas watching a movie marathon.

We spend the day in Manhattan anyway, going to one shop after another, eating lunch at our favorite cafe. Although I love this—seeing my best friend happy and having a good time, especially after being in tears on the phone with me the other night—I'm not enjoying it. Not as much as I should be.

At five o'clock, Hilarie finally decides to call it a day. As we walk over to the nearest subway station, my thoughts return to last night, when she told me that people who are depressed stop doing the things they love. Most of my smiles today have been fake. It's not like I am depressed—I'm definitely not. It's just that coming home has been a real eye-opener, especially after I've been staying in such a peaceful town where I can relax by the lake and daydream all day long if I want.

Being here jolts me back to reality. The reality of remembering all the mistakes that I've made in life, and knowing that no matter where I go, I am still the same person with the same imperfections. The same past that will never be erased.

Hilarie and I are quiet during most of the ride back to Brooklyn. My mind continues to wander, and I actually find myself wishing I could be back in Lake Lure.

I'm trying, I really am. Trying to be a friend to Hilarie. Trying to act happy, make things the way they used to be.

But I can hardly stand it anymore. I look around at all the people with blank expressions sitting near us on the subway, most either staring down at the floor, reading a book, or looking out of the windows. No one is speaking, just listening to the sounds of the subway rushing down the track—screeching metal, rattling doors, the conductor announcing the upcoming stops.

Everyone seems to be in such a rush to be somewhere they're not. Or they've already given up trying and have turned to begging on the streets just to get by. A struggle to get ahead and make it to the top as fast as possible, or a struggle for survival. Either way, it's a fight.

Where's the peace in life? The peace I once had as a kid living in Kentucky with my family and without a care in the world?

Dad had painted such a beautiful picture of life in my head when I was little. It wasn't until I moved to New York when I realized that was an unrealistic fabrication. I came to this conclusion when Mom and I were walking home from a restaurant one evening when I was eleven. A group of young boys appeared from nowhere and ran in front of us, cursing and fighting with each other. One reached down, picked up an empty glass bottle from the ground, and threw it at another guy. Mom grabbed my hand as the glass shattered near my feet, and we ran to hide behind a large trash can until they were no longer in sight. I could hear my heart pounding inside my chest.

If there is a God, why does everyone on the subway train look so gloomy, as if their entire life has been a struggle? If there's a God, why are there so many homeless people on the streets, begging for money, begging for mercy?

Many of the kids at my school come from broken families. What about them?

The kids I went to school with in Kentucky all came from good, Christian homes. Or at least that's what I thought. It's easy to be a Christian when you're living the perfect life. It's easy to live a perfect life when God seems to be showering you with blessings.

I realize my eyes have been closed when I feel Hilarie nudge me with her elbow. "Are you okay?"

I nod. That is probably the one question that I absolutely cannot stand to be asked, the one that forces me to lie. "I'm fine."

"Come on, Selena. What is it?"

I swallow. "Just thinking about my mom and all." There's no way I could tell her that coming here has put such a damper on everything for me.

That coming here has made me crave a cigarette more than anything.

* * *

After our hectic shopping day in the city, Hilarie and I stay up until three in the morning watching *The OC* reruns and then fall asleep on the couch—only to be awakened five hours later by Ms. Ross.

We drag ourselves off the couch and into the kitchen to make pancakes. I can't remember one time that I spent the night with Hilarie when we didn't make breakfast together in the morning, even though she's always the one who does most of the cooking.

Since Hilarie seems to have had such a great time, I haven't mentioned the pregnancy to her, afraid it'd make her uncomfortable. But the last chance I have to bring it up before I leave is at the table as Hilarie, Ms. Ross, and I eat breakfast. No one is talking, and Hilarie already has a gloomy look on her face as she stuffs her mouth full of pancakes.

"So, Hilarie—" I take a long sip of my orange juice. "Have you decided if you're keeping the baby or not?"

"I've looked into placing it up for adoption." She places her elbow against the table, resting her chin on her hand. "I don't know what I'm going to do. I don't want the baby to think it wasn't wanted if I decide to put it up for adoption. You know?"

"Mmm-hmm. Trust me, I know what it's like to not be wanted by a parent." I stab a fork into my pancake.

"What do you mean, you know what it's like?" Hilarie's mom joins the conversation, narrowing her eyes at me as if I'm not speaking English. "You aren't referring to your father, are you?"

I lick the sticky syrup from my lips, not sure of how to respond to that question. She and my mom are best friends; how would Ms. Ross not know about my dad kicking us out?

"Of course he wants you back," she says when I don't respond. "Why wouldn't he?"

I glance at Hilarie, hoping she'll answer for me like she always does when I need a rescue. But she seems just as confused as I do. "What do you mean?"

"Your dad—" Her mom cuts her pancake into small sections, acting normal like she always does even when she's cracking jokes. But I don't think she's joking this time. "That man would've done anything to keep you there with him. Why else would he have tried so many times to get you back?"

A bite of pancake sticks to the back of my throat. I swallow hard, but this doesn't take away the lump. "I haven't heard from my dad in eight years."

She has to be wrong. There is no way Mom would lie to me about my dad all this time.

The thought alone causes my heart to skip a beat.

Ms. Ross' eyes widen. "Oh. Well, you know. I probably have the story wrong." She gives a nervous laugh and shoves a bite of pancake into her mouth, still talking, even though her mouth is full. "It was years ago when your mom told me everything. Plus we were at a party I think, a little tipsy. Never mind what I just said."

Hilarie glances at me, her eyebrows curved downward in concern.

"Anyway, Hil—" Ms. Ross clears her throat—"there's nothing bad about adoption at all," she says, obviously in a quick effort to change the subject. Her voice trails off as she continues to talk about her thoughts on adoption, but her words become a blur.

Did Dad really want me? Could she be right?

She couldn't be. My mom and Ms. Ross were at a party, after all, when they talked about this. And I know from first-hand experience that Mom can say some pretty crazy things when she's drunk.

Plus, Mom knew Dad was my best friend. I was a Daddy's girl; there's no way she would've taken me away from him on purpose. He's the one that changed, anyway. The arguments I overheard from my bedroom between them always had to do with him and how much time he spent working at the church. He stopped paying attention to us. He stopped paying attention to me.

Mom wouldn't have just taken me away from him and lied about it to me for all these years. Right?

When we're done eating, I take a quick shower and drag my suitcase to the front door. The sting of goodbye brings tears to my eyes as Hilarie gets up from the couch to give me one last, tight hug.

"I'll see you at the end of summer," she says, her voice quivering.

"Try to cheer up a little, okay?" I look at her now. I'd give anything if I could just stay with her for the rest of the summer instead. "Things are going to turn out for the best."

If only I could convince myself.

Chapter 17

The stormy weather causes my flight to be delayed, but finally at noon, we're on our way. It's exhilarating watching as the plane rises above the storm below.

Everywhere I look I see layers of majestic buildings and skyscrapers stacked next to each other as if they're building blocks. All of the graffiti, dirt, and piles of trash on the side of the roads are no longer in view. If only real life could be this way—I would be able to rise above any storm in my life, and all of the ugliness would suddenly disappear, revealing only the beauty.

I only doze off for a little while before our plane hits turbulence. Most of the flight continues to be choppy and unstable; however, the weather finally begins to clear as we approach North Carolina. When the plane descends and the pilot's voice comes over the intercom, I glance out the window—but, even from above, the tranquil view of the mountains and the lake fails to capture my attention.

The twenty minute ride from the Asheville Regional Airport to my summer home in Lake Lure is silent. Uncle Ben doesn't have much to say, listening to an oldies radio station playing music from the seventies. If I didn't know that he is always this quiet, I would think that maybe he is irritated that he had to leave his work early to come and pick me up. And if I have to listen to another Bee Gees song on this trip, I think I'm going to scream.

I check my phone, realizing that I have an unread text message.

Austin: *When are you getting back from Brooklyn again? Don't forget skit practice tomorrow.*

I let out a huff. I had completely forgotten about the skit, and honestly I'd just rather not have anything to do with it anymore. I wonder how Brooke and Austin would treat me if I suddenly backed out of the whole thing. It shouldn't be that big of a deal, considering it just started.

I pull out my sketchbook and just stare at the pictures I've drawn. The soft colors in my watercolor fairy tale sketches give the pictures a serene appearance.

Yet it's fake. It's not reality. Because nothing in life can be that perfect, that peaceful.

What's the point of trying to sketch it anyway if it's not a reflection of life? Perhaps I should just rip out all of the pages.

All of my innermost thoughts and emotions expressed within the pages of this sketchbook—only to be ruined.

The thought alone makes me shudder.

* * *

I'm almost convinced that I'm back in Austin's boat on the lake as I close my eyes and feel the wind blow through my hair—until I remember that I'm only in Whitney's car, on the way to Erica's party. I don't even bother to say anything about speeding—not because I know it's useless, but because it surprisingly doesn't bother me as much.

I take my phone from my purse to text Richard and let him

know that I'm on my way, tilting the screen so Whitney can't see who I'm texting. He responds almost immediately:

Richard: *Great. How was NY?*

Me: *It was alright. I'm excited about tonight though.* =)

Richard: *Me too. We'll need to stay away from where ever Whitney's hanging out so she won't see us together.*

I don't reply. It bothers me how much he wants our relationship to be so secret.

Whitney broke up with *him*, so why should he care?

"So what made you want to come tonight?" Whitney yells over the radio.

I shrug. "It's summer. I have no other plans for tonight."

I try to push back the guilt of knowing that I am really coming to spend time with Richard, especially since I know that being there will only make me want to smoke and drink again.

But I'll only be there to have a good time. What's so wrong with that? Besides, I deserve it. Why are Austin and Brooke making me feel so bad about hanging out with Richard? I thought Christians were supposed to be accepting of *everyone*.

When I see the amount of cars parked in the driveway of Erica's house, I straighten my posture. No longer am I going to allow fear from the past to force me to recoil from having a good time.

That's a lot easier said than done. There are probably twice the amount of people here than there were at the birthday party a few weeks ago. Most of them are girls, and I assume that many of the guys here are their boyfriends.

I feel like I stick out like a sore thumb as I stand awkwardly in the midst of everyone dancing, searching for Richard. He's nowhere in sight.

Everyone here is having fun and laughing with their friends. Why can't I just pretend that I'm different for once, and make a few friends? I am thankful that I'm not getting the "new kid" stares anymore, but instead I'm invisible, watching as everyone else dances with their friends, boyfriend, or takes pictures of each other. My palms start to sweat and my heart races as I begin to feel claustrophobic. It's not the crowded house full of people but the feeling of alienation that always triggers these anxiety attacks.

I step into the kitchen for more space to breathe. As I'm about to search the cabinets for cups to pour myself some water, I feel an arm wrap around my waist.

I spin around, coming face to face with Richard. "There you are." I smile. Never before have I met anyone who can both calm my nerves and make me feel anxious just from one look.

"Wow. You look—incredible." He studies me up and down, seeming to approve the outfit I chose today, a green dress with sandals. "Care for one?" He raises his right hand, holding a red plastic cup. Right in front of my face.

I almost take it without even thinking, until I remember my promise. "Oh, no. Thanks."

I can hardly hear my own voice over the loud music.

"You sure? I mean, you don't have to." He leans back against the kitchen island, resting on his elbows. "I don't want you to feel pressured or anything. It's not really my thing, either, but every now and then I have a drink or two. Parties are just better that way." He raises a cup to his lips and takes a slow sip.

This is not the path I want to walk again.

"Well, I guess I'll put this one back, then." He turns around, places the cup on the kitchen counter and begins looking around the house, almost as if he is bored with me and trying to find other people to hang out with. People who are more *fun* than I am.

Forget it. I am not going to allow myself to be rejected again. "You know, one little drink won't hurt, will it?" Besides, I've already broken the promise anyway.

He turns his attention back to me as he flashes his Crest white teeth at me, then reaches behind him for the other drink. "How about we go outside?"

"Sure."

Pulling on my arm, Richard weaves us past the group of girls in the kitchen until we're on the back porch that apparently has yet to be discovered by the others.

As I lean against the railing, I wonder if Richard is trying to hide me from everyone because he doesn't want Whitney to know that we're together, or if he just doesn't want to be seen with me at all.

"So," he says, placing his cup on the railing. "Tell me about your art."

I can't help but laugh. "My art?" If he wanted to talk to me about art, why didn't he take me someplace like a bookstore or coffee shop? Or even better, an art museum?

"Yeah. I wanted to come out here so we could discuss your art more freely, you know." Richard folds his broad arms across his chest.

"Oh, right." I clear my throat. "Well, what would you like to know?"

He scratches his head and leans over the porch railing, looking across the lawn. "What kind of stuff do you like to draw? Who are your favorite artists? I never get to talk to anyone about this stuff."

I cringe at the bitter taste of the beer. Perhaps if I sip it slowly, it'll last longer, and I'll be less tempted to get another. "I really like Flavia's work. And fairy tales are my favorite." I can't believe I just told him that.

"Oh yeah?" His smile is bright. A little too bright. "And why, exactly, are those your favorite?"

I have to set my cup on the railing so he can't tell how much I am shaking right now. Why am I so nervous? It's not the kind of nervous someone gets when they're in love. This is the kind of feeling someone experiences before approaching something risky—like knowing they're about to endanger their life by diving off a cliff into the water below, but they do it anyway, perhaps for the midair thrill.

Right before hitting the water.

"Because. They're about, well, princesses."

"Beautiful princesses?"

I give a crooked smirk. "Mostly."

The longer Richard's greenish-blue gaze pierces through me, the more I want to back away. "I think all fairy tale princesses are beautiful. How do the stories end?"

"You know. They find their prince and fall in love." I pause, forcing myself to take a deep breath. "Then live happily ever after."

"Well, what about stories where maybe the prince and princess don't end up together, or the story doesn't end happily?" His mouth forms a sly grin. "Those are actually my favorite."

"Really?" Confused, I try to think of an example that fits Richard's description. But I'm distracted as he moves closer to me, filling in the gap that was between us.

"Well, yeah. Because that's life. But at least, for the moment, the prince finds his princess and they have a good time together while it lasts, no strings attached."

Heart racing, I raise the cup to my mouth and take a long sip this time, keeping my eyes focused on Richard as he continues to move even closer to me.

His alcohol-breath makes me take a step back as he lifts my chin with his finger. I set down my drink.

"Am I right?"

"Richard—"

Before I can even get out another word, he places his large hand on the side of my head and brings his lips to mine. I try moving my head back, but he continues to press my mouth against his. And when I take a step back, he pushes me against the railing. It's impossible for me to make any kind of escape.

Instead of fighting it, I finally relent to his wishes and force myself to enjoy this moment—even though, in the back of my mind, I know this isn't right. It reminds me of the first time I tried a cigarette. It was a new sensation, and I hated it. But I didn't stop.

This kiss with Richard is the same kind of thing—it doesn't feel right. Doesn't even feel safe. But I remind myself that however this ends, Richard is right. At least for the moment, the prince and princess can have a good time.

And that's what happens. I have more fun tonight than I've had in months. I even find myself laughing out loud over how I was actually afraid of Richard earlier.

After our extended make-out session on the back porch, he decides the party would be much more enjoyable if we join the others inside. This makes me feel good, realizing that he is probably no longer ashamed to be seen with me.

By now, I've stopped counting my drinks. I don't even feel guilty. For once. Nor do I care if Whitney sees me.

I haven't felt this fearless and carefree in what seems like forever.

Around midnight, I stand in a huddle with Richard and a few of his friends, laughing over something one of the guys said about being a Christian—or maybe it was about being with Kristen, I'm not sure—until I hear someone behind me call my name.

I turn around, relieved to see that it's only Hayden and not Whitney.

"You should've told me you were coming!" she says, then points at Richard talking amongst his friends. "Wait a second, you're with him?"

"Mmm-hmm. He's mine." I grab Richard's hand and stand on tiptoe to kiss his stubble cheek, bursting out laughing that I had to stand up tall in order to reach him.

"Wow. You're drunk."

"I know." These giggles will not stop. "It feels great."

"I thought you said that you didn't drink?"

My eyes widen as I look down at the cup in my hands, but I just give a shrug and flash a smile, hoping that my sudden flush of shame isn't noticeable. "It's summer," I say. "Here's to *summer.*" I raise the cup and drink until there's none left.

"Baby," Richard says to me once Hayden has disappeared back into the crowd. He looks down at me in a way that makes me feel beautiful, as if I am his girl—and the way he called me baby gives me butterflies. The good kind. "Why don't we take a break from the party and head upstairs?"

I know what this means.

I feel my head start to nod, but quickly turn it into a shake when the horrible flashback returns.

"Actually, can we just stay here? Where the music is, and all the drinks."

The excitement in his eyes fades a little, but then he leans down to plant a kiss on my forehead. "Whatever you want, beautiful."

I love how understanding Richard is, certainly not pressuring like Jeremy was.

"Thanks," I say, then stand on my tiptoes and pull his head toward mine for another kiss. When we pull away, I accidently knock his drink and some of it spills on his gray shirt.

He glances down, but shows little concern over this. Instead, he interrupts my flow of giggles with another kiss.

Yes. I've lost all control of myself.

But it feels good, considering I can't feel a thing.

And, honestly, I don't mind if this doesn't end "happily ever after" like most fairy tale relationships. I'm having fun.

At least, for now.

* * *

"Thanks for the ride," I say to Richard as he pulls in the Huiets' driveway. I snatch my purse off the floorboard and get out of his car—not in as graceful a manner as I'd like.

After blowing Richard a kiss as he backs away, I spin

around. The front door is so small, it seems so far away. I take a step, but somehow trip over my own feet, and burst out laughing as I hit the driveway, thankful only my hands are scratched up a little from the pavement.

"Have a good time tonight?"

I jump at the voice, then my uncontrollable laughter starts all over again. A hand reaches down from above. I hold on to it as it pulls me up to my feet.

I come face to face with the curly-haired geek who wears one of his usual plaid shirts and his camera strapped around his neck.

"You're always scaring me, Four-Eyed-Brewer," I say, swatting at him. I grab my purse from him after he picks it up for me.

I start taking some more steps toward the far-away front door, but then stop to pull out a cigarette. "Why are you out here?"

Austin stands with his hands on his hips, watching me.

"It's late, isn't it?" I light the cigarette with a lighter Richard gave me at the party.

Austin takes slow steps toward me, not stopping until he is hovering over me. "Why are *you* out so late?" he asks. "Where've you been?"

Okay, he's not funny anymore. To show him that I do *not* appreciate his tone with me, I take another drag of my cigarette and blow the smoke. Right in his face.

"Why do you care? You're not my father." I try walking past him, giving him a shove, but he stands firm and strong, keeping me from taking another step.

"Move!"

) Tessa Emily Hall

"You're drunk."

"And you're a geek."

He laughs. He actually laughs. "We're not in third grade anymore, Selena. You know what alcohol is?" He leans over to where his mouth is next to my ear. "It's poison. Pure. Poison. Not to mention it's illegal for a sixteen-year-old."

Clenching down on my bottom lip, I shake my head. He stands looking at me as if I am a disgrace.

"You could kill yourself with that junk. Same with the cancer stick you're holding."

His sermons are *seriously* getting old.

I take a drag of my cigarette just to show him that I really do not care about his opinion. My head throbs in pain, and I could swear I hear my bed calling my name.

So I push him again. "Just move, Brewer! It's my life. Let me make my *own* decisions!"

"Fine. You're right." He holds up his hands, finally stepping out of my way. "And I'm sorry. Don't listen to me. Just go and make your own stupid mistakes."

I throw my cigarette—I mean, *cancer stick*—down and stomp on it with my sandal. "See, that's—that's your problem, Austin. You think that you're just so holy, so righteous, and that everyone should follow your way of life. Psshh. You know what? Your way of life isn't for everyone. It certainly isn't for me." I let out an angry sigh. "I like Richard, okay? So take your little immature jealousy, and just leave me alone. For the rest of the summer."

"All right." His hands remain in a surrendered position as he backs away. "That's fine with me."

I raise my eyebrows, a little shocked at his response. I was kind of wishing he would fight for me.

Stomping up the front steps, I let out another huff as I search through my purse for the key.

"You know Selena, I thought you were different."

I turn back around, preparing to hear Austin's final sermon of the night. Hopefully.

"Even when we were kids, there was something about you—something different. An innocence, an inner beauty that no other girl had." He runs a hand through his thick curls, dropping his voice level down a notch, almost as if he is being sincere rather than trying to make me feel like a terrible person. "But I guess I was wrong. You're just like all the other girls who turn to guys and partying to cover up their problems and pain. I just hope one day you'll finally realize it's God you should be turning to."

My fingers tighten around the porch railing as he slowly backs away and turns around, vanishing out of the moonlight and into the darkness.

Chapter 18

Everything is foggy as I shuffle down the stairs the next morning, my head pounding with each step. After fixing myself some coffee, I plop down on the recliner in the living room where Whitney lies on the couch, flipping through channels on the television.

"How'd you get home last night?" she mumbles without even giving a glance in my direction. "You didn't walk home again, did you?"

I squint, trying to piece together the mess from last night. "I can't remember. Oh, yeah—um, my friend drove me."

I watch steam rise from my coffee as the pieces from last night begin to come together. It all feels like a dream: making out with Richard, acting crazy, laughing uncontrollably.

The bitter coffee burns my tongue as I take a sip, remembering my fight with Austin.

Whitney and I remain in the same position in her living room, watching reruns of the show *Friends*, when my phone lights up with his name.

The only reason I decide to answer is so I can apologize.

But for some reason, once I hear Austin's voice come through the phone, the word "sorry" just won't push through my lips.

My eyes shut at the sound of his voice saying my name.

"I'm calling just to see if you're still going to skit rehearsal tonight."

"Uh yeah." My fingers try to comb through my tangled hair. "I guess so. When is it? Are you driving?"

"I think Cole will pick us up. Starts at seven. Make sure you're ready," he says, then hangs up without a goodbye or a chance for me to apologize. I'm surprised that he didn't say he's sorry first.

I let out a sigh, wishing so desperately that our fight had never happened. I know I ruined our relationship, or whatever it was. But it's too late to fix it now.

I glance at Whitney, who is wrapped underneath a fuzzy blanket and sipping on hot tea. How is it that she looks so perfect even when she's not trying? Her hair is up in a messy ponytail and she's not wearing any makeup; even her pajamas look more appealing than mine.

I'm sure she's never had any insecure feelings.

If I could be confident like that, then maybe Austin would like me more, and maybe this tension between us wouldn't hurt as much.

When Whitney asks me if I want anything from Chick-Fil-A, I don't accept her offer. I'm disciplining myself by not feeding the hunger that builds inside of me.

Perhaps Richard wouldn't be as embarrassed to be seen with me if I was a stick like his ex-girlfriend.

* * *

Brooke turns her head away from me as soon as I slide in next to her in the back of Cole's truck. Does she really think that her anger makes me feel bad?

Because it doesn't.

I tune out the conversation between Austin, Audrey and Cole as I scroll through the text messages on my phone, wondering why Richard still has yet to respond to the good morning text I sent him hours ago.

"Congratulations for getting the part of the main character, Selena," Audrey tells me, her smile actually genuine.

"Thanks, I'm looking forward to it." I make sure to say this cheerfully for Brooke and Austin, adding a flip of the hair at the end of my sentence. A little fake show of confidence.

In the youth building, Lexie stands next to the platform sorting through papers. When she sees me sitting next to Audrey on the couch, she walks over and leans down to give me a hug. "We missed you last practice! Here's the script. It doesn't have any dialogue, but I just thought you would like this since we aren't having many rehearsals. You were chosen for the lead role."

"Yeah, Brooke told me," I say, taking the papers from her hands. "Thanks so much."

Brooke glares at me as she takes a seat on the chair next to Audrey.

She *seriously* needs to get over it.

"Great, looks like everyone is here," Lexie says after taking roll call, adjusting her glasses as well as her posture. It's annoying how confident and happy she always appears to be. "Today we're going to learn the beginning of the skit. I need Jesus and the main girl—played by Austin and Selena—to come and stand right where I'm standing."

Austin gives no glance toward me as we both get up from our seats and step up on the platform. Lexie plays the beginning of the skit for us on the church's video screen, then shows Austin and me the first part of the choreography. Personally, I think it's odd. I have to mimic the moves of Jesus—played by Austin—then appear excited when he shows me the "wonderful things that he has in store for me," as Lexie explains.

Once we've gotten through that part of the choreography, Lexie plays more of the skit video that portrays the main girl and Jesus dancing together. "I want you to try this. It doesn't have to be perfect," she says, pressing the pause button on the remote.

I want to look away from Austin as he stares at me for what seems like forever before finally reaching for my hand, twirling me around the way Lexie instructs. Thanks to my dad who used to dance with me when I was a kid, I already know this dance move.

Lexie tilts her head. "Not too bad. There just needs to be more smiling. You two are happy, everything is perfect. And then, after you do this twirl, Selena, you step here."

After showing me where I need to stand, she places my hand back in Austin's and says, "Pull Selena closer to you, Austin—in and out. Here, let's try it all from the beginning."

He drops my hand as if I am contagious, then goes back to the beginning, with the music playing this time.

Once we're done with that part, Lexie calls Sam—the guy who plays the "bad guy"—up onto the platform to learn his part, which is to pull me away from Austin and dance with me instead.

I'm not supposed to look as happy when this happens. Which, believe me, I'm not. Sam is a rather bulky guy who hardly says a word or makes any type of expression at all.

"Great!" Lexie says after the three of us practice the

beginning one last time. "This already looks amazing. Needs a little work, but you're just learning this, so it's okay. Cole, now this is your part for the greed role."

We turn our attention back to the screen behind us to watch the part of the skit where the "money dude" is tempting the main girl as she attempts to take the dollar bills from his hands. Once Cole learns this part, Lexie calls up Tara who plays the role of the drunk girl tempting me to drink by shoving a beer bottle at me.

Austin shakes his head. I swallow and look away, knowing what's probably going through his mind right now, something to do with how I am such a hypocrite.

Brooke is next on the platform to learn her role of the high fashion, worldly girl—which she plays perfectly since she's a model. While we rehearse, she struts past me with a snooty glare. I have a strong feeling that she's not just acting.

Audrey is the last person called onto the platform. She plays a "spirit" that is supposed to lure me into cutting myself and almost committing suicide.

"That's all we're going to learn for tonight," Lexie says as we all go back to our seats. "You guys did so well! I can't believe how much we accomplished in only an hour and a half. I'll teach the ending at our next practice. Before we leave, do any of you guys have anything you'd like for me to pray about?"

I fidget as people discuss their prayer needs: travel safety, a lost dog, and a couple other small concerns.

"I have a prayer request," Austin's voice says behind me. "Let's just say I have a friend going through a hard time right now who could really use some prayer."

His gaze catches mine, and I narrow my eyes at him, then

turn back around as Lexie begins to pray, but I still can't get over Austin's prayer request. Why can't he just let me live my own life?

When the prayer ends and everyone starts to leave, Lexie asks if she can talk with me for a moment.

"Oh, sure." I stand up and follow her to the edge of the platform.

"Sorry, it won't take long." She sits down. "I just wanted to see how everything was going since you accepted Christ into your life. Things can be a bit confusing at first, and I know how hard that is."

I nod, forcing a smile on my lips. "It's been fine. Thanks for asking."

She doesn't smile back, which is very rare for her. "Look, you can be honest with me. Some Christians have a tendency to judge others, but I don't. You can trust me on that one."

My hands tap nervously on my legs. Either she has a sixth sense, or someone has been talking to her.

She takes off her glasses and sits up a bit straighter, not allowing her gaze to be taken off of me. "Well, you don't have to talk about it if you don't want to. Just know that you can call me any time you need someone to talk to. Okay?"

"Thanks." I flash a shy grin, proof that there are some unspoken things that I am still holding onto. "I appreciate it."

* * *

It's not that hard to fake sick the next few days, since I haven't really been feeling too well anyway. I only allow myself to eat two small meals a day. It's been pretty easy, considering the knots that have formed in my stomach due to anxiety.

I don't get much sleep, either—not because of my growling stomach, but because I can't stop thinking about Austin.

I wish there were more skit practices so I could have a reason to get out of the house and see him, not to mention put my hand in his.

Richard and I have only texted a little back and forth since he's been working at a football camp all week. I don't mind that I haven't seen him, but I am looking forward to seeing him at Whitney's pre-July Fourth party tonight. I'm not even nervous either, because I'm ready to just let go of everything and have a good time. Parties seem to bring out the best in me, so I guess that's one advantage to having a popular cousin.

Now that I think about it, the only time I was truly happy this week was at Erica's party.

With Richard.

Drunk.

I carefully apply lipstick as I'm getting ready for the party. This shade isn't too bright, but it isn't natural, either. I'm hoping that it'll cause Richard's attention to be brought to my lips when he sees me.

"Selena," Aunt Kori's voice calls through my closed door. "There's a letter for you from your mom."

I swing open the door and almost yank the letter from Kori's manicured fingernails.

"Well, you're all dressed up," she says, eyeing the new blue top I got from Urban Outfitters. "Going somewhere tonight?"

I open my mouth to answer—but then realize that Whitney probably doesn't want her parents to know about the party. "Yeah, just out with a few friends."

"Well, you have a good time, Miss Popular. Ben and I won't be back until pretty late tonight, but you can always call or text if you need us."

"Alright. Thanks." I practically shut the door in her face, not able to wait any longer to hear what my mom has to say. I sit down at the window seat and rip open the envelope.

> *Selena,*
>
> *You have no idea what of a relief it was to hear back from you. I was afraid that you wouldn't write back.*
>
> *The first weeks of being here has been difficult. I dream of a new life, and I will try everything I can for it to happen.*

I let out a groan when my cell phone starts ringing, a picture of Hilarie lighting up the screen.

"Hey, Hil. How's everything—"

"Selena! Please, help!"

"Hilarie?" I hold the phone closer to my ear and lean forward. "What's wrong?"

Her sobs are interrupted with a few deep breaths. "My mom and I just had a huge fight. She kicked me out, Selena. She said that she can't deal with my problems anymore, and to go find a friend to stay with."

"Oh my gosh, Hil. I'm so sorry. What did you argue over?"

"That's beside the point. I—I don't know what I'm going to do, Selena." Her crying starts up again. "What about my baby?"

My heart breaks for her. "Have you looked into the adoption agency?"

"I've thought about it, but I really don't want my child to be raised by people I don't know. Maybe even thousands of miles away. I'd never get to see it again." She catches her breath, then mumbles, "I'm going to move in with him."

I lean forward. "Wait—what? You're—you're moving in with Josh? The guy that got you pregnant by practically *forcing* himself on you?"

"See," she raises her voice over a siren in the background, "this is exactly why I was so hesitant to tell you about my pregnancy. I knew you would be the one to judge, considering you would *never* do *anything* as major as getting yourself into this kind of predicament."

"What? Hilarie, I—"

"No. I'm fine. Just stay in your beautiful lake house mansion with your rich aunt and uncle who pay for anything you want, and don't worry about me or my problems."

It takes a while for me to take the phone away from my ear when I realize she hung up. Considering how I just spent three days with her makes what she just said even more pathetic.

Why does she suddenly hate me? It seems like everyone has been so against me recently. What's scary is the fact that I probably hate myself more than any of them.

My phone beeps twice, letting me know I received a text message.

Richard: *Hey gorgeous. Can't wait 4 tonight. Miss you.*

I smile before typing a response.

Me: *I miss you too. Like crazy. And I know. I'm ready to have some fun.*

* * *

"Excuse me." Whitney's dancing and drinking friends glare at me as I push my way through their huddles. It's been an hour, and Richard is once again MIA.

My stomach knots. Crowds seriously make me feel claustrophobic.

The entire house is filled with partying teenagers, and not one of them is my potential boyfriend.

I stomp toward the back door, desperate for some fresh air. As soon as I grab the brass handle, the door flies open, admitting a girl with long, black hair and dressed in an all-black outfit.

"Hayden? I didn't know you were invited."

She looks up at me as if I am crazy for talking to her. As if she had no idea who I was. Maybe I was mistaken, and this is only someone who looks like Hayden, but Patrick is next to her, his arm draped around her neck.

"Anyway, have you seen Richard?" I ask.

"Richard Steyne?" Patrick asks, half drunk. "Yeah. He went—over there." He motions toward the kitchen.

"Um, okay. Thanks."

"Who are you looking for?" I hear someone ask behind me, followed by giggles.

Three girls stand with drinks in their hands, laughing. The brunette says, "Oh, there's no need to hide anything! You're looking for Richard Steyne. You know, the guy you've been sneaking around with behind your cousin's back." She glances at one of the other girls. "I can't believe she actually fell for that."

"Fell for what?" I ask, my voice coming out weak.

"The idea he would actually like someone like you." They explode with laughter.

I bite down on the inside of my cheek, wishing I had the guts to take up for myself. What do they mean, *a girl like me?* They don't even know who I am.

Perhaps they're only saying this because they saw us the other night at the party. Of course. They're just jealous. "Excuse me," I say, walking past them. I head upstairs, away from the dancing. Away from the partying, loud music, and rich little snooty girls to whom I will never be able to measure up.

I dig my phone from my pocket and, fingers shaking, enter Richard's number. A ringtone goes off. As I approach my bedroom, it grows louder.

I slowly open the door, pulling the phone away from my ear.

Found him.

Chapter 19

Richard presses Whitney against the wall next to my bed. Making out.

The music from downstairs has faded. The only thing I hear now is the pounding of my heart.

I blink. Perhaps I'm only hallucinating.

When Whitney notices me at the door, she stops kissing and crosses her arms. "So it's true."

Richard turns around and just stares at me with those blueish-green eyes of his.

Whitney giggles at my shock. "You actually thought you could steal my boyfriend from me, and that he would *actually* fall for you?"

I clench my fists, my gaze landing on Richard. "How could you?" My voice trembles from a mixture of anger and hurt.

"Selena—" His expression is difficult to read. He looks at Whitney, then joins her laughter. "Come on, girl! It was a joke. You know, just for fun."

"Everyone was in on it." Whitney's evil smile lets me know how amused she is by my disappointment. "Everyone except you, I mean."

Anger burns in my chest, making it hard for me to inhale.

"Aw, the poor little baby wants to cry." Whitney grabs Richard's arm and pulls him toward the door. "Come on, Richie. She can't take a joke."

I spin around. "Your boyfriend pretending to love me is a *joke?*" I shake my head. "You're both just immature little rich kids with a sick sense of humor."

"Selena," Richard's voice is lower than usual. "Wait—"

I slam the door in his face, my sweaty fingers struggling to lock the door. Why am I always the one that gets shoved around? And since when has playing with a girl's heart been considered just a joke, just a silly little game?

My hands catch my tears as I slide down the wall to the floor. Those girls downstairs were right. It was dumb of me, thinking that I could actually be good enough for someone like Richard. Whitney has been right from the beginning. I am just an inexperienced little girl, in search of the fairy tale life I have been wishing for since I was a kid.

That's so silly of me, still thinking that princes and happy endings exist. That a jock like Richard would actually be interested in a girl like me.

I stomp over to my bed and yank my suitcase from underneath it. I'm sick of myself, sick of this place, sick of trying to find a new beginning. Every time I do, things just get worse.

I pause from cramming my clothes into the suitcase and take a few deep breaths before spotting the crinkled paper laying on my window seat. The letter from Mom that I never finished reading.

After wiping the tears from my eyes, I open the letter and continue reading where I left off.

Selena, there is something very important that you need to know. My intentions were to talk to you about this a long time ago, but I have procrastinated for fear of your reaction when you hear what I have to say. I feel that now the time is right and I'm ready to let you know the truth about what happened in Kentucky.

Your father never kicked us out of the house like I've led you to believe. He was not an evil monster like you thought that he had become.

It was useless, wiping my eye. Because now, as my heart pounds even more than it was before, tears blur my vision. I swallow the dryness in my throat and sit slowly on my bed, trying to keep the paper steady and focus on the words.

No matter how hard they are to read.

He was a gifted pastor, Selena, and the church was beginning to grow extensively. With the continued demands of a large congregation, he had to stay at church for longer stretches of time, sometimes not returning until late at night. I began to feel abandoned, jealous even. I became so angry at him and angry at God for allowing the church to grow, taking away our family time. I began to secretly start drinking. I wasn't a loving or supporting wife during those times and used alcohol to rebel. I had a drinking problem in college, you know. I decided alcohol was the only way to handle the extra stress and sudden feelings of loneliness.

One night he came home early, so excited to tell me that the board had made a decision

) Tessa Emily Hall

to build a larger sanctuary. But he caught me drinking and, of course, I was not happy, which is how the fight began. I lost my temper. I didn't want to deal with the stress of building a larger church. I felt like—the more the church grew, the more time I'd have apart from my husband. I couldn't take it anymore. That night, I started packing. I've never been one to resolve conflicts. I tend to run away in hopes to avoid them instead.

Selena, your father tried to stop me. He did everything he could, sweetie, because he wanted us to stay. You were daddy's little girl. I regret making this sudden decision more than anything, but please understand that I couldn't deal with the pain of feeling like our family life was being replaced by his church. I realize now that having a larger building would have meant a larger staff and his responsibilities would have been shared. He was only trying to make our life better, but I couldn't see it. I wanted a new life and didn't even feel cut out for being a preacher's wife anymore either. Because I didn't want to be lonely, I decided to take you with me, knowing that Drake wouldn't want to go with me since he was old enough to understand the truth.

There isn't anything else to say except that I am sorry, and I hope you can please try to understand at least a little and find it in your heart to forgive me someday. I truly do love you, sweetheart, and am sorry for all the pain that I've caused you through the years.

The letter goes on, but my reading stops there. I'm not able to take any more of it. I go over to the trash can beside my dresser and tear up the letter, hot tears pouring from my eyes as I watch the pieces fall. The fact that Mom decided to wait until I am sixteen to tell me this news—through a letter rather than face-to-face—makes me even more upset.

I shake my head in disbelief. How could she have kept this from me for all these years?

Trembling, I sit back down on the bed. Everything is her fault. All of these years, I could've been living in Kentucky, without any of the problems I'm dealing with now. Why would Mom drag me into the mess of her life?

I would still be Daddy's little girl if it wasn't for her.

I catch a glimpse of my reflection in the mirror as I look up. Black eye makeup smears my face, but for once, I don't care.

I'm sick of being naïve. I'm done.

I zip my suitcase and grab my purse, then pause, realizing that I have nowhere to go. No one to take me. Austin definitely won't talk to me, and Audrey can't even drive.

Suddenly an idea pops into my head. Deceitful, yes. But revenge.

I open the door then remember my sketchpad on the window seat. I almost decide to just leave it there, but grab it before heading down the hall.

Whitney's door is wide open, revealing a room almost as big as the den downstairs. She and Richard sit on the edge of her bed, just casually talking and flirting.

Whitney snickers when she sees me at her doorway. "Where are you going? Back home? And how are you getting there, Selena? You don't have a car. You probably don't even have your learner's permit."

Richard rubs the back of his neck. "Enough is enough, Whitney," he mumbles. "You're taking this joke a little too far."

She looks at him as if he is a *horrible* person for saying that. "So now you're on her side? This was mostly *your* idea. I told you how much I wanted to get back at her for screwing up my summer, and you came up with this one yourself!"

"Yeah, but I didn't know—"

They continue to argue as I scan the top of Whitney's dresser, searching for her keys.

Of course, they wouldn't be on her dresser—they'd be in her purse.

Just before I'm about to give up searching, I spot them. Right behind a picture frame on her dresser.

Perfect.

After glancing up to make sure they're not paying any attention, I slip the keys into my purse. I'm just about to walk out of her bedroom safely until her voice stops me.

"I see you're taking your sketchpad with you. How sweet. So, what—you're going to like, hitchhike over to a creek somewhere to sketch it, as if you're some kind of artist?"

I turn around, wanting to slap that stupid smile off her face. Instead, I flip open the sketchbook and carefully rip the pages filled with my artwork, one by one, crinkling them and throwing them at her. "There you go, Whitney. Something you two can remember me by."

Whitney's laughter fades as I slam her bedroom door and run down the stairs, back into the crowd of dancing, drunk teenagers. Everything seems to be spinning as I reach the kitchen, and I have to pause a second to regain focus.

It would feel really good if I could pass out right now. An escape from this nightmare I'm living.

My shaking hands shove everyone out of the way as I open the front door. The fresh air helps my light-headedness only a little. I run down the porch steps, but turn when I hear the door open and slam shut again.

"Selena, wait. Please." It's Richard.

I am *not* going to give in to whatever lies he has for me this time.

"Listen," he says, a little out of breath as he catches up with me. "I can't get away from Whitney. I've tried, okay? She's not the one I want anymore. I want you."

I back away as he tries to touch my face.

"That's why I came up with this plan in the first place. I had no idea it'd end like this." His voice lowers to a whisper as he continues. Almost as if he were afraid Whitney would overhear him from inside. "The movie, that wasn't planned. It wasn't part of the joke. Whitney doesn't know about it, and she doesn't know that I kissed you. That was all me, Selena!"

It's crazy how the same person I was drooling over now makes me want to punch him just by looking at his face. What's even more crazy is how I almost find myself wanting to believe everything he just said.

"Richard!" Whitney's shriek comes from the top of the porch steps. "What are you doing?!"

The pace of my heart becomes more and more out of control. I remind myself to breathe in through my nose, out through my mouth. The anxiety medicine that I took this morning isn't even coming close to helping me this time.

Richard lets out a frustrated groan, keeping his focus on me. "Hold on, Whitney. I'll be there in a second."

"Well, hurry," she snaps back, glaring at me. "You're wasting our time." The door slams shut behind her as she goes back inside.

I look back at Richard, who is now clenching his jaw in a familiar look of determination that reminds me of Jeremy. "Look, Selena. I can explain. I mean, she bribed me." He lets out a heavy sigh. "I'm sorry."

"Sorry?" I laugh, forcing his hand off my arm. "You lied to me, Richard. You played the part of some innocent guy when the truth is ..." I stare at the ground, not able to come up with the rest of my sentence.

It's really not even him I'm most frustrated with. It's myself—for giving in, for imagining I am actually a princess and once again thinking that I might've found my prince.

"Whatever," I say, my voice quivering. I grab my belongings from the grass and press the unlock button on Whitney's keys. "You're not even worth it."

I take off running to Whitney's car in the driveway, throw my bags on the back seat and slam the door. But just as I'm about to open the front door, Richard catches up with me and grabs my hand, jerking me away from the car.

"You're not going anywhere, Selena." His tone—as well as his grip—is way more firm than before. "Not until you listen to me."

"Leave me alone, you jerk." I try to pull away, but his hand squeezes my wrist even tighter.

"Don't call me a jerk!" he shouts.

Tears burn my eyes. "Let me go, Jer—I mean, Richard! Stop! Just sto—"

He shuts me up by leaning forward and pressing his

mouth against mine. My shaking knees want to collapse, but Richard's left arm wraps around my neck, pulling me even closer.

"Get off her!" a voice yells in the distance.

I gasp for air as Richard finally unlocks his mouth from mine, then starts laughing as he looks behind me. A wave of relief calms me at the sight of Austin running toward us.

"Let her go," Austin says in a calm voice, panting as he catches up with us.

"Why?" A grin slithers across Richard's lips. "I'm not hurting her. Am I, Selena?"

Tears fall from my eyes, but I don't have a free hand to wipe them.

"She's safe, okay, Austin? She loves me. She said so herself. So how about you just—"

"I never said I loved you." I force the words out of my mouth.

"Let her go." Austin's expression darkens with anger, an emotion I've never seen from him. He shoves Richard's arm, trying to free me from his grip.

"Oh, so you want to go *there* now," Richard says. Blood rushes back in my arm as he lets me go. "All right, then."

Austin takes a step back, but it's too late. Richard punches him in the face with the same forceful hand that was just wrapped around my wrist, causing Austin to fall to the ground.

Without a second thought, I jump up onto Richard's back, my arms wrapping around his neck as I try my best to choke him using all the energy I can muster.

I hear the front door open and look over my shoulder,

watching as Whitney runs toward us. "Get off my boyfriend!" she yells, then pushes me off his back and onto the grass.

"What were you doing, trying to kill him?" She kicks me in the stomach with those evil stiletto heels of hers. "Stay away from him. It was a joke, for crying out loud." She turns to Richard now, placing her hand in his. "Come on, Richie. My party is going on without me. We'll deal with these two idiots later."

Richard's piercing stare causes the hair on the back of my neck to stand straight up. Whitney tugs his hand, and they finally go back inside the house.

"Selena, are you okay?" Austin asks. He stands up, covering his face with his hand.

"I'm fine. What about your nose?"

Blood oozes from his nose and upper lip as he uncovers his face. I gasp.

"Don't worry, it's probably not as bad as it looks." He offers a hand to pull me to my feet. "What did he do to you before I got here, Selena?"

"Nothing. You didn't have to let him hurt you. I could've dealt with him myself." With Whitney's keys still in my hand, I run toward Whitney's convertible before Austin has a chance to catch up with me.

I open the door, but Austin swoops in front of me and slams it shut again. "Whoa, Selena. Where do you think you're going?"

"Stop worrying about me, Austin! I'll be fine. Go back to your house and get some help with your nose. Quit trying to constantly fix me and my problems."

He still blocks me from grabbing the door handle. If only Whitney had left the top down.

"You really think I'm going to let you drive in a car that's not even yours? Especially when you've been drinking?"

"I haven't been drinking."

His face hovers over mine. "Are you sure?"

Tears flood my cheeks as I tremble uncontrollably. I feel as if this is all a bad dream. I just wish I could wake up.

"Your face is pale, Selena. You aren't going anywhere."

I wipe my tears before trying to shove my way past Austin, but he is relentless, and just shoves me right back. Clasping the keys in my right hand, I dash for the convertible's back door. In a split second, I squeeze behind the door, slam it shut, and quickly lock it.

Out of breath, I climb over to sit in the driver's seat. Attempting to slide the key into the ignition, I realize it's not the right one. My hands fumble as I try the second. Too fat. The third key slides right in. I start the car and turn off the music that starts blaring, and just as I back out into the road, headlights appear behind me.

I reach into the pocket of my jeans when my phone starts ringing. Austin's name lights up the screen.

"Why are you doing this?" he demands, blinking his headlights from behind me.

"You're going to get blood all in your car, Austin."

"Yeah. Like that's my main concern right now."

I drive right past a stop sign, refusing to hit the breaks. "Being on the phone while driving is really dangerous."

"Answer my question."

Whatever. He's going to get the truth out of me one way or another. "I've made a mess of my life, Austin," I yell into the receiver. "I just want to start a new one, okay? I'm turning into my mom. And I'm scared."

"Are you sure you're not just giving up?"

"I've tried for years to keep pushing through. I've tried to make things better, but when I do, I end up making another stupid mistake that causes my life to shatter into a million pieces." I force a deep breath. "Things will never change. The only way to get rid of the pain is to keep running, because it won't be long before something bad happens again."

I jerk the steering wheel to avoid hitting a mailbox. What is wrong with this car? Why is it swerving?

"When bad stuff happens, you can't just run away. You have to trust God! And fight *against* it. Fight the good fight of faith." He lets out a deep breath. "Now pull over, Selena. *Please.*"

I laugh. "Sorry, Austin, but that God stuff just isn't for me. I've tried to get to know Him better, but things only got worse. He's the one screwing up my life."

There's a long pause. I swerve around an unexpected curve in the road and glance out the window, noticing how dark the sky is. Pitch black.

Not a single star visible.

"Selena." Austin's tone is now calm. Firm. "Pull over."

Tears stream down my face, blurring my vision. "No."

"Selena, pull over. Now!"

My heart pounds faster as it becomes more difficult for me to breathe. I gasp for air, but there's a tightness in my chest, and I hear a familiar buzzing sound in my ears. The same noise I always hear when I become lightheaded.

My sweaty fingers drop the phone as I start to hyperventilate, too weak to calm my anxiety. I try to focus on the road ahead, but everything spins in circular motion.

Then fades into darkness.

Chapter 20

A light shines through the surrounding fog as my eyes peel themselves open. Everything seems upside down, yet I can't tell whether I'm standing up, sitting down, or lying down.

Panic rushes through me. Where am I? I can't be dead. My chest is heavy and burns inside, making it impossible for me to cough.

I vaguely hear someone yell my name. Struggling to turn my neck in the direction of the voice, I realize that my effort is futile. My head throbs.

"Austin," a hoarse voice in the distance calls out. Or was that me?

A dim figure above me—or in front of me—suddenly punches a fist through cracked glass. I cringe as the glass shatters from the force.

Maybe I've been kidnapped. I try calling for help, but it only hurts my head worse.

"Selena, thank God, you're alive." A figure crouches down in front of me. "I'm coming. An ambulance and fire truck are on their way."

Tears burn my cheeks as the smoke becomes heavier, forcing my eyes to close.

"Try to stay awake," the male voice yells frantically.

A few more shouts, then I feel his arms wrap around me. I'm not sure if this person is saving me or hurting me.

My body goes limp as everything slips away.

* * *

"Mom?"

She leans over me, dried tear stains on her cheeks. Am I dreaming? I can't remember where I am, how I got here.

I want to pull away as Mom touches my hand.

"Oh, sweetie."

"Why are you crying?" It's a struggle for me to push words out. My voice sounds husky, the way a heavy smoker's sounds after years of smoking. "What's going on?"

The beeping noises, the smell of ammonia, and the clipboard that hangs at the foot of my bed above stark white sheets…

I'm in a hospital room.

Mom strokes my hand again, tears creating more tracks on her cheeks. "I love you so much. Oh, I was so scared." She covers her mouth as if trying to hold back from crying. When she finally regains the strength to continue talking, she says, "Don't be alarmed, sweetie, but you were in a car accident. I thought my world had ended when they told me you were in a serious accident. Oh, you're so beautiful with your eyes open. I was so worried." Her voice trails off into sobs.

"Serious? How serious, Mom? How long have I been in here?"

My head throbs as I try to recall the last thing I remember. I gasp at the vision: me behind the steering wheel, on the phone with Austin as he followed me. "Austin ... what about Austin, Mom? Is he okay?" Unable to lift my head, I touch my neck and realize I'm wearing a brace.

"Yes." Mom touches my hand. "He saved your life, Selena."

I blink several times and look away, trying to block the unwelcome memories flooding in all at once: the party, Richard, Austin chasing me in his car, telling me to pull over.

I could've killed him. "How is he, though? Please, tell me he's okay."

"Yes, he's fine, sweetie. He only broke his wrist, and had to get stitches on his hands from the glass." She leans down and plants a kiss on my forehead. "The nurse should probably know that you're awake now. I'm so glad you're okay, baby. I missed you so much."

She pats my hand before pressing the nurse's button.

My eyelids grow heavy. I force to keep them open, although it's very tempting to keep them shut.

I attempt to swallow dryness, which only makes me more thirsty, but this discomfort can't even compare to how bad I feel about Austin.

I didn't deserve to live. Why couldn't Austin have just left me in the car?

A blurry nurse floats through the door a few minutes later, but I close my eyes and allow myself to be swallowed up into the darkness once again.

* * *

The sun is almost blinding as a nurse pulls open the curtains. She smiles when she sees me. "Good afternoon,

Selena. Glad to see that you're awake. Your mom just went to the cafeteria to get some lunch. She should be right back, though. Try to stay awake until then, okay?"

I try to nod before remembering there's a brace choking my neck.

The nurse walks out of the room, leaving me here alone on this bed, unable to move because of the tubes that connect me to machines. The pain and soreness in my body makes me want to just lie here anyway.

I don't care that the nurse wants me to stay awake. I want to go back into unconsciousness. That's the only place where I feel relieved—emotionally and physically.

"Selena, you have a visitor," someone says a few seconds later. Opening my eyes, I see the nurse standing at the doorway. "Stay awake now, honey."

In walks Austin. My heart comes almost to a complete stop. I watch him, not able to make out his expression. He takes slow steps toward me, then stops.

"Hey. How you feeling?" Austin takes a seat on a chair next to my bed. A gauze bandage covers his nose. When I don't respond, he says, "The nurse said you should be ready to go home soon."

His fingers fidget on his knee. That's when I realize that a cast is on his right arm, and scratches and stitches cover both hands.

"Did I cause you to get in a wreck?" I ask in a barely audible monotone.

He shakes his head, and his eyes hold mine for a second. "I'm not sure if I'm actually allowed to tell you all the details right now, though. You know, since you have a concussion and everything."

"I have a concussion?"

Mom comes through the door, taking over the conversation by talking about whatever, as if trying to lighten the mood.

I interrupt her—"How long have I been here?"—my voice raising in frustration and confusion. "Why won't anyone tell me what's going on?"

Austin stands. "Ms. Taylor, I think it'd be best if I leave you with her. She's still a little fuzzy." He looks at me, as if he's not able to deal with my sudden outburst. "Call me when the nurse releases her."

Mom nods, then takes Austin's place in the chair next to me once he leaves. She sighs before speaking and places her hand next to the IV on my arm. "X-rays show a few fractured ribs, sweetie, but your lungs are fine. You have a concussion and whiplash. Your neck has an ugly gash from the glass, but not nearly as bad as it could've been. Nasty cuts and bruises." Tears pool in her silver-blue eyes. "Selena, if Austin hadn't been there, you could have died."

"What did he do?"

She hesitates. "When you lost control of the car, you swerved off the road, hit a tree, and landed in a ditch. Your head hit the driver's window, shattering it and knocking you unconscious. Austin was right behind you, witnessing the entire thing." She pauses and glances at the wall behind me, as if trying to gain enough strength to continue. "Austin said black smoke started to come out from under the car, and he knew he had to get you out as soon as possible. He managed to punch his fist through your shattered window to unlock your door so he could drag you out and away from the car as the smoke kept building. He called 911 and stayed with you until an ambulance and a fire truck came." She wraps her hand around my arm.

"The police said that your foot had continued pressing down on the gas pedal after you were unconscious in the ditch, until Austin pulled you out. The tires had been spinning so fast against the dry leaves that a fire ignited under the car. Austin got you out just in time, Selena. If he had waited for the paramedics, it would've been too late."

"You mean—I could've *killed* Austin?" My voice comes out harsh and scratchy, and I swallow. I try to contain myself. In reality, I want to scream. "You didn't have to leave your rehab to come see me."

"Don't blame yourself, sweetie." Her eyes soften, as well as her voice. "This was a God-thing, don't you see? What if Austin hadn't been behind you or had just waited until the paramedics came instead of going ahead and pulling you out?" A hint of a smile forms on her lips for the first time today. "I really like him, by the way. Saved my baby's life. A real gentleman. Not to mention, he's a cutie."

I can't help smiling, too—but a smile doesn't cancel the overwhelming guilt eating me up inside.

* * *

The nurse is never going to give us permission to leave, I think as I listen to her going on about how I need counseling for my anxiety. She even mentions that I'm "a tad underweight for my height and age." Good thing she says this while Mom is out of the room, answering a phone call; otherwise she would probably decide not to go back to rehab in order to take care of my "problems". The nurse tells me that people who suffer with anxiety disorders tend to overeat—or, in my case, not eat as much as they should.

Before finally giving us permission to leave, the nurse hands Mom some papers and discusses how I need to stay home and get lots of bed rest for at least three days, but cannot take my neck brace off for five days.

So—with the brace around my neck, more than my share of bandages, and an extremely tight Velcro-fastened belt strapped around my ribs—I am pushed in a wheelchair through the long hallways of the hospital and into an elevator. It seems a little silly that they make me leave in a wheelchair since the hospital is responsible for my safety as I leave, but right now my ribs are in such excruciating pain that I'm thankful I don't have to walk the long distance.

The ride home from the hospital is silent. On my part, anyway. Mom still goes on and on about how thankful to God she is for sending Austin to save my life. Although I'm glad that she's not giving me lectures about the actions that led me into this predicament—such as stealing Whitney's car— hearing her say all of this, especially after reading the letter yesterday, makes me wonder if she's genuine. I'm not fully convinced that I can trust anyone right now, and her good mood just seems to annoy me.

Because technically, if it wasn't for her, I wouldn't have gotten into this wreck in the first place.

"Oh, no," I say, cutting her off as she tells me how she heard the news. "Where's my purse? And my suitcase? They were both with me in Whitney's car."

She gives me a sideways glance. "I'm sorry, Selena. Your suitcase is gone, and so is your cell phone. Austin was able to get your purse out, though."

I lean my head back on the seat. I don't have a choice really, thanks to this neck brace. "That means all of the new clothes I just bought are ruined." My sketchpad wasn't in the car, but I'd thrown the torn pages at Whitney anyway.

Everything is destroyed.

Just like the rest of my life.

"I'm sorry, hon," Mom says, driving the car once again through the winding roads leading to Whitney's neighborhood. "Let's plan to go shopping tomorrow, okay? I don't have to leave until Monday."

Great. That means she'll be here to watch the stupid performance I'll be forced to be in on Sunday. Or maybe this neck brace will be a good excuse for me to just resign from the skit.

The Huiets' house becomes closer as the familiar dread returns, perhaps even worse than it was when Mom and I first arrived. At least then I wasn't having to prepare myself for whatever revenge Whitney has planned.

Aunt Kori's excitement to see me only makes my head hurt. She offers to make soup. I almost don't take her up on the offer, but food will probably help to ease my headache. At least a little bit, anyway.

But eating soup with them around their kitchen table actually makes me wish I am back in the hospital.

I stare at my linen placemat with its matching linen napkin all rolled up neatly in its own little designer napkin ring. Why does everything here have to always be so perfect?

"Hilarie's pregnant," I blurt out, hoping to create a diversion from the obvious issues that need to be discussed.

Mom pauses, her mouth open wide. "*What?*"

"Ms. Ross kicked her out, so Hilarie decided to stay with Josh. Hil got sort of upset with me when I asked why she'd go to him."

Mom places her spoon back into her soup. "Well, where exactly do you expect her to live? On the streets?"

"I just wish she'd at least talk to me." I glance down at my tomato soup. "She's kind of upset with me for no reason at all."

"Why don't you call her?" Kori offers. "It's hard going through something tough and not having your best friend there to help you out."

Just then the front door opens, and I glance up, my heart sinking as Whitney struts through the door.

"Thanks, Mom, for dropping me off at Erica's house— since, you know, I don't have a car or anything." She shoots a glare at me before running up the stairs.

"Sorry about that, Selena," Aunt Kori says with a sigh. "Whitney hasn't been in a very good mood since Ben put her on restriction for throwing a party without permission."

Must be some kind of new *unrestricted* restriction, seeing that she just got back from Erica's house.

I drop my spoon on my napkin. The soup isn't taking away my headache, nor will it take away this emptiness. I stand carefully, protecting the fractured rib. "I kind of just want to be alone right now."

"Are you sure you're not hungry, sweetie?" Mom asks. "You hardly ate any soup."

"Yeah." I pour the soup down the drain. "I'm fine."

After getting permission to borrow Mom's phone, I take it with me and cautiously ascend the stairs. With every step I take, pain shoots through my chest, knocking out my breath. But I don't want any help. I deserve this.

It's difficult to sit in the window seat with my neck brace on, but after getting situated, I dial in Hilarie's number.

"Hello?"

"Hilarie—" I stumble for words, trying to remember the reason I called her. "I'm sorry. I should've supported you and not criticized your decision to—"

"I've been trying to call, but it keeps going to your voicemail. I also wanted to apologize. Josh is a jerk, and you were right. I don't want him to be part of the baby's life. Or mine. I'm staying with Sarah until Mom gets over the shock and lets me come back. If she doesn't, then I'll probably have to start working full-time so I can afford to rent a place of my own." She sighs. "Don't worry about it. I should've listened to you. I feel horrible for yelling when you were only trying to help. I've just been sort of on edge recently."

I work my fingers through my hair, piece by piece, in an effort to untangle the matted mess. "I understand, Hil." I clasp the phone tighter, wondering if I should add to her burden by telling her the reason I haven't been responding.

"Wait, how are you calling from your mom's phone?"

I look out the window. The same bird that built a nest in the tree a couple weeks ago is now feeding her baby chicks. Watching this scene, I tell Hilarie about the wreck, starting from the beginning: Richard, the party, the humiliation, the crash, the hospital—Austin.

It's weird. Telling her all of this almost feels as if I'm just hearing it for the first time myself.

It's sunset before we hang up, and I stand to join my mom downstairs. But something stops me.

I squat down to peek through the window and watch as the mama bird in its nest encourages her baby bird to fly. The fledgling tests its wings while the mama stands by, chirping before nudging her baby out of the nest.

The baby bird starts falling toward the ground, desperately flapping its wings. And just as if I were watching a cartoon, the mama bird swoops down to the rescue. I watch in awe as this process is repeated again and again until the little bird finally flies away.

Chapter 21

"Help! Austin, help me!" I struggle to catch my breath through my screams. My heart pounds as if I have just run a marathon.

The familiar, hazy darkness has returned. My hands scurry, touching everything that surrounds as I try to figure out where I am. Perhaps I am running? That would explain the sweat that pours from my body.

"Selena, I'm over here."

I turn to the sound of Austin's voice, the darkness fading to gray. Smoke—along with the broken glass around me—makes it apparent that I'm in Whitney's crashed car.

Blood drips from Austin's hand reaching toward me through a shattered window. "It's alright. You'll be safe now."

I'm able to see him more clearly as the smoke fades. Although blood oozes from his nose and is smeared all across his face, he looks down at me with a faint smile, yet there is anguish in his eyes.

"Why, Austin?" I ask as he cries out in pain. I'm sobbing, but somehow at ease—no longer out of breath or anxious. I believe his words. I'm safe. "You willingly put yourself in danger just so I could be safe. I didn't do anything to deserve that! Why would you do that for me?"

"It's called love, Selena." It seems as if just saying those words intensifies his pain. But he says it again. *"It's called love."*

I can't bear to watch as he suffers. If only I could take back my mistake. Erase everything. "I'm sorry! I shouldn't have fought with you. You were right all along. I'm sorry. I'm sorry!"

My eyes open. I gasp for air as if resurfacing after being held underwater. It's dark again, but this time I'm in my bed rather than a car.

And Austin is nowhere in sight.

Wiping tears from my cheeks, I pull the covers over my head and try to calm myself down. Why must my dreams be so intense? I wonder if it's common for those who suffer from anxiety attacks to also suffer from nightmares. That has to be the explanation for this.

Yet, even though that makes perfect sense, there's still something inside of me that knows these nightmares are more than just dreams.

* * *

The opportunity for Mom and me to have a real heart-to-heart discussion doesn't arrive until after Whitney leaves the house the next day. It's getting harder and harder for me to ignore Whitney's evil glares without clenching my fist—or even worse, opening my mouth.

Mom and I sit on the couch and drink hot tea rather than coffee. She says that decaffeinated tea would be more calming for me with all I've been through.

I try not to act as irritated with her as I was yesterday while listening to her go on about her new rehab life. I know she means well. It'd only be harder for her if I truly showed how upset I am with her for keeping the truth from me for so many years.

And I'm not planning on mentioning it, either. So when she brings it up—asking if I received the letter she last sent—I swallow, unsure of what to say.

"Yes, I did."

She wraps her hands around her tea cup before taking a slow sip. "And?"

"How could you do that, Mom?" I focus on her unpolished nails. I don't have the strength in me to look her in the eye right now. "Hide it from me all these years?"

She places her hand on my arm. "I'm sorry, baby. I really am."

I don't pull away from her touch this time. When she apologized in the letter, I wasn't convinced that it was sincere.

But now, watching her, hearing her say this in person, I know she's being honest.

I only nod and glance down at my tea. "Being here in Lake Lure has made me really miss our family. The way that we used to be. Have you tried to get in touch with Dad or Drake at all?"

"Here and there, you know," she says, in her own nervous fashion. "I didn't want your father in your life, so I never passed along the phone calls or letters."

"There were letters?" Tears rush to my eyes. "Daddy—he tried getting in touch with me?"

Part of me wants to respond the way I would've if Mom had told me the truth a few weeks ago: escape to my bedroom, slam the door, and not come out for days.

But as I watch her head drop in shame, I know that's not

the way I should react. It still doesn't take away the fact that I'm not happy, though. How could she have kept this from me all this time?

I set my tea down on the coffee table, keeping my voice level. "Do you think I could try to get in touch with him now that I know the truth?"

She looks up at me now—but I can tell it's a struggle for her eyes to meet mine. "I'll see what I can do."

Her phone buzzes on the coffee table, playing its annoying ringtone. I let out a frustrated sigh, knowing that if anyone calls Mom, there's a possibility they'll never get her to stop talking.

"Hello? Oh, hi, Austin—"

She offers the phone to me, but I shake my head.

"—Yes, sorry I forgot to call you back last night. She's not allowed to go anywhere for a few days. Well, I'm sure you could come over—"

"No!" I say in the best yelling-whisper I can. There is absolutely no way I can face Austin. Especially after the accident.

"—wait, actually, Austin, coming over wouldn't be such a great idea. Selena still doesn't feel too well—okay, I'll have her call you then. Bye, bye, sweetie." She closes her phone. "Why couldn't you at least talk to him, Selena?"

"I can't. I can't talk to him, I can't see him." I brush a strand of hair away from my face. "We had a fight a few days before the wreck, but even though I was a flat out jerk to him, he saved my life."

"At least apologize to him."

I remember my dream last night, how I repeatedly told him

that I was sorry—yet despite his look of anguish, I somehow knew that he had forgiven me.

"Not any time soon."

Her silver-blue gaze takes hold of me. "Can I ask you something?"

"Mmm-hmm?"

She pauses, stirring the spoon around in her tea. "What caused you to have a wreck in the first place? I haven't had a chance to ask you about this yet. Why were you running away? Where were you going?"

Great. I knew she would ask this at some point, but I wasn't prepared to answer it right now. "Mom, I've always been the overly-emotional drama-queen. It's just who I am. I take things too seriously." Stalling, I take one last sip of my tea. "I was angry at myself. And I found out that the guy I had been talking to was only using me as a joke. I found him making out with Whitney—in *my* bedroom. Which is why I took her car. I just wanted to get away—I didn't really have a plan."

I continue regurgitating the events that led up to the wreck—or some of them, at least. This tea is supposed to help calm nerves. However, I can't help thinking that the anxious knots inside of me are untangling themselves because I'm talking with my Mom.

While she shares tidbits of advice, I drown out her words only to take in this moment.

I really have missed out on a great relationship with her all these years. I've been so bitter about our family being split, and all of the problems that we've had to deal with because of it, that I never allowed myself to realize what a great mother

I have. Sure, times have been tough, but she really does love me.

For once, I allow myself to believe that this love is genuine, almost forgetting about the letter and the reason why I'm not so happy with her right now.

* * *

I sleep much better tonight than I did last night. I don't have any bad dreams, either. Even when I see Whitney in the morning, I feel more at peace. No, it's still not easy being around her as she throws flaming spears toward me with her hateful expressions—but at least I don't feel as if I should fight back anymore. That'll just make things worse, anyway.

To my surprise, Kori decides to stay home from work today. She makes Mom and me breakfast, and the three of us watch one of her favorite movies. I'm not sure exactly what it's even about, but it's fun being with them together. This is probably the only sister-bonding time my mom has ever experienced with Kori—at least that I've witnessed. Seeing them beside each other on the couch is pretty humorous. One is decorated with tattoos and an overabundance of make-up, fiery red dyed hair, and a few extra piercings. All of the pain and hardships she's had in life are cleverly disguised under the layers of "extras" where no one would ever notice.

Her sister, my mother, cannot be any more opposite. She hasn't worn jewelry or make-up in years, her untamed hair has a mind of its own, and all of life's struggles are clearly outlined on her face in the form of unhidden wrinkles.

Watching them laugh together makes me feel gratitude for the family I have. For once.

In the evening when I'm by myself in my bedroom, I go through my purse, making sure I didn't lose anything in the wreck. Everything is still there—everything, of course, except my cell phone. Which is actually somewhat freeing instead of disappointing. I don't think I'm ready to talk to Brooke or Audrey yet.

Gathering the miscellaneous gum wrappers, crumpled receipts, and typical purse trash in my hands, I notice that the crinkled-up napkin has ink on it. I open it, assuming it's Hayden's number that she gave me the night of my first party here. Although the ink is smeared, I realize it's actually the letter Austin wrote me the night I "got saved".

> *Selena,*
>
> *I just wanted to let you know how proud of you I am. I'm also really happy you were able to stay here for the summer. You mean a lot to me. Just remember that just because you're saved, doesn't mean only good things will happen. And it doesn't mean you have to be "religious", either. Just be yourself, because I like you better that way.*
>
> *Austin*
>
> *PS: Look up Isaiah 60:19-22. I read it last night and thought of you.*

I smile, and re-read the letter a couple more times. Placing it on my dresser, I have the sudden urge to call Austin now and apologize.

I grab Mom's phone and sit in the window seat, trying to gain the courage to dial his number. But what would I say to him?

Five minutes pass. The only things that come to mind sound cheesy and corny. Finally I decide to stop procrastinating and just wing it.

Four rings, no answer. What was I thinking? He probably knows that it's me calling from Mom's phone, and is ignoring me on purpose.

"Hey, it's Austin—"

I start to say hey back, but my heart drops when I realize it's only his voicemail. Still, I smile at the sound of his voice.

"—sorry I couldn't get to the phone. You know what to do."

"Um, hey, Austin. It's me, Selena." I pause for a few seconds, not even able to come up with my next sentence. What was I thinking, leaving a voicemail?

Too late now. "Look, I know that you probably don't want to speak to me, and I understand. But I really just—oh, never mind, you're calling me. Well, um, bye."

I quickly click send, hoping that's the right button to answer the call waiting. "Austin?"

"Selena? Or is this Miss Taylor?"

My hand fidgets with the fuzzy pillow in my lap. "No, it's me. I, um, was just calling because I wanted to apologize. But I don't blame you if you never want to speak to me ever again."

He laughs. "What are you talking about?"

"You know what I mean. Anyways, I just wanted to let you know that tomorrow I'll finally be able to get out of the house."

"Yes, I'd love to go somewhere with you. In fact, let's make it a date."

My heart skips a beat as I lean forward. "Um, what?"

"Date it is. Pick you up at seven. Is that okay?"

"Well, I—"

"Great." I swear I can hear him smiling through the phone. "See you then."

Chapter 22

If it had been my choice, I would've worn casual jeggings with a dark purple flowing top and cute but simple sandals. Instead, Aunt Kori forced Whitney to let me borrow one of her nicer outfits for my date. Although it's not really my style—a way too tight yellow ruffle top, and faded blue jean shorts that end just above my knees—this may be just the look I need to feel confident. I actually feel beautiful for once rather than just comfortable.

"Getting ready for your big date tonight?" Mom asks, peeking her head around my door.

"I'm so nervous, Mom." I let out a breath I've been holding. "Should I get Whitney to give me another outfit? One that's more—me?"

"I think yellow looks nice on you, Selena. A change from your usual dark green, gray, and purple." She places her hands on my shoulder, her gaze meeting mine in the mirror. "You know, I've never seen you try to make your appearance so perfect for a guy before."

I laugh. "Trust me, you never saw the way I tried to pamper myself up for Richard." I twist the curling iron to wrap my hair around the rod. "But that was because I knew he would reject me if I didn't look like a Barbie doll."

"You always look perfect, sweetie. I can't believe it. You've grown up right before my eyes, and I never took the time to truly appreciate you and be with you."

"Mom, you've done fine. Please stop regretting things, okay? Gosh, why did I have to inherit that trait from you?"

She shakes her head. "I have no idea. It's miserable. That's why I think we both feel hopeless and end up making poor choices. It's because we're so critical and down on ourselves all the time."

I place the iron on the vanity, turning to my mom. "Let's not do that anymore. Okay?"

"You've got it, girl." She wraps her pinky around mine, sealing our promise.

* * *

The moment I open the door for Austin, our gazes lock. Time freezes. I wish so bad that I could collapse into his arms and tell him I'm sorry over and over again.

"Well, don't you look beautiful," he says, sticking his hands in his pockets.

I feel my cheeks blush, and drop my head in embarrassment. It's the second time Austin has called me beautiful. Not hot, but *beautiful*.

Mom appears from her bedroom to greet him, and insists on taking our pictures in front of the fireplace. I actually don't mind this—standing next to Austin with his arm around me. Our outfits seem to complement each other, too. He's wearing yellow, brown, and blue plaid shorts, with a brown T-shirt. It's kind of funny that in the pictures of us going on our first date, I'm wearing a neck brace and Austin is wearing a cast on his right arm that ends at his elbow.

"So where are we going?" I ask Austin once Mom finally lets us get out the door.

His eyes smile with cleverness, as if holding a special secret. "It might take us a while to get there," he says, putting the top to his Jeep down. "So just trust me and relax."

I lean my head against the back of the seat as Austin pulls out of the driveway. I've never had a guy take me on a surprise date before.

"You have just about every song that I love on your iPod," I tell Austin. "This song by Secondhand Serenade is one of my favorites."

He glances at me with a smile, and turns up the volume. The next few songs to come on Austin's iPod are Christian. I relax and enjoy the scenery while Austin sings along with the music. The distant mountains are stacked on top of each other, the evening sun's rays beaming down and highlighting their peaks. Austin and I don't speak for a while—but it's a nice kind of quiet. And, just as I have noticed a change in my relationship with my mom, I can also feel a shift between the two of us. Maybe it's because he saved my life. Or maybe I just like what he said on the napkin.

Looking at the cast on his right arm, I notice his strong fingers peeking out just enough to clutch the steering wheel. I remember my dream from the other night, and realize I don't feel so guilty anymore, but instead, appreciative.

Houses begin to disappear, along with the lake, as we drive through areas that seem to have no civilization—only a few scattered cottages. I try to guess where Austin might be taking me. Chimney Rock, maybe? Or canoeing? No, not canoeing. That was definitely a bad guess.

We sing along as another song plays—a free-spirited ukulele song—and I smile that I'm with Austin, riding around on uncivilized roads with the wind rushing through my hair.

"You're not too bad of a singer," I say when the song comes to an end.

"Same to you, Selly." He gives me a sideways glance before swerving off the main road and onto a dirt road. We ride only a minute more before suddenly coming to a bumpy stop. "We're here."

As I look to my right, my jaw drops. I turn back at Austin and shake my head in amazement, hoping that the tears in my eyes are enough to tell him how much I appreciate this.

I would've never guessed that he was romantic enough to bring me to a lavender field.

I inhale deeply, the smell reminding me of the lavender-scented bubble bath I use at home.

"So, you like it?" Austin asks.

I still can't speak. Instead, I keep my gaze on the field, realizing just how similar this scene looks to a watercolor picture of a field of purple flowers I painted last year.

"Austin, how did you know?" I look back at him as he takes the keys out of the ignition. "I've always wanted to visit a lavender field."

He grins. As we get out of the car, I have a sudden urge to kick off my shoes and run barefoot through the lavender.

"This is just like a dream," I say, gazing out at the endless blanket of purple. "Fields are my favorite. There's something so mysterious about them."

Austin opens the back of the Jeep, still smiling at my reaction. "Actually, your aunt is the one who told my mom about this lavender farm a few years ago. She knows the owners, and uses their products at her spa. Mom called ahead to make sure it was okay for us to come here today. Lavender is a sedative, you know. Helps to calm anxiety and speed healing." He shrugs. "Thought you might need it."

I turn my head away so he can't see the tears forming in my eyes.

This is real.

I really am in a glorious lavender field right now, in the mountains, with probably the most perfect, caring guy in the whole world.

"And I brought a picnic basket for us."

I turn back to him. "Why are you doing all this for me, Austin? This is too much—it's just crazy."

His gaze locks onto mine as he places a blanket in my hands. "Because I want to, Selena." If only I could stare into his brown eyes forever, allowing all of my anxieties and insecurities to melt away. "Don't ask questions."

A peaceful calm settles inside of me. He locks his car, and I follow him into the field and through long rows of lavender, where we stretch out the thick blanket.

I can't help but giggle as I kick off my shoes and feel the long grass between my toes. A warm, soothing breeze orchestrates a ripple of bends through the flowers, almost as if they're bowing in approval.

I still can't get over how much this seems like a dream—a *fairy tale* dream. Perhaps it is.

"This really is too much, Austin," I say as he places a wrap on my plate. "You didn't have to do this, you know."

"Selena, I know I didn't have to. But I did, okay? So now we're going to enjoy it." He bows his head slowly before praying over the food. He also prays for me, thanking God for saving me in the accident—however I want to say that it was him who saved me, not God—then he prays for my "walk with Him." This part irritates me somewhat, since I told him that I never really got saved. After the prayer, Austin and I eat our wraps as he gives me the update on Audrey and Brooke, and tells me how much they miss me. "I thought Brooke was mad at me, though."

He takes the last bite of his wrap, making me feel ridiculous for only eating half of mine so far. "I told you she'd get over it. She was really worried about you. They both wanted to come and visit—and Cole—but they thought that you should probably recuperate and spend some quality time with your mom before she has to go back. They've been constantly asking about how you've been, though."

I swallow a big bite before asking, "How's the youth group? Oh, and the skit?"

"We've only had two practices since you've been in the hospital, so you haven't missed too much. And we prayed for you at both practices. I mean, for your health and all."

"Are you serious?" A strand of hair falls in front of my face as I lean over to grab the potato chip bag. "Why do you guys care so much about me? I was a fake. I prayed the prayer of salvation, but only because I thought that maybe things would get better if I said those words. And I was a jerk to you, Austin." My laugh is bitter. "I still can't believe that you'd want to be my friend after all this."

"Selena, you know we've already gone through this." The softness of his voice sends chills down my spine.

But it's too difficult to look him in the eyes right now.

"It's called forgiveness. None of us are perfect! We all make mistakes. Don't you know that?"

❯ Tessa Emily Hall

I catch a glimpse of Austin running a hand through his curls in my peripheral vision.

"Don't you know that God's grace is so powerful and it covers all sins no matter what?"

I set down my plate. There's still a bite of my wrap left, but I'm not in the mood to eat anymore. "That's easy for you to say. You don't know what all I've done, Austin. How can His grace, just with a snap of the fingers, cause all that stupid stuff I've done in the past to be gone? Vanished—just like that?"

He looks out into the distance, then back at me. "It's possible. God doesn't limit us based on what mistakes we've made or how good we are. Trust me. I would know. He still loves us, and He sacrificed His Son for us." The dimples on his cheeks multiply as his smile widens. "That's why He's so great!"

"I haven't practiced the skit in so long—"

"So what? It's simple. There's no dialogue to memorize or anything." He puts a clip on the potato chip bag, and places it back into the basket. "We're going to have one last practice before the performance. Plus, you can practice it at home by yourself."

"By myself?" I let out a light laugh. "Wouldn't that be a little weird?" I can understand rehearsing lines by myself, but not weird movements, acting as if other people are with me.

"Are you saying you'd like someone to practice it with you?" A grin slowly makes its way to Austin's lips. "Right now, maybe?"

"Oh, no." I shake my head quickly. "I didn't mean that—"

I giggle, because his expression is serious. And, actually, it wouldn't be too bad of an idea. "We don't even have the music, though."

"And your point is?" he stands, and offers me a hand. I smile as he pulls me up, and we come face to face, but only for a moment.

"You're sitting on the ground first, remember."

I clear my throat. "Right." I don't know what sounds more awkward—doing this skit by myself in my bedroom, or practicing it with Austin in a lavender field with no music.

Although I'm kind of glad he's insisting on practicing it now.

I squat down in between the rows of lavender as Austin gets behind me, then causes me to rise up. He speaks the lyrics out loud as we go through the beginning movements. It's still surprisingly familiar to me.

"Do that with more of a smile," Austin instructs, reminding me of Lexie's instructions when she was telling us to look happier when we were in an argument. I laugh and smile big—a little too much, over-exaggerating for Austin.

I look around at the lavender field and the mountains and the sun setting, then realize that my smile is actually not fake like it was during our first rehearsal. This is the happiness I felt in Kentucky, when everything around me was beautiful.

I miss being this happy, being this peaceful.

Austin continues to recite the lyrics, then grabs my hand and spins me around to face him.

"I can't really remember this part," I say, nervous as his other hand grabs mine and pulls me closer to him.

"We spin in and out," he says, his voice gentle. "Like this." He spins me around slowly, then grabs my other hand so that we're face-to-face again. "Then I spin you out, and that's when Sam grabs you from me." He looks disappointed when he says this.

I laugh at Austin's deflated expression. "But I try to get back to you, right?"

He nods. "Of course. The whole time you want me, but are too distracted with everything else. But don't worry, you'll get me back by the end." He takes my hand again, and pulls me back to him. "And we're back together again."

I swallow, nervous again at our closeness. "I think I've got it now."

The dimple deepens in his cheek. "Good."

My heart sinks as Austin releases his hands from mine. It's weird how much I'd like to lay my head on his chest, feel his arms around me, and never let him go.

Instead, he sits on the picnic blanket as if he's not thinking about the same thing at all; as if our closeness was nothing more than practice.

"You can study the rest at home," he says as I sit back down. "There are several videos of the skit on YouTube." He looks at my plate. "You done with that?"

I nod, and lean over to hand Austin my plate. I have to turn my face as his comes only inches from mine. Every time he watches me with that look in his eyes, my heart pounds. He seems to know more about me than what I expose on the surface when he looks at me that way.

It's terrifying. I'm afraid that the longer his eyes stare into mine, the more flaws he'll find. The more secrets and hurts I've buried will be discovered.

I'm just not sure if I'm ready for him to know me quite that deeply. Once he discovers who I really am, he'll run as fast as he can in the opposite direction.

And I'd rather not go through yet another rejection in my lifetime.

I lean back, watching as pink clouds join together in front of distant mountains as if begging me to sketch them.

"What are you thinking about?" Austin asks. I turn to see him sitting in the same position, still watching me with that expression I both love and hate at the same time.

I shrug. "Just wishing that I could sketch like I used to."

"What are you talking about? You're incredible, Selena."

"You haven't even seen my sketchbook."

"I know. You haven't let me. But Audrey told me. She said you're unlike any other artist she's ever seen."

My cheeks warm over the compliment. "Well—"

He gives a light laugh. "Well what?"

How is it that he always seems to have a knack of getting the truth out of me? "I haven't exactly told anyone this yet, but I basically stopped sketching a year ago. I've tried since then, but the inspiration seems to have left me. I came here this summer in hopes that I might get inspired again and sketch like I used to."

"Wait a second." He tilts his head, looking at me curiously. "So you're saying that inspiration left you?"

I nod.

"But you just told me that you wish you could still sketch, correct?"

"Of course." Where's he going with this? "This is probably the most inspiring place I've ever been. Not just this lavender field, but Lake Lure in general. The scenery makes me want to start sketching and never stop."

Austin's mouth curves into a smile again, one that makes me think he has just come up with a great discovery. "Sounds to me like your inspiration is still there, Selena Taylor. It never

❭ Tessa Emily Hall

left you. You *have* been inspired. That's not the problem, though, is it?"

I try to make it look like I'm following him, but sometimes his words just go way over my head.

Austin leans forward, bringing him a little closer to me. "The problem is, you've closed yourself up. You say that you want to sketch, yet you don't allow yourself to open the artistic vein God has given you." His powerful gaze draws me back in. "It seems to me that *you* have left inspiration."

He pauses, waiting for my response.

Nothing comes out of my mouth. I don't know if it's because what he's saying is just so ridiculous and absurd, or if it's completely true, and I'm just afraid to admit it to myself. And to him, especially.

"Do you have your sketchbook with you?"

A breeze flips my hair behind my shoulders. "I don't have it anymore."

He raises his eyebrows in concern, as if I just told him that I lost a family member. "What do you mean?"

I sigh. "Before the wreck, I caught Whitney and Richard making out at the party, and—"

"Oh." He shakes his head slowly. "I'm sorry. I'm sure that must have hurt."

"Believe it or not, the whole thing was a set up. I should have listened to you, Austin, and I'm sorry that I didn't. The night of the wreck, I was really upset—not in my right mind— so I ripped out the pages in my sketchpad, crumpled them up, and threw them at Whitney." My voice quivers. I'd really like it if I were able to talk about something slightly emotional, for once, without breaking down in tears. "I didn't think I'd be back, and I wanted to leave that behind. I thought I was running away. For good."

He reaches over and uses his left arm to spread out the corner of the blanket that the wind has folded over. "Well, why don't you ask her to give them back to you? Do you know what she did with them?" He leans back on his hands, stretching his legs out in front of him.

"I don't even *want* to know. She probably burned them, or threw all of them into the lake or something." The image of my artwork completely destroyed by flames or water fills my head.

"I thought I was actually starting to fall for Richard." I almost choke on my laughter. It sounds silly just coming out of my mouth. "I tried to create a fairy tale out of my life, but there's no such thing as a fairy tale. Fantasies are just myths."

"Well, I don't think that's completely true."

I tilt my head, unsure of what he means by that.

Before I can ask, he reaches for his camera. "Hope you don't mind, I have to take some pictures of this field before the sun goes completely down."

I nod. "Sure."

Another evening breeze pushes my hair back, bringing with it a stronger sensation of the soothing aroma lavender. As Austin gets up to take pictures, I pluck a lavender from the ground, and place it in my purse.

I watch as Austin crouches down, balancing his camera with his left hand to take a picture of the purple fields, mountains, and the sunset all around us. As I glance over to my left, making sure that we are alone, I hear a click next to me.

Austin is right next to me, looking down at his camera with a clever smile.

"Please, Austin," I say with a laugh. "Let's not start that again."

"That was a good picture, though. Oh, that reminds me." After putting his camera back in its case, he reaches into the picnic basket and pulls out two glass jars. "Here you go," he says, handing one to me, and holding the other between the fingers of his hand with the cast.

Tiny holes are poked into the lid of this jar. "Firefly jars?"

"Yep. But the rule is that, after you catch some, you have to let them go after a few minutes."

"Oh, don't worry. I've learned that things eventually die if you hold on to them for too long."

He smiles. "Let's see who can catch ten of them the quickest."

"Okay." I stand up as we both put on our game faces and prepare to sprint. "Ready, set, go!"

Austin and I spend the next few minutes running around the field, chasing the glowing insects all around us. If a car were to pass by us right now, the passengers would probably be a little concerned—me with my neck brace and Austin with his cast—both of us running around aimlessly in a field of flowers. Every time either of us catch another bug, we yell the number that we have in our jar. After a while, though, I am lost in the game and have to pause a moment. The last time I did this with someone, I was with Dad. The night of the purple moon.

That is a night that I will *never* forget.

A dark blanket creeps across the sky as Austin announces

he's reached ten."Wait!" I yell to him from the other side of the field. "That's not fair. I have eight, plus you stole one of mine!"

He laughs. "I did not! You were trying to catch one, I clearly saw it first."

We meet at the picnic blanket. The only light that shines is the moonlight and the lightning bugs milling around in our jars, as well as the ones flying in the field around us.

Austin holds up his container, and I hold mine next to his, taking in the beauty.

"Keep it there," he almost whispers. "I've gotta get a shot of this." He sets his jar down before grabbing his camera from the blanket. "Actually, would you mind taking a picture of us holding our jars next to each other? I seem to only have one good hand."

I smile as I take the camera from him. "Sure."

Our jars clink together as we hold them up again. "Thanks," he says, grabbing his camera from me after I take the picture. "How should we release these?"

"Just unscrew the lid, I guess."

He sets his camera back on the blanket and smiles. "On the count of three."

"One, two—"

Before he can get to three, both of us have already unscrewed the lids. There's a hush between us as we stand in awe, watching fireflies escape and scatter throughout the field.

"This has always been my favorite part," I whisper; speaking louder would only spoil the moment. "Releasing the bugs. Although it's probably the hardest part, too. But it's especially beautiful in the pitch black darkness."

Austin and I glance at each other before sitting on the picnic blanket, closer to each other than we have ever been before.

"See?" he says, his head still faced in the direction where we released the fireflies. "There's beauty in letting go. It doesn't have to be so painful."

"I know."

Austin's arm has somehow snuck around me, and he pulls me close, face to face. I can't see his eyes clearly, but my heart leaps, doing all sorts of tumbles that I've never felt it do before.

He opens up his left hand and gently touches the palm of my right hand. Our fingers are slowly woven together like two puzzle pieces that have finally found where they fit.

I should be afraid that he can feel me shaking, but I don't think about this as his hand squeezes mine, promising security. There's something about him—something alluring and tempting—that makes me want to lay my head on his shoulder. With his fingers clasping mine and his arm around me, I feel more connected to him now than I ever have before. Than I have with anyone, ever. It's beautiful and frightening and so many other feelings I have never felt before.

His hand is smooth but rough in a way a teenage guy's hand should be, and his touch is gentle—not forceful like Jeremy's or Richard's. It just feels right, holding hands with him. I feel safe, my small hand fitting perfectly into his.

Yet there's a part of me that is still afraid to trust him.

Austin's moonlit eyes look down at our hands. "What's that scar on your wrist?"

"What scar?" I raise my eyebrows, completely taken aback at this question. "I mean—how can you see it? It's too dark."

"I've noticed it before. I've seen you look down at it many times. And every time you do, you don't look too happy. As if the pain from the scar is still there." He touches his finger to the scar on my wrist. "Is that why you're afraid?"

I straighten. No one has ever asked me what caused the scar. It could be anything, really. "Afraid of what?" Often people think it's a scar from cutting my wrists—although it's in the shape of a square. Not a line.

"Of getting too close to someone."

"I already told you why I'm scared of getting close to God, Austin. It's hard releasing things into His hands, giving Him the broken pieces of my past."

"I'm not talking about God, Selena. I'm talking about getting close to a person. Relationship-wise."

"Relationship?" I swallow, trying to get rid of the lump in my throat. "How do you know?"

There's a pause. He doesn't have to tell me how he knows—he knows the way he knows everything else about me. "Who hurt you?"

I turn my head, watching as the lights of a car pass. "My ex-boyfriend, Jeremy. Um—"

"Did he *abuse* you?" Austin's tone lowers, as if the thought alone makes him angry.

"The way that you know these things about me is just too freaky. Jeremy *tried* to rape me. I didn't let him succeed, though."

Austin is quiet, as if he is trying to mentally calm himself down before speaking again. "Talk to someone about it Selena," he says, his voice still deeper than usual. "You need to allow yourself to let go of the pain and start building trust toward people again."

He rubs his thumb over my knuckles, but the memory has erased all the magic.

"I have an idea." Austin stands up, pulling me with him. "Come on."

"What's your idea?"

The light from the moon shines down, revealing that clever smile once again. "Just trust me."

Chapter 23

"We would like two medium Luna Bonita Lattes. In to-go cups, please." Austin pulls a ten dollar bill from his wallet and places it on the counter.

"I should've known you'd be taking me here," I say as the cashier hands Austin the change. "Not that I'm complaining. But you could've at least let me pay for my drink."

He looks at me like I'm crazy for thinking such a thing. "Yeah, right. I could never let you pay even a cent on our first—and definitely not last—date."

I smile as Austin and I go to the other end of the counter to wait for our drinks to be made. The quote by C.S. Lewis above the cash register reminds me of the first time I came here, so annoyed that a religious quote was posted in public.

It's funny how one's opinion about something can change within such a short amount of time.

"Why did you order these in to-go cups?" I ask Austin as the guy making the drinks hands us our lattes. "We aren't drinking them here?"

"There's one more place I'd like to take you tonight," Austin says as he holds the door open for me and we step into the secluded parking lot of Brewer's Coffee. The warmth of the cup in my hands is soothing, despite the thick humidity outside. It's not easy going for three days without any coffee whatsoever.

My fingers tap along to the beat of the unfamiliar song playing from Austin's speakers as the view of Lake Lure comes back into sight. I lean my head against the seat and peer through the window, watching the reflection of moonbeams dancing along the rippling water.

I've always loved late night drives, but being here in Lake Lure with Austin—and especially on a date that a girl would only dream about—makes this one even more special.

"Okay, Austin, I told you something that I've never shared with any guy before, so now you have to tell me one of your secrets. Unless, well, you don't have any. You've probably never done anything risky before." I pause, feeling the sting of the words on my tongue as soon as they've escaped. It's too late to reel them back now.

He glances at me. "And how can you be so sure?"

"I didn't mean that," I quickly say. "It's just—you're such a good Christian. You probably don't really have any 'dirty' secret that nobody knows about."

"Am I a human?"

"Yes?"

"Am I a teenager?"

"Well, according to your birth date you are."

"And am I a guy?"

"Um, I hope so."

Austin comes to a stop sign and takes a sip of his latte, keeping his eyes focused ahead. "Just because someone has a relationship with Christ doesn't mean they're perfect. We're all faced with temptation. We all sin." The tone of his voice becomes really serious. "And yes, we all have secrets we're ashamed of."

"So tell me." I survey his face and can't help but get irritated as his expression grows more hesitant. Shouldn't I have the right to ask that question? I mean, he knows just about every ugly secret of mine.

Almost, anyway.

"The thing is, it's a *really* long story." He runs a hand through the back of his hair. "I'll begin by saying that, in middle school, after my parents divorced, I was completely broken. Mad at God, you know. Felt like He no longer cared about me anymore. I didn't have many friends either, since I had grown so distant from everyone. This put me in even more of a state of loneliness. So eventually I got tired of being alone, and tried gaining friends by hanging out with the wrong crowd. I never drank, but I did start to smoke cigars because I thought that maybe they weren't as bad as cigarettes." He lets out a long sigh, clasping the steering wheel tighter as he leans forward. "It's going to be really difficult admitting to you the next part."

"You can tell me." It can't be that bad.

He gives me a sideways glance at a stop sign, his forehead creased, almost as if he's not sure whether or not he can trust me. "Well, these so-called 'friends' of mine eventually introduced and got me hooked on pornography."

My mouth forms an oval when the word *pornography* escapes his lips.

"You have no idea how miserable I was, Selena," he says, his voice all shaky and quiet now. "I just wasn't myself. I felt so convicted every time I went to church, every time I opened up my laptop. I hated it. Hated who I was—who I had become."

Austin turns into his driveway, not speaking again until he presses the brakes. "Let's just say that I was reborn about a year and a half ago. My relationship with God did a complete 180 and filled me with a love that I have never felt before. I'm a completely different person than I was." He puts his car into park, then his gaze finally meets mine. "It feels incredible. I also think it's no coincidence that—just after I've gone through my healing process—God is bringing you into my life."

Goosebumps rise on my arm. "Wow. I would've never guessed that you could go through something like that, yet still be the person you are now."

"It's all because of God," he says, his face lighting up as he unbuckles himself. "Everyone makes mistakes, but it's what you learn from those mistakes that help you to grow as a person."

I grab my purse from the floor of his Jeep as we get out of the car. Austin shuts my door for me, then reaches down and places his hand in mine, causing all sorts of tingly stuff to happen inside of me.

"I thought you said you wanted to take me to one more place?"

He squeezes my hand as we walk past his house toward his backyard, then he looks down at me and smiles. "I did."

"Oh, you're creative," I tease.

As Austin continues leading me by the hand through the grass in his yard, I lean my head back to gaze up into the sky. The dark swallows up the tiny dots of light scattered here and there, but I imagine the night sky overflowing with all different colors—purple, blue, orange. Like the northern lights almost.

The heels of my sandals click as we walk up onto the Brewers' dock. For a moment, Austin and I stand holding hands at the edge, watching as a couple of boats slowly pass by on the water. The only noise that surrounds us is the croaking of toads and chirping of crickets—causing this moment to be even more peaceful.

"Austin, there has to be more to life." I shake my head, studying the way the mountains are perfectly outlined around the lake. "Sure, bad stuff happens, but what about all the good stuff?" I glance up at the half moon now, a smile finding its way to my lips without my realization. "This summer I've felt something I never have before. I know that I'm a daydreamer, but I don't think I'm only imagining this."

"That's God." He lets go of my hand as we sit down on the edge of the dock, our feet dangling just above the water. "He's been answering my prayers."

"Prayers?"

"I've been praying that you'd feel Him. That it'd be indescribable. Unimaginable."

I lower my head, staring at my blurred reflection on the water below us.

"Selena." Austin whispers my name as if it is the most beautiful name in the world. "God has an incredible life laid out for you. In those fairy tales, was there ever a heartbreak? Were the characters perfect, or were most of them broken?"

"Well, they were broken—" I stop my sentence and smile, realizing where he's going with this. "That's what made the happy ending so much more satisfying." It's so obvious; why have I never realized this before?

"Exactly. Now think about my own testimony I just shared with you in the car. I was *completely* broken, but God put me back together. I haven't been the same guy since then."

Austin keeps his gaze on me as I take off my sandals and

dip my feet into the cool water. "By the way, did you ever look up the scripture that I wrote down on the napkin I gave you?"

"I don't have a Bible." What an embarrassing statement to make to such a strong Christian.

He doesn't seem to care, though. He reaches in his pocket and pulls out his Droid. I watch while he goes through some apps, clicking on one that has a Bible icon. After entering in a scripture reference, he hands the phone to me.

I read out loud the passage from the book of Isaiah. *"The sun will no more be your light by day, nor will the brightness of the moon shine on you, for the LORD will be your everlasting light, and your God will be your glory. Your sun will never set again, and your moon will wane no more; the LORD will be your everlasting light, and—"* I scan the following line, pausing a moment before gaining the strength to acknowledge the verse with my mouth—*"and your days of sorrow will end. Then all your people will be righteous and they will possess the land forever. They are the shoot I have planted, the work of my hands, for the display of my splendor. The least of you will become a thousand, the smallest a mighty nation. I am the LORD; in its time I will do this swiftly."*

I look up from the Droid, slowly placing it back into Austin's open hand. "The load I've been carrying around is too heavy for me. I can't go on."

He waits for two jet skis to pass by us before responding. "So what are you saying?"

I think back to the beginning of the *Everything* skit. Just like in the skit, there was something I experienced in Kentucky that was beautiful, peaceful, happy. I thought it was fake. But being here this summer reminds me that it's not. I've been too distracted in New York; I didn't realize it was still possible. But I know it is now. I've felt that peace. I've seen it on their faces.

Satan stole it from me.

And I want it back.

"I've been giving up because I thought that, by ignoring the heaviness, it would eventually just go away by itself. That's why I wear a sleep mask every night. Not to block out light, but to block out reality." I pull my wet feet out of the water and cross my legs. "The thing is, though, when I wake up in the morning, all of my problems are still there. Ignoring this extra weight hasn't made them disappear. It's because—I need to release them to God." The stars above us glisten like diamonds against the darkness, and the moon is half covered by trees that surround Austin's house. "I just, can't manage life on my own anymore. It's too heavy."

His mouth widens into a smile, and I'm almost convinced that it's the biggest grin I have ever seen in my entire life. "So you trust Him now? As in, for real?"

I consider this question as little snippets of my past hurts rise to the surface. With my eyes closed, I watch as images from these scenes play through my mind.

My dad, when he first started ignoring me and putting his church before his family.

My mom, when she took me from Dad and Drake in order to live a messed up, depressing life in Brooklyn. Her lies to me for all these years, convincing me that my dad was the bad guy. *Not* her.

And the nights when she would come home drunk, doing more damage to me with her tongue than she ever would with her hands. Using words that she probably has no idea she has ever said to me, causing me to develop an anxiety disorder and an extremely low self-esteem.

Then, of course, Jeremy. Making me believe that I was

a princess and that he was Prince Charming, until that night when he ended up scarring me forever—inside and out.

"Selena?"

My fingers wipe away tears that have somehow escaped my from eyes. "Mmm-hmm?"

"Are you ready to experience the fairy tale that God has written just for you?"

I exhale slowly. "It's tempting to say no, once again. Tempting to allow the stupid scars from my past to hold me back from ever opening myself up again."

I shiver as Austin places his hand on top of mine, his palm covering the scar that Jeremy placed there just months ago.

"But I know now that the only way I'll ever be able to get past all this—and to be healed completely—is by submitting myself to God. So yes." I nod my head with all the determination I have in me. "I'm ready. I trust Him for real now. In fact"—reaching behind me, I grab my purse and pull out my pack of cigarettes—"to prove that I'm ready to give God my broken past and move on now, I want to destroy these."

I was wrong. The smile Austin has *now* is the biggest I've ever seen.

"Do it."

I laugh. "How?"

"Just do it. Tear them up."

My hands shake, but I don't let this stop me. I hold the cigarettes above the lake and rip the pack open.

"This is one of those moments that needs to be captured forever," Austin says, unzipping his camera.

I laugh, although there is nothing funny about this moment. It's actually pretty serious. But I'm not laughing because I think it's a joke. It's the laughter of genuine happiness.

Relief rushes through me as I tear the cigarettes apart,

watching as the broken pieces fall into the water below. I can't help but giggle once more as Austin takes pictures until the final cigarette has been released from my fingers.

I look down at my addiction—my past—that is now shredded into tiny fragments, being dispersed and carried away with the water.

I have never felt so free. Not just because it's the end of my addiction, but because it's the end of that lifestyle.

"That was beautiful." Austin's voice is almost a whisper, and he gives me the same look that I have seen in movies but never experienced in real life.

I clear my throat. "How do I do this?" I ask, hoping to wake him back into reality. "You know—get saved?"

He looks away and puts his camera back into its case. "You just say it. I can't lead you. Well, I can say the prayer and you can repeat after me, or—"

"At SummerThirst, I repeated the words Lexie said to me and considered myself saved, although I didn't mean what I said. I'd rather do it from my heart this time, if that's okay."

He shrugs. "Sounds good."

Pulling my knees up to my chest, I close my eyes to focus only on the words I'm about to speak. For a moment, nothing comes out. The silence of the night thickens around me as I inhale deeply, feeling the familiar sting in my nose, the one I get right before I'm about to burst into tears.

My voice shakes as I begin my prayer, pretending as if it's only God and me. And for some reason, I'm not ashamed that I've never spoken a prayer in front of anyone before. I'm not exactly sure that I've chosen the right words for this kind of prayer, but when I say amen, I feel a million pounds fall off my shoulders and into the lake below, along with the rest of my shredded past.

"Amen," Austin repeats after me, wrapping his arms

around me in a long hug. I slowly inhale the soothing smell of his cologne, and when he pulls away, it surprises me how much I long to be back in the comfort of his arms.

I smile, although I'm sure he can see the tears that glisten in my eyes.

"You don't have to be so strong, Selena." He places a hand underneath my chin.

"I'm sick of crying, though! It makes me feel so weak. When I said that prayer, I was pretending as if I was tearing up the broken pieces of my past and placing them in God's hands, like I did with the cigarettes. So everything, all the hurts, all the memories—" The images come flashing back, and I pause, afraid that if I go on, tears will start streaming down.

And I *refuse* to cry in front of Austin.

"This is an emotional time." He leans his head next to mine as he puts his arm back around me, his hand on my shoulder calming me down. "It's the most important time of your life! Don't be ashamed of crying. Many people do when they accept Christ into their life. I know I did."

My neck brace makes it difficult to bury my head in between my knees, but I ignore this as the dam breaks and tears flow down my cheeks like pelting rain.

"Lord, I give Selena's life to You. Whatever she does. Wherever she goes. Thank You for coming into her heart, and guide her steps as she begins her walk with You. Help her to never lose her focus, and bless her in everything that she does. Thank You for the beautiful fairy tale that You have written just for her. It's in Your name we pray. Amen."

Chapter 24

What they say is true, about how you never know how good you've got it until you've lost it. Well, in this case, it's the opposite—I didn't realize how horrible wearing a neck brace was until I finally took it off. Being free is such a new thing for me to experience.

And so is going to the mall with my mom. Even though I want to stay home to go over my skit, she insists we go shopping—a little mother-daughter bonding time. I don't argue with her. It's very rare for her to want to go on a shopping trip with me.

"Oh, my. Come here and look at this dress, Selena. It's just *perfect* for you." Mom pulls a pastel-colored flowery dress from a rack at JCPenney.

I blink, trying to tell whether she's joking or not.

Apparently she thinks I wear old-lady clothing.

"What?" she asks when I laugh. "I thought you liked vintage?"

I take the dress from her and place it back on the rack. "Mom," I say, dragging her over to the teen section. "These are the clothes that a 21st century *normal* teen wears. Just because a dress was made for an old lady doesn't exactly mean that it's vintage."

"I guess I'm not into fashion much these days. Funny, considering I used to want to be a fashion designer."

"You? A designer?" The only fashionable outfits I've seen her put together were on my old Barbie dolls. Even the inside of our apartment is plain.

"Now, don't look too surprised. It wasn't until high school that I, well, took the wrong turn and ended up where God didn't intend for me to be. But believe it or not, my senior year of high school I took a sewing class and won first place in a contest for fashion design." She grabs a hanger off the rack and holds the oversized T-shirt up to me, tilts her head, then—thankfully—puts it back. "You didn't get all of your artistic ability from your father, you know."

She looks away, still going through the clothes on the racks.

"Why don't you go back to college then, Mom? Who knows. You could still have it in you."

Her hands freeze for a moment as she considers the bizarre idea. "You know, that might actually be kinda fun." She shrugs. "Heck, with all the new stuff happening in our lives right now, why not throw in a little somethin' else?"

I smile, wishing I could believe that she will actually go back to college to become a fashion designer. It just seems too far-fetched to be true. However, I used to think the same thing about her being free from alcohol. I would've never guessed a year ago that she would actually be going to rehab.

If there's anything I've learned this summer, it's that God likes to throw a few surprises into our lives every once in a while.

* * *

"Chick-Fil-A sounds good to me," Mom says as we enter the food court after visiting a few more shops. "I don't think I've had their food in years."

After giving our orders to the cashier, I can't help but notice Mom's unpolished nails tapping nervously on the counter.

"Are you okay?" I ask her. "Why are you shaking so much?"

"I'm not sure what you're talking about." She snaps her wallet shut, then holds out her hand to me in an effort to prove that she's not shaking, but fails at the attempt. "Well, I guess I just must be hungrier than I realize."

I continue observing Mom as she grabs our tray from the counter. I'd like to believe that the reason she's suddenly acting so anxious is because she is hungry, or even that it's due to the amount of money she's spending today, but I've been around addicts long enough to recognize their nervous habits as they go through withdrawals. Her agitation as she follows me to a table kind of scares me.

"Stay right here." She places our tray down on the table. "I've gotta run to the bathroom real quick."

Mom makes no eye contact with me as she spins around and hurries to the restroom as if she is about to have an accident in her pants.

While she's gone, I scan the cafeteria, spotting teenage girls who look as if they are gossiping as they huddle at their table. Four scary-looking guys with tattoos and bulky shoulders appear as if they could be part of a gang. Two business men sit at a table, leaning over an iPad. A family sits next to them, with two hyper kids and baby that will not stop screaming.

It all reminds me of the time I was here with Whitney and

Erica just a few weeks ago. It made my stomach churn, the way I thought everyone was looking at me then. I just couldn't stand to be around fake people any longer. So I pretended I had to go to the bathroom, just like my mom, but only to get away from everyone.

I wasn't secure enough in who I was.

I'm still not completely secure in who I am, but I don't want to be overpowered by those feelings anymore.

It takes a while for me to eat a bite of my chicken nuggets since a bitter feeling has now settled into the pit of my stomach. Mom keeps telling me this is a new beginning, but we are both very much alike: we never continue to pursue what we start.

When she returns to the table, she begins asking questions about my "new life". I tell her all about youth group, Austin, my new friends, and SummerThirst. She even congratulates me when I tell her I accepted Christ into my life last night.

I would've loved to answer all of these questions just a couple hours ago, even enjoyed hearing her forced advice about following my heart concerning Austin, but now it's as if something has stolen the joy from me.

Although neither of us mention it, we're both putting on a front.

I try to remind myself that I have Christ in me now. I don't have to relive the past.

But it's hard. It's as if Satan has his hands wrapped around my wrists like Richard had once gripped them, and is whispering to me over and over again that my chance of starting over does not exist.

I've been trying to push him away from me, to take my hands back. The more I try, the tighter he grips.

But I am determined not to let him win this time.

* * *

"Text me and let me know when I should come get you." Mom turns her car into the parking lot of the church's youth building. "Do good, sweetie. I love you."

"I will," I say, opening the car door. "Love you, too."

Although church wasn't on my agenda for today, I couldn't just ignore Lexie when she texted me while Mom and I were at the mall, asking if I could meet her here to go over a few things. Considering I have a commitment to this skit now—not to mention I'm the main character—I agreed. Although I'd much rather be spending my time with Mom since she has to leave soon.

Lexie flashes her bright smile when I walk through the door. Never has someone I hardly know been so happy to see me. "Hey, Selena!" She wraps me in a hug. "You don't even look like you were in a car accident. How are you feeling?"

I try to hide the sudden shame. If she knows about my wreck, then of course she knows what caused it.

"Much better." I clear my throat before continuing, unable to reason why her excitement makes me feel intimidated. "Just a little nervous about this skit, I guess. I haven't performed in front of a crowd since I was a kid."

"Well, that's why you're here." She opens her lime green laptop and plugs a chord into the back. "I was actually hoping that we could watch the skit once more before going over some stuff."

"That's fine," I say, collapsing into one of the empty chairs in front of the platform. "But to be honest, I didn't really catch the message that you were talking about the first time you showed it to us."

She pulls the video up on the screen. "Well wasn't that before you became a Christian? It might be clear to you now. Just try watching it once more, and feel free to ask me any questions you might have afterward."

The familiar song by Lifehouse begins, and on the screen a spotlight hits the stage, revealing a guy dressed in a white robe, who is supposed to be playing Jesus. He walks over to a girl sitting on the stage—which is my part—and helps her to stand up.

They begin to dance, the girl's face gleaming with happiness as He shows her what I'm guessing is supposed to be the beauty of life. I can't help but be reminded of my dad, how close we used to be. Especially as another guy comes up and steals the girl from Jesus as He spins her in and out. The girl's face transforms into a frown as the new guy dances with her instead, and she seems unable to escape from his grip. Either that, or she isn't sure whether or not she wants to be free.

My palms feel clammy. I've become captivated after only a few minutes of watching this, overcome by the powerful message. Even though we already learned this at practice, it's all finally coming together for me. It's different now. Much different.

It's as if I am watching my life story unfold on the screen.

One after another, just as we rehearsed, people come onto the stage, tempting the girl with various things—money, alcohol, fame—and Jesus stands to the side, waving His hands to get her attention. She doesn't even glance in his direction or pay a bit of attention to Him, because she's completely distracted with these other things around her that's keeping her from the joy she once knew.

The role that Brooke has been assigned—the tall, thin girl—struts past the main girl now, tempting her to change her appearance, then leading her to make herself throw up.

I lean forward in my seat, watching as a dark figure comes onto the stage and places a knife in this girl's hand. Blood—fake blood, I have to remind myself—appears on this girl's arm as she slices herself with the knife.

I know this isn't really happening. It's only a skit.

But there's something so real about it—something different about watching it now that I'm a Christian. I can't exactly put my finger on it. How did Lexie know this would happen?

What occurs next in the skit causes me to clench my teeth. The dark figure slips a gun into this girl's hand. For the longest time, I watch as she just holds it to her head, apparently considering the decision.

Her eyes squeeze shut as the bridge of the song begins to play. Chills run down my spine. She throws the gun on the ground, running to all of the people who tempted her. She fights against them with all of her strength so she can get back to Jesus, but they push her to the ground. She doesn't give up.

Then, just as if I am that girl, I silently thank Jesus as He steps in, taking the pain away from the girl and putting it on Himself instead.

The girl drops to her knees and raises her hands to praise Him as the temptations fall to the ground. Jesus takes the girl by the hand, lifts her to her feet and they walk off the stage together, just as happy as they were at the beginning.

Almost as if none of that had ever happened.

Chapter 25

The sound of Lexie closing her laptop reminds me I'm not alone. I wipe tears from my eyes, wondering at which point in the video they escaped.

"You remind me a lot of myself when I first watched this," she says, sitting in the chair next to me.

"Good to know I'm not the only one to bawl while watching a silent skit. I had no idea it related so much to my life."

Her smile makes me feel a little less stupid for my sudden emotions. "That's one of the reasons I love writing and acting so much. God can use the arts to speak in many different ways to our audience."

She pauses, waiting for my response. Yet nothing comes.

"Same with you and your sketching," Lexie continues. "Audrey told me how gifted you are."

I let out a light laugh. "Hardly even a gift. Just therapy, really. If it was *really* a gift, I would still be able to draw right now. But I can't. It's as if my creativity has left me."

"Well, when's the last time you were able to sketch?"

I look around the room, knowing eye contact will be difficult while answering this question. "About a year ago. Just before my boyfriend and I broke up. That's when I stopped."

Lexie doesn't say anything for a while, but I can tell that she's thinking. She stands up to unplug her laptop. After returning to her seat, she types in a website address and presses enter. A sunflower-themed blog with a photo of her at the top covers the screen.

"I want you to read this," she says, scrolling through her archives. She hands me the laptop, and I silently read the posts she indicates.

September 7th, 2002

Hi ya'll. I apologize for the lack of posts these past few weeks, but to put it bluntly, I haven't been inspired to write or do anything since becoming diagnosed with Crohn's Disease. I hesitate whether or not to post this, knowing that I sound depressing, but I have to be honest with you guys. I have been beyond confused at why God has chosen to put this illness on me, angry at him for allowing me to go through this. Due to everything I've been dealing with currently, I will be putting this blog on hiatus and keep it that way until I have gained the strength, the courage and inspiration, to write once again. I'm not sure when that will be based on how miserable I feel, but I'd appreciate it if you would not post any sympathy comments at the moment. Thank you.

March 18th, 2003

These past several months have been the most overwhelming time of my life. As mentioned in my previous post, I had become angry at God after being diagnosed with Crohn's Disease, because it had left me no choice but to come face-to-face with all the brokenness I was feeling, and I wasn't prepared to deal with it. I wasn't ready to completely trust in God's strength and rely on Him as much as I have been forced to these past several months. Neglecting to write and keep up with my blog is not at all like me, as you probably know. The reason I refused to write was because I didn't want to allow my feelings to be exposed, and not just to ya'll, but to myself mostly. I tried the best I could to avoid having to look inside myself, confront how I truly felt. To put it short, God has been doing a change in me these last several months, and I can honestly say that I am beyond thankful that he has allowed me to go through this tough season. I have felt His love more than I ever have before, and I have finally come to the realization that I have been handling this situation all wrong. From now on, rather than using my weakened condition to pull me away from God, I will allow it to make me grow stronger in Him. Thank you, everyone, for your prayers.

I set the laptop back in Lexie's lap, shaking my head. "That's incredible, Lexie. I had no idea you've had to go through something like that. I definitely wouldn't have enough strength to deal with it. I hardly have enough strength to face my own problems."

Her eyes soften. "What do you mean?"

I clench my teeth down on my bottom lip. Am I ready to vent—to share my past with this strong, always-happy-and-perky youth leader?

When I don't answer, she leans forward and places a reassuring hand on my knee. "You can tell me anything, Selena. Like I told you before at skit rehearsal once—I'm not going to judge you."

I bring my knees up to my chin and stare at the floor. "I just found out that my mom took me away from my dad—my best friend—when I was only eight. All these years she's led me to believe that it was his fault—*he* was the bad guy. I thought he kicked us out, but he didn't. It was my mom. She's the reason I haven't had a relationship with my dad all these years." My thumb catches a tear before it slides down my cheek. "So instead of living a happy life with all of my family together, I've grown up living far away in Brooklyn, having to be the caretaker of my mom. And it seems as if I've followed her example in turning to alcohol and cigarettes to cover up the pain."

I glance up at Lexie now, who still looks at me intently. As if she actually cared about what I was venting. "I've been trying to have a relationship with my mom these past few days since she's been in town. But there's a part of me that's still angry with her, you know? Just thinking about all that could have been different these past eight years. It really upsets me, especially since she kept it a secret from me, not allowing me to have a relationship with my own father." I drop my head again. "It ruined everything."

There's a pause, and I know she's waiting to make sure I'm done talking before she begins to speak.

"Nothing comes by surprise to God, Selena. Do you think your mom taking you away from your dad could ruin His plans for your life? He wrote out your entire life before you were born. His plan can still prevail in spite of any mistakes made along the way."

I turn back toward her, trying to smile at her encouraging words. "I don't understand how you can have such a good perspective of life after what you've gone through."

"Trust me, I'm not perfect, Selena. I still have my doubts, and have to fight being angry at God, but I've made the decision to not let my past ruin my future. Do you know what I mean?"

I nod, feeling a rush of relief. The kind that comes with a hint of joy. "Things are starting to make so much more sense now. And watching this skit really made me realize just how badly I want to be totally free from the partying lifestyle, free from wishing that I was a different person, from bitterness and unforgiveness toward both of my parents."

"Confession is a good step! It's all part of the healing process."

"Speaking of—" I glance down at my hand fidgeting in my lap. "I told you I stopped being able to sketch a year ago, but I didn't tell you why."

Lexie's eyes fill with concern. "What happened?"

Readjusting myself in the chair, I prepare myself to relive the memory. The one that left a big scar on my wrist—and on my heart. "It was almost a year ago. My boyfriend and I were at his apartment, hanging out like we did every weekend, but this time no one was home. He was drinking, but I didn't realize how much he had. When we were in the kitchen getting popcorn during the movie, we started making out. Which wasn't unusual, of course. But then he dragged me to the bathroom and tried taking my clothes off, even though he knew that I was a virgin and wanted to remain one until I got married."

I swallow as the scene replays in my mind. "I tried opening the door, but he grabbed me by my wrist and squeezed it so tight that I couldn't get away. I was wearing a charm bracelet that my dad had given me when I still lived in Kentucky. As Jeremy squeezed, I could feel one of the charms cutting into my skin. When he finally released me, he grabbed my bracelet and yanked it, breaking the chain."

I tuck the hair hanging in front of my face behind my ear, and force myself to glance up at Lexie. "He apologized later, saying that he just had too much to drink. I almost gave in to his apology, until I looked down at my hand. Every time I see that scar, I'm reminded of when he hurt me."

Lexie's eyes study my wrist. "You know, scars can actually be proof of a healing wound."

I smile. "I've never thought of it that way before."

"Believe it or not, I used to be extremely insecure in who I was." She stands. "Instead of appreciating that I was different from other girls my age, I pretended to be somebody I wasn't in order to blend in with everyone else. I put on an act." She gathers papers from the platform. "Not to brag or anything, but I'm a pretty good actress. That's another thing I learned from having Crohn's disease. You can't live in fear of being rejected. You can't be afraid of getting hurt again. So, you ready to begin?"

I stand, and grab the papers she holds out for me. "Yes. Very much."

"That's what I like to hear. Now, what I usually try to do when I'm acting is find ways that I can relate to a certain character, and portray that relation as strong as I can. I have a feeling this won't be too difficult for you. Remember, this isn't a big skit, but it's a powerful one, so it has to be authentic in order to express the message to the audience. Do you think you can do that?"

"I'll do my best."

She smiles, then gives me several tips on how to get into character. As I perform alone, I feel my shell beginning to open up. I feel my insecurities falling aside as I do what Lexie suggests, and use my painful memories to help me relate to this role.

When I get home, I keep those same techniques in mind as I sit in the window seat with a pencil and a paper to draw the picture of Lake Lure that's been in my mind since I arrived. Instead of allowing myself to become frustrated, I look at the paper with everything Lexie taught me still fresh in my memory, and it's all suddenly clear.

I've been trying too hard to cover my feelings and suppress them ever since Jeremy tried to rape me, rather than opening up and allowing myself to heal so that I can finally feel again. Hiding a wound can cause a serious infection without healing. It has to be exposed and washed. Sure, the cleansing may cause pain at first—but, in the end, it brings healing, as well as relief.

I smile at this realization. That's what's been holding me back from sketching, and that's the reason I was able to draw something the night after receiving that first letter from my mom. Because I was finally able to feel again.

With a pencil in my hand, I am swept into my drawing as it takes me all over the page for the next hour, opening the vein that's been closed too long. Using the advice that Lexie gave me, I draw from my emotions rather than from my mind.

I wouldn't have thought a simple sketch of a lake could have so many emotional strings attached to it.

But it does. For me, at least.

* * *

"Can I ask you something?" I peek into the guest bedroom

bright and early, where my mom stands at the vanity mirror, getting ready for Sunday morning church service.

"Sure, sweetie. Anything."

I sit down on the edge of the bed, studying her reflection in the mirror as she slides on a necklace. It's always been difficult for me to confront my mom about something. Perhaps because of the fits that she usually throws afterward.

"Yesterday, at the mall, you seemed, well, as if you were having a hard time. You know, with the whole alcohol thing. You were shaking, like, a lot." My eyes struggle to meet hers. "I could tell that your mind was elsewhere."

She nervously plays with her necklace. "I told you this hasn't been easy for me, Selena. Recovering from alcohol addiction is especially not an easy thing for someone who experiences frequent anxiety attacks. Your wreck made my stress level rise—"

I look away from her as she turns around to sit next to me. "I don't mean for you to feel bad about it, sweetie. I really don't. That's not my point, anyway. My point is that maybe this is what I needed. You know, a little test to see how I will react if something like this happens when we return home."

Her silver-blue eyes are outlined with a thin line of eyeliner, for the first time in years.

However, that's not the biggest difference about her that gives me hope.

It's the way that she's looking down at me as she strokes my hair, just as she did when I was a kid and would look up at her. In my eyes, she was perfect.

"Just please don't turn to alcohol anymore, Mom."

She smiles. "I can assure you, sweetie, I won't let you down again."

* * *

❯ Tessa Emily Hall

I had no idea getting ready for a skit would involve so much preparation. It takes two different relaxation exercises, two cups of chamomile tea, and an anxiety pill to completely ease my nerves as I go over the skit by myself a final time before leaving for church.

I'm not even nervous about the acting part.

I haven't been to a Sunday church service since Mom and I were with Dad. When he preached. When we were a family.

The tension in Uncle Ben's crammed car doesn't help, nor does the oldies rock music coming through the speakers. It's obvious that no one except Mom wants to go to church today.

When we arrive, I'm surprised at how church fashion has changed over the years. I'm more in style wearing my jeans and T-shirt for the skit than Ben, Kori, Whitney, and Mom are in their traditional dressy church clothes.

After leaving my purse on the seat next to Mom, I rush to the back to find where the skit group is supposed to meet.

"Selena!"

I spin around. That shriek can only belong to one person.

Before I'm able to respond, Brooke's arms fly around me and smother me in a tight squeeze. Austin said she missed me, but I didn't really believe him. The last time I talked to her, she despised me.

She finally releases me so that I can breathe again, but keeps her hands on both of my shoulders. "Don't ever get in a wreck again, okay? I was worried sick when Austin called and told us everything that had happened."

I laugh. "I'm not planning on it."

"Are you feeling any better?" Audrey asks, dressed in a

black long-sleeved shirt and matching black pants. She's wearing this for the skit, but it certainly looks out of character for her wearing black from head to toe.

"Yep. Still a little sore, but I'm fine."

Brooke practically cuts off my sentence. "Austin told us about your decision to re-dedicate your life to Christ. That is *so* awesome. Please forgive me for what I said about your being fake. That was dumb. I was wrong."

"No, you weren't. *I* was dumb for pursuing Richard and ditching my commitment to the skit. He turned out to be a liar, anyway."

"Come here." Audrey tugs on my arm. "We want to show you something."

I follow her and Brooke into a small dark room next to the nursery. "What are we doing in here?" The room is completely empty, except for a long white table that stretches from wall to wall, several chairs tucked underneath.

"So we can show you this."

Audrey pulls something out of her oversized purse.

My sketchbook? That's impossible.

But it has to be mine. It has my initials, SJT, on the cover, and heart doodles scribbled next to it. But how?

I take it from her hands and eagerly flip through the pages. This is one of the few times in my life that I have actually been speechless.

At first glance, it almost looks as if nothing ever happened to it, until I realize that the sketches are photocopies of pieced together pages. It appears that there were a few stains on some of the pages. The photocopies are glued onto the blank pages from my sketchbook. It's not perfect, but it's mine.

❯ Tessa Emily Hall

Tears form in my eyes. "How in the world were you guys able to get this?"

Audrey sits on top of a stack of chairs that stand against the wall. "Before I received the call that you had been in the wreck, I was already headed over to the Huiets' house because Austin's phone had gone straight to voicemail when I called to tell him it was time for supper. I couldn't find either of you inside the house, but I saw Whitney holding your sketchbook and laughing. My heart sank when I saw that she had torn and wrinkled pieces of your artwork, and was showing her friends how you had ripped out the pages and thrown them at her. She went into the kitchen and threw the sketchbook along with the ripped pages into a huge garbage can filled with trash from the party, as if it was also trash." She shakes her head.

Brooke's long legs cross over each other as she sits next to Audrey. "Audrey waited until Whitney and her friends left the room, then she dug through disgusting empty beer cups and pizza crusts to find it."

"No, I didn't have to dig that much. I'm just glad that I was able to get it while it was still on top. I'm not so sure I could've salvaged pages soggy with beer and smeared with tomato sauce if I had waited much later." She shakes her head. "It's not as perfect as it was before, but it's the best I could do to restore it. You have a gift, Selena. Don't ever give it up, okay?"

I nod. Very rarely do tears of joy run down my cheeks.

"I won't," I say, closing the sketchbook and looking up at my two new friends.

* * *

Fortunately for me, the skit team does one last walk-through in the cafeteria without an audience before heading to perform. It's a rush of both nervousness and excitement that I feel as I line up with the others in the hallway, closing my eyes while Lexie whispers a prayer. Then she instructs Austin and me to walk through the doors and into the dimly lit sanctuary.

I step up onto the stage and force myself not to look out into the crowd of people as I get into position. I'm just about to say a final prayer, but before I can begin, the music plays.

And the spotlight is on me.

Chapter 26

"You have to remember to perform from your heart, Selena. Not from your brain."

The spotlight shines in my eyes as I raise my head. Austin's hand brushes against mine as we act out the beginning of the skit, but I refuse to allow this to distract me. Right now, I am completely convinced that I'm a kid again and that Austin is my dad, telling me beautiful fairy tales and all of the spiritual analogies about life that he once taught me. As we dance, I fall in love with this guy that Daddy tells me is named Jesus.

The skit continues, and—just as Lexie and I had rehearsed—I pull everything from deep inside of me and lay it out onto the stage.

The pain.

The guilt.

The insecurities.

As each temptation comes onto the stage, so does a memory. Of drinking and partying. Of rejection, the striving to become good enough. Wishing I were someone different. Regretting decisions that I've made.

Longing to return to the love that I once knew.

Audrey comes on stage near the end of the skit and hands

me a knife. Even though I've never hurt myself before, I feel overwhelmed with emotions I have experienced of self-hatred as I pretend to cut myself. The emotions only multiply when she places a gun in my hand.

My character does her best to resist. But she can't. Aiming the gun toward my head, I close my eyes.

Chills run down my spine as the song's bridge begins— the turning point. I throw the gun on the ground, and with all of my strength I run back to Jesus. Temptations throw me to the ground. I fight against them, and I don't give up. I fight until Jesus comes to my rescue and forces the spirits off me, taking the pain upon himself.

I drop to my trembling knees and lift my hands to praise God, and His presence—the same presence I just days ago refused to believe in—overtakes me as I close my eyes. The evil spirits finally drop to the ground, then Austin raises me up again, and we give one last hug before walking off stage.

* * *

Mom pats my leg when I sit down next to her, her teary-eyed smile tells me that she's proud of me.

That thought alone causes me to smile back.

I had expected to feel uneasy during the church service— awkward, as if everyone knows that my family and I don't go to church—but we don't seem to stand out at all, and for once I don't feel as if all eyes are on us.

During the sermon, I take notes on the back of the bulletin we were given and listen intently, trying to soak in every word. My focus drifts occasionally, though, when the pastor says something that sends my thoughts elsewhere. *Now isn't the time to daydream, Selena!* I shift my attention and begin taking notes again.

My mom seems tense; however, the pastor has a way of getting his message across while lacing it with humor to lighten the atmosphere. He isn't the kind of preacher who points at someone and calls him a sinner, or tells someone she's going to hell if she doesn't repent immediately, neither is he scary or intimidating. I wonder if Dad preaches this way.

Everyone stands, and the praise and worship team plays a couple of songs at the end of the sermon. Even though I don't know the songs, I read words on a big screen and sing along as God's love completely fills my heart. I shut my eyes once again, focusing on Him and only Him.

After the service, Mom and Aunt Kori congratulate me and Austin on the skit. Mom especially is stunned at my acting skills. Whitney, of course, spots some friends of hers and struts off to socialize, while Uncle Ben just stands there expressionless.

"It would've been terrible if I didn't meet with Lexie the other day," I tell Mom and Aunt Kori. "That was when I realized that this is actually the story of my life. I didn't even have to act."

Mom's hand covers mine as she says the exact words I knew she was thinking after the skit. "I am so proud of you. So, very proud, Selena. And I'm so glad I was able to come here today. I've missed going to church."

Ms. Brewer, my mom, and Kori begin talking amongst each other. I feel someone tap me on the shoulder, and I turn to see Lexie right before she smothers me in a hug.

"Selena, that was the most powerful performance of that skit that I've seen. I'm not even kidding. It was very well done, so incredibly touching." Her ponytail flies as she shakes her head. "You're extremely talented."

Her sincere compliments make me smile. "It's only

because of you, really. Trust me, it's a lot more person being in it than watching it. Thank you so much for casting me in this role, Lexie."

"You don't need to thank me. I've heard nothing but good things from everyone about your performance. I hope you realize what an impact you've made here."

Chills multiply on my arms as that realization sinks in.

Everything was orchestrated by God: coming to Lake Lure, attending SummerThirst, and even surviving the wreck. Sure, falling for Richard and wrecking the car may have been my doing—but finding God through all this was definitely His doing.

God has been with me the entire time, knowing it all— Mom coming home, the mall, Whitney, practicing with Lexie, shredding my cigarettes over the lake—would lead to my performance this day, so I can find Him again. And, in the process, leave an impact on others.

"No, not me," I say. "God. I couldn't have done this without Him."

* * *

"Selena!" A familiar voice calls my name as I set my tray down next to Austin in the cafeteria where the skit group is having lunch.

I turn around, spotting Hayden rushing up to me to give me a hug. "Hey! I didn't know you went to this church."

She wears a yellow shirt today instead of black—the first real color that I've seen her wear, ever.

"It's my second time. My grandma just moved in with my mom and me, so we have no choice but to come here. It's actually kind of nice. By the way, that skit—it was really

---

touching. And believe me, I'm not easily moved by something like that. Especially if it's Christian."

"I know what you mean." I sit down and Hayden sets her tray next to mine.

"I heard a rumor that you got in a wreck after Whitney's party. I knew it wasn't true, though."

"Actually, it was true," Brooke volunteers for me. "She's okay now."

Hayden's jaw drops as she widens her eyes at me. "Are you serious? What happened, Selena?"

I shrug. "Nothing too severe. It could've been a lot worse, actually," I say, then give her a condensed summary of the accident.

She shakes her head. "By the way, sorry for ignoring you at the party. Whitney was going around telling lies about you. I feel like a complete idiot for believing her."

"Oh, don't worry. Hey, these are my friends," I say, then give her a quick introduction to everyone at the table. "And this is the youth pastor's wife and skit director, Lexie."

"Nice to meet you," Lexie says, offering Hayden her usual bright smile. "You know, we'd love to have you at our youth group meetings on Wednesday nights here at seven."

Hayden smiles. "I'd like that."

* * *

"I have something to tell you, Selena." Mom raises a Luna Bonita Latte to her lips, glancing out the window next to our table at Brewer's Coffee Shop.

"What?" I ask, my voice sounding slightly apprehensive. Why do I always expect the worst with her?

"I told you this before. It's not as easy as I thought it'd be, having to give up drinking and all. It was very tough for my therapist to allow me to stay for as long as I have while I waited for you to heal completely."

I fidget with the pendant on the necklace that Aunt Kori let me borrow. "Yeah?"

Mom taps her nails on the table. I am unable to make out the expression in her eyes: happiness, fear, maybe sadness.

"They suggested that I stay in rehab for a few extra weeks. Or months, really. It all depends. But at the pace that I'm going, it'll most likely be a few extra months. You saw me the other day, how unstable I became while we were at the mall around so many people."

"Seriously? You may be staying longer?" I allow this news to sink in, not sure if I should be excited or disappointed. "Wow."

"I'm going to strive to recover sooner so that we can move on with our new life, but until then, the Huiets have agreed to let you stay with them. They were also talking about the school for the arts that Whitney attends. It sounds like the perfect fit for you, Selena." She smiles and winks at me, as if she knows that this will somehow make up for having to live with Whitney longer than planned.

"That's the school all of my friends go to, also," I say, trying not to sound overly excited. "They said I would love it there."

Mom's hands wrap around her mug as she takes a sip of her coffee. "You need to pursue your art. I wish so badly that I could go back in time and pursue my talents. Anyway, I'm going to see if you can get into that school. It's a little late to apply, but their website said they're still taking applications."

"But what if I don't get accepted?"

❯ Tessa Emily Hall

"Then you would go to public school. But don't worry, hon. I'm sure you'll get in. The Huiets insist on paying your full tuition if you do. I still think that we should pay at least a portion of the cost. Since I can't earn an income right now, I think it would be a nice idea for you to get a job and give a percentage to the Huiets. So, what do you say?"

I look over at the counter and watch as Ms. Brewer smiles politely at a guy as she hands him his coffee.

"I know the perfect place."

* * *

I don't think I'll ever be able to get over the pain of saying a goodbye.

Mom and I give one last wave to each other before her car disappears out of the driveway, fading behind the distant trees.

I swallow. *Be strong, Selena.*

"Looks like we're going to have to keep you for a while longer," Uncle Ben says, patting me on my head before returning to the house.

Just as I'm going up the steps behind him, another car roars up the driveway, and I turn around. Whitney steps out of a black Porsche, shopping bags in her hands, her blond hair flapping in the breeze as she walks toward me.

"Nice new car."

She passes me without any remark.

"You know, I would say something mean back," she says, opening the door. "But as much as I hate to say this—" she continues walking without even a glance in my direction—"I really am sorry."

I follow her inside the house, surprised at even her meager effort to apologize. "I am too, Whitney. I feel horrible for doing what I did."

Whitney abruptly halts, her Gucci purse swinging around and hitting her shopping bags as she turns my direction and speaks in her spoiled brat voice, "Besides, my parents told me that the only way I could get a new car is if I apologize to you." She turns back around and then mumbles, "And I'm not a liar—unlike *some* people."

"Oh, of course not."

Whitney continues to walk, and steps into the kitchen. "Playing a little joke on your cousin is *not* lying." She drops her bags onto the counter and looks at me. "Stealing, that's like, way worse than lying." She reaches into one of the bags and takes out her new assortment of Bath and Body Works products, lining them all up side by side on the counter. "By the way, the skit you were in yesterday wasn't too bad, though." She flips open the lid to a sparkly pink gel and sniffs. "You did pretty good. But that does not mean I'm excited about you staying here."

I laugh. "Yeah, well, I'm not so happy about that either, *cousin*."

* * *

"Happy freedom day." Cole sits on a wicker chair on the Brewer's patio, licking an orange popsicle as it drips onto his white shirt.

"Thanks. Sorry I'm late. Audrey, do you need some help with the food?"

"Actually, that'd be great." She glances up from flipping a burger on the grill and calls for Brooke, who holds a fishing pole over the lake.

After Audrey gives Cole, Brooke, and me instructions on what she needs us to do, the three of us go inside the Brewer's house to find the paper plates and hot dog condiments.

"Hey, Selena." Austin pours Pepsi into plastic cups on the counter. "Stay here, I have something I want to show you."

"You two love birds better hurry," Brooke says, grabbing a stack of paper plates from a high shelf. "I'm getting pretty hungry."

I glare at Brooke, but she just shrugs. "What? Isn't it obvious?"

"Brooke, you're digging yourself deeper." Cole closes the refrigerator, juggling ketchup, mustard, relish, mayonnaise, barbeque sauce, and salad dressings.

"Hush, condiment boy."

Austin laughs, almost spilling the Pepsi on the counter. "Thanks, Cole, but I don't think we really need barbeque sauce or salad dressing to eat hot dogs."

"Uh, I might." He turns around—almost dropping the ketchup—and pushes the patio door open with his elbow.

When they both finally leave the kitchen, I turn to Austin, hoping my cheeks aren't still showing how embarrassed I am at Brooke's remark. "Sorry. What is it you wanted to show me?"

He sets the two liter of Pepsi on the counter. "Be right back."

I walk into the den and take a seat on their couch as Austin goes into their hallway, then reappears a few seconds later with a shoe box in his hands and a big grin on his face.

"What's that?"

Rather than responding, he sits next to me and puts the

box in my lap. "Go ahead, take off the lid."

I slowly remove the lid, not knowing what to expect.

"Another sleeping mask?" I pick up the mask, running my finger over the small purple moon painted in the corner. "Wow. This is beautiful, Austin."

"It's a prayer mask. From now on, instead of putting on your old mask to escape from your problems, put this one on and pray about them. The moon is your reminder that God is never-changing and you can always depend on Him to hear your prayers."

Not quite knowing what to say, I look down at the shoebox again, which now reveals neatly stacked Polaroid photographs. On top of the stack is a picture of a young girl with dark hair blowing bubbles into a little boy's face. Another little girl stands in the background, hugging her baby doll. "Hey, is that us?"

Holding the photograph closer to my eyes, I take in every little detail. My mom only has a few pictures of me when I was young. I can't help but admit I look adorable with my long, silky hair falling down in waves to my shoulders, and my eyes smiling as I blow the bubbles in a not-so-happy geek's face.

"Love your thick glasses."

"Gee, thanks," he says with a laugh. "They were pretty stylish back then for an eight-year-old."

"Oh, I'm sure they were." I tuck the picture back under the stack, then look back up at Austin. "I looked up the meaning of your name on the Internet the other day."

He raises his eyebrows. "Oh, you did?"

"Yep. It means 'great'. Ironic, isn't it?"

Austin's grin widens, then falls slowly, his dark eyes

shifting their focus to my lips.

"Um, was that your dad?" I ask, looking away from Austin and at the next picture in the shoe box.

He runs a hand through his curls. "Yeah."

"Wow. I remember him." I stare at the guy in the picture. He has dark hair—just like Austin—and his eyes are very similar to Austin's, too, as well as his stature. He stands at their dock, fishing. "Oh, I completely forgot to tell you. My mom told me more about the incident between my dad and her."

His eyes light up. "Really?"

I nod, then tell him everything my mom told me—the *real* story of her taking me away from Dad.

"At least now you know that he wanted you to stay. Are you mad at your mom for doing that and not telling you the truth until now?"

"Well, of course I was." I look down at my sleeping mask, remembering how angry I was while reading that letter. Just before I got into the accident. "But I talked to Lexie about it. Our family just—"

My words come to a halt as I look back up at Austin. His gaze has grown way more intense. His eyes are soft, only focusing my lips.

My heart beats faster. He touches my chin, lifting it slightly—then leans in, pressing his lips to mine.

Chapter 27

When Austin and I pull away, his eyes stare into mine, searching my face.

"Sorry," he clears his throat. "Was that too soon?"

I open my mouth, but realize my lips are far too numb for any words to fumble out of them. I hear the door behind us open, but I can't seem to take my eyes off Austin.

"What's taking so long?" I hear Cole ask. I look over my shoulder and see him holding the door open with his foot, a meatless "hot dog" in his hand. "The food's ready."

"Be right there." Austin shifts his attention from me to place the lid back on the shoebox, then stands up, leaving me sitting on the couch as he walks back into the hallway.

I want to get up and grab him before he disappears into a back room, hold him and tell him everything I'm feeling right now, everything I've felt this entire summer with him. But I'm afraid to admit these feelings to him; maybe even to myself.

My knees tremble as I stand up. Rather than following Austin, I go through the door and join the others at the picnic table on the back patio. When he comes out with the drinks, he avoids eye contact with me completely.

I try to enjoy the lunch, but seem to be just as quiet as

Austin. Why didn't I say something—*anything*—after he kissed me? When Richard kissed me, I never acted that way. Instead, I smiled, only pretending to enjoy it.

But when Austin kissed me—

My lips still tingle as I take myself back to the moment we shared earlier, and suddenly my hot dog starts tasting more like mint-flavored gum.

After spending the entire afternoon in the sun—going tubing, swimming, and talking with Audrey and Brooke while trying to get my mind off Austin—the three of us stand in Audrey's bathroom, doing the best we can to get the lake crud off of us before heading to the park for the evening and to watch a fireworks show.

"There is no way that I am stepping out of your house looking like this," I say, turning off Audrey's hair dryer and setting it down on her bathroom counter. My reflection reveals that my hair is a mess. A stringy, wavy mess, begging to be washed.

Brooke's head pops into the mirror as she stands from her seat on the clothes hamper. "Alright, the prissiness between you two is seriously starting to wear off on me."

I laugh, watching as she snatches a comb from the counter and runs it through her damp hair. "Well, you better get used to it. Who knows how long I'm going to be staying."

"What are you talking about?" Audrey asks as she stops applying mascara to her lashes. Reflected in the mirror, her eyes meet mine. "I thought you said you were staying through the summer?"

"Oh!" I let out a gasp and drop the clip in my hand, turning to face my friends. "I didn't tell you guys yet, did I?"

Brooke narrows her eyes at me. "What?"

My smile grows, along with the eagerness on their

expressions. "My mom has to stay in rehab for a few more months. I'm not leaving!"

"What?" Brooke's comb flies out of her fingers as she throws her arms around me. "Oh my gosh!"

"Are you serious, Selena?" Audrey's doll-like eyes light up. "So does that mean you'll be attending our school?"

"If it works out and I get accepted, then yes." I face the mirror again, gathering my hair to one side and wrap the elastic around it. I had no idea they'd be this excited about me staying a while longer.

"You don't even need to worry about being accepted. With your talent, of course they'll accept you," Brooke says. "Oh my goodness, I cannot believe this! God is *so* awesome!"

"What are you girls screaming about?" Cole asks, suddenly appearing at the bathroom door.

I turn around and see Austin standing next to him. But his eyes refuse to meet mine. "Ya'll better hurry. We don't want to miss the fireworks show."

"Selena gets to stay longer!" Brooke says, clapping her hands together in excitement.

The once tired-and-bored expression on Austin's face is now transformed as his eyes light up and he finally looks at me for the first time since the kiss. "Really? For how long?"

"Probably at least a semester, maybe more," I say.

"She's going to try to get accepted into our school," Audrey squeals.

"Ah, too bad." Cole leans against the door frame and swishes his wet, blond hair away from his eyes. "I was really looking forward to you finally leaving us."

I laugh. "Oh, I'm sure you were."

* * *

Cole pulls his truck into the lot of the same park I had gone to with Hayden and Patrick. Today, there are many more people—families eating at picnic tables, and kids running around on the playground or feeding ducks at the pond.

I step out of the truck and into summer warmth that holds the promise of an enchanted evening.

This is a summer that I will never forget. The summer I found true friends. The summer I found myself. The summer I found God.

And it isn't even over yet.

"Are you okay?" Austin glances at me as I join the rest of them climbing onto the back of Cole's truck. "You seem to be in another world today."

"Selena is always in some other world," Brooke says, opening a container of hot dogs leftover from lunch.

I settle next to Austin in the corner of the truck. "So what? I'm an artist. Artists can't just stay put in the real world." A grin plays on my lips as Brooke shakes her head at me. "And where do you think we're supposed to get our inspiration from if we weren't always daydreaming about things, Brooke?"

She pours Pepsi into Austin's cup. "I'm an actress, and a model. You never see me in a daze, do you?"

"I actually have to agree with Selena on this one," Austin says. He takes a quick sip of his drink before the fizz settles. "Brooke wouldn't understand, of course, since she's always been under the impression that this world revolves around her."

"What does that have to do with anything?" she asks, her eyebrows crinkled together. "I think you're asking me to pour this two liter of soda on your head. Of course you'd agree with your girlfriend. I'd just rather stay in this world, in reality."

I hold my drink out as she fills my cup with Pepsi also. "That is, until I get to heaven."

Austin laughs. "Whatever. Let's just eat, I'm hungry. Should we pray?"

We all close our eyes as Austin blesses the food. As soon as he says "amen", Cole stuffs his condiment-filled hot dog bun into his mouth as if he is starving to death.

"Slow down there, Cole," Brooke says.

Audrey laughs, eyeing his plate. "Wow, Cole. Five hot—I mean, *condiment*—dogs? How could you possibly eat that much after already having at least a dozen earlier today?"

"'Cause," he mumbles between bites, "I'm a beast."

She smiles. "Well, I can't argue with that."

"Okay, how come I never got the couples-only memo?" Brooke asks, popping a chip into her mouth.

Audrey's cheeks turn a bit pink as she glares at her. Brooke sure does know how to embarrass people. Of course, I have been wanting to bring that up with Audrey—how she and Cole have been flirting so much today—but, unlike Brooke, I've decided to just keep my mouth shut.

We all climb out of the truck and clean up our mess while my thoughts seem to—as Austin said—take me to another world as everyone else indulges themselves in conversation. I can't help it that I'd rather watch little kids play on the playground and chase ducks rather than be involved in a normal conversation.

As the five of us are walking back to the truck after throwing away our trash, Audrey points toward the sky. We all pause walking for a moment to take in the sunset. The sky is transformed, and it almost takes my breath away: an intense orange fills the sky with streaks of pink offsetting the purple evening clouds. Sunlight peeks through the trees and plays on the ripples from the pond below, outlining the silhouette of a family of ducks in the distance.

It's as if God has painted a sunset just for us.

"I've got to take some shots of that." With the camera in his hand, Austin sprints over to the pond and crouches down to take a picture of "God's art"—the term he had used a month ago when I first arrived.

After the rest of us have climbed into the back of the truck again, Brooke opens a box filled with games. I settle into the corner where Austin and I have been sitting and get comfortable. Cole passes out the deck of cards when Austin returns from his sunset photo shoot.

"Come here, you guys," he says. "I want us to get a picture together before it gets dark."

We hop down from the truck and form a huddle as Brooke—the one with the longest arms—reaches out as far as she can, turns the camera toward us, and snaps a picture. After several unsuccessful attempts to get all five of us in the shot, a stranger stops and offers to take the photo for us.

"Thanks," Austin tells him.

I can't help but feel nervous as he places the expensive camera in the guy's hands. I would never trust a stranger back in New York with my camera, especially a nice one like Austin's.

But the man politely returns the camera to Austin after he takes the picture, and we all climb into the back of the truck to play games. Austin takes a few more shots while we play cards, but our game comes to a halt as soon as the fireworks begin.

Without saying anything, the five of us stare into the sky

in sudden silence. There's an immediate hush throughout the park as the sky lights up, exploding into multi-colored raindrops sprinkling above the pond and then fading as they fall.

I feel a tickle on my shoulder and turn to see Austin slipping his arm around me. My gaze moves down to his lips that I wish so bad to kiss again.

Instead, I turn my attention back to the fireworks and rest my head on his shoulder. We gasp in awe at the grand finale—the grand finale that not only wraps up the fireworks show, but also wraps up a perfect July Fourth in Lake Lure.

Very few words are spoken as we leave the park. It's as if the fireworks brought with them a magical sense of peace.

"Bye, y'all," Brooke says as Cole stops in front of the Huiets' and Brewers' houses. We say our goodbyes before shutting the truck door.

"See you guys tomorrow," I say to Austin and Audrey as I walk through the Huiets' lawn. "Thanks for the food, Audrey."

"It was no problem at all," she says. "I had a great time today."

"Yeah, I did, too." My voice becomes a whisper as I notice the look in Austin's eyes.

He smiles, the same, dimpled grin that has captivated me from the time we were eight. "See you."

Chapter 28

He made the moon to mark the seasons…

\- Psalm 104:19 (NIV)

Aunt Kori and Uncle Ben sit around the table in the kitchen, sipping wine with a few of their friends. They all stop talking and look at me as I come through the front door, and I suddenly feel as if I interrupted something.

"You're home early," Uncle Ben says. Is it just me or did I hear a hint of annoyance in his voice?

Kori takes a sip of her wine. "We weren't expecting to see you home so soon. Whitney probably won't be here until late." She introduces me to the others, then says, "Did you have a fun July 4th?"

"Yes ma'am. I had a great time." I give a polite smile—this time, not fake.

"Glad to hear that no accidents were involved." Ben winks at me, making it difficult to tell if this is sarcasm or genuine concern.

"There are firework displays on the lake that you can see from the backyard if you wanna go out there and watch," Kori says. "You may want to hurry, though."

I nod, taking this as a hint that she probably wants me away from her and her friends.

I run up to my bedroom to change into some cozy clothes before heading outside. As I enter the room, I have to take a second glance at my bed. A purple sketchbook lies near the bottom, a silk ribbon tied on the cover.

It can't be mine. My sketchbook is green.

I study the sketchbook before picking it up, tears welling in my eyes. Audrey and Austin must have snuck it up here somehow.

A folded piece of paper falls out as I flip open the cover. After unfolding it, I sit on the edge of my bed, noticing cursive handwriting scribbled along the lines. This has to be a female's handwriting. It's too fancy to be written by a guy.

> Selena,
>
> Happy July 4th, cuz. Sorry for being a brat to you. No, I'm not just saying this so that I can keep my new car. I really feel bad about the whole prank thing. Especially about your sketchbook. So, I decided to buy you this. I'm not sure if it's the certain brand you use or whatever, but I bought the one with your favorite color. Yeah, I'm more thoughtful than you think I am. Besides, I thought you'd be needing a new sketchbook if you'll be going to Lake Lure Academy. I'm sure you'll be accepted.
>
> From Your Favorite Cousin (or am I your only cousin?),
>
> Whitney

PS—I just saw that your old sketchbook has reappeared. I won't even ask how that happened.

* * *

A summer evening breeze welcomes me as soon as I open the back porch door. I brush hair away from my face and hold my new art diary close against my chest. I now have a whole new set of pages to sketch. A new life to begin.

Fireworks burst in the night sky as I step down from the Huiets' back porch. I start to head for the hammock, but then decide to sit on the dock so I can get a closer look at the firework display.

Plenty of boats are out on the water tonight. Most of them aren't moving, though—just sitting there, probably filled with folks watching the fireworks. Instead of the usual calm lake, tonight the air is filled with the laughter of children, and music playing from various boats. This is occasionally interrupted with the whistles of sky rockets and the crackling of fireworks nearby.

After kicking off my shoes, I allow my bare feet to hang off the edge of the dock and grasp my pencil. This is the first page of my sketchpad—the first of many.

I sweep my gaze across the lake before beginning my picture. Everything is magical, beautiful. Since I received Christ, life has seemed to have so much more significance and value. It's mind-blowing, really, knowing that all of this beauty was actually handcrafted. Not handcrafted by some false god who doesn't care, but by my *Father.*

The earth is His sketchpad.

Sure, I may have gotten my love for drawing from my

Tessa Emily Hall ☾

mom, and my romantic side from my dad. But I definitely inherited my creativity from my Heavenly Daddy.

I say a short prayer, then draw whatever comes to mind: a picture of one of Jesus' bleeding hands from when He was crucified. When He allowed himself to go through torture, just for me. He might even still have the scars on His wrists.

A distant firework show continues its magnificent display as I add finishing touches to the picture, thinking of what Lexie told me the other day. How scars can actually be proof of healed wounds.

"Wow. You're very multi-talented."

A smile creeps to my lips before I even look up. A figure sits in a row boat a few feet from me—a teenage boy with dark, curly hair.

"But I'm not smoking this time," I tease back to Austin.

"That's true." He rows closer to me. "But you're watching fireworks and sketching at the same time. That's pretty impressive."

I laugh. "Well, thank you."

"Would you mind joining me in my boat tonight?" He gives a crooked smile. "Or are you 'too exhausted' like you were the last time I asked?"

"Don't I need like a life jacket or something?"

"Ah, don't worry 'bout that. I'll be sure to rescue you if you start to drown."

"Oh, I'm sure you will," I say with a grin. I close my sketchpad and slide my pencil into the spiral edging.

"So is that a yes?"

"Well, I guess. But only to get a better view of the fireworks."

Austin rows closer to the dock, then reaches his hand out for me. "I'm sure that's the reason."

After allowing him to pull me into the row boat, I sit against one of the seats across from him. He rows away from the dock, and when his eyes meet mine, we both smile. Then he nods toward the sketchpad in my lap. "Is that the one Audrey was able to put back together for you?"

"Nope." I hold it up so he can see the purple cover. "It's a new one. Whitney bought it for me today."

"Wait, I'm sorry. I don't think I heard correctly." He leans his head forward, clearly joking with me. "Did you say *Whitney*?"

I nod. "Apparently she felt bad about the whole thing."

"Wow." The boat sways back and forth as Austin continues to row. "Would you mind if I take a look?"

I bite my lip, opening the cover. If he had asked me that just a couple weeks ago, I wouldn't have allowed him. It seems like he'd be more critical since he's a photographer; he should know the difference between good art and bad.

But I place it in his lap anyway as he continues to row the boat. His eyes open wide in amazement as he studies my new sketch. "Did you just do this?"

I nod. "I don't even know where it came from."

"It came from God, Selena." He shakes his head, then sets the open sketchbook back in my lap. "It's beautiful."

I smile, my heart overwhelmed at this new realization. Lexie was right.

It is a gift. A gift that the Creator of the Universe has given me.

And I've always thought it was just a silly little hobby. Something else to distract me from reality.

I close my sketchbook and look back up at Austin. "So how'd you know I'd be out here tonight?"

He gives a light shrug. "Had a feeling."

I inhale deeply and gaze up toward the sky, watching the specks of white lights shoot upward and then burst into millions of colors twinkling above the water. The stars, I notice, are unusually bright against the darkness tonight. This night is one of those moments in time I'd like to tuck into my heart forever so I can pull it back out every time I need inspiration.

I look back at Austin, watching as he studies the same scene. His eyes meet mine, and the way he smiles almost makes me blush.

"Oh yeah." I clear my throat. "I have something I've been meaning to ask you."

He raises his eyebrows. "What's that?"

"What you said at the lavender field, after I told you that the fairy tales—the bedtime stories my dad made up every night—are just myths."

Austin nods.

"What did you mean when you said you didn't really agree?"

"Well, you know that stories have a lesson in them that can help teach us better about life, right? Just like the parables Jesus taught his disciples. They were fiction, yes. But they were more than just little stories. Can you remember any of the stories that your dad used to tell?"

I look out into the distance where the moon plays hide-and-seek behind the clouds. "There's one in particular that was my absolute favorite. He told it to me just about every night as he would tuck me into bed." I smile as the memory fills my mind. My dad's voice plays in my head as I begin the story, turning on my book light and doodling as I tell it. "It was about a spoiled little girl who always wanted the best of everything. No matter what she was given, though, she was never satisfied. One day when this girl became a teenager, she decided that she wanted the most valuable diamond in the kingdom, knowing that being in possession of this diamond could be the key to having any man she wanted. So she set out on a journey to search for it. But every time she thought she finally had found the best diamond there was, she would meet someone who had an even more valuable one."

I doodle diamonds around a girl while continuing the story. "After many years of endless searching and never being satisfied, she eventually became an ugly old hag with a sour attitude. Feeling defeated and worthless, she finally gave up and went home to her family that missed her. They all threw her a welcome home party when she arrived, and she saw how much they loved her.

"She went straight to her room, where she threw herself across her bed and began to sob in exasperation— overwhelmed by the love she felt from her family, and by the peace she felt from finally releasing her struggles. Her tears filled the room and spilled out through the window, forming a stream that flowed into an old dry well in her backyard. The water swirled around and around inside of the well as it became larger and larger, brighter and brighter, until finally it was so bright that it was almost blinding to look at, melting her bitterness, restoring her youth."

I realize I'm staring at the lake water, deep into the story. "The water settled into the ground, leaving a large crater filled with tremendous diamonds. A crater filled with the largest diamonds in the world had been in her backyard all this time, on the land that she had inherited. Immediately she was visited by all the most important men in the kingdom. However, she decided that she would only be happy marrying her best friend from her youth." I pause for a moment, noticing what I just said. "The one who she had known and loved all of her life." Austin's eyes catch mine as I look up from my sketch. "Because he offered something that those other guys could never offer—unconditional love. And acceptance."

Nervous, I speed through the ending, turning off the book light and closing my sketchbook. "So she marries the guy, and they live happily ever after."

My heart pounds as Austin looks at me, expressionless.

He blinks, then finally looks away for a moment before saying, "You know—I think your dad was telling fairy tales that had spiritual meaning. Do you know the prodigal son story? He left home to live a life full of sin, but when he realized that he had made a mess of his life, he came home. His dad, rather than being upset with him, welcomed his son by throwing a party. Those stories, Selena—they're more than just silly little fairy tales."

The sky grows dim as I try to think back on Daddy tucking me in at night. Right before turning out the light, he would read me a Bible story and tell me a fairy tale. They probably corresponded with each other, but that never even crossed my mind.

"So they weren't just lies he told me to make me feel better about life and love," I say, sitting straight up as everything starts to make sense to me now. "They were real—a reflection of life." I smile at this realization. "Just like all art is."

Another realization hits me. My own life is a fairy tale story—one that has already been written by the hands of God. All this time, I have been trying to write it myself.

I look back at Austin, at the peaceful way he just sits there and rows the boat. I have never felt this way about any guy; all of the other relationships I've been in were forced.

---

310   ❯ Tessa Emily Hall

Yet this happened so naturally with Austin. "I don't want to write my love stories anymore," I blurt out, not afraid to share what I'm thinking with him. "I want God to write them from now on."

I would usually never have the guts to be this open with a guy—but I feel as if Austin deserves to hear the truth. Especially after all that he's done for me.

Not to mention, I still feel bad about not kissing him back earlier today.

"I've tried to ignore the way I feel toward you." I feel my cheeks flush, but I don't shy away from saying what I feel right now. "I can't. And I'm through fighting with what I know—what I feel—is right."

There's a sudden twinkle in his eye. "Meaning?"

"You and me, Austin." I nod my head with confidence. "It feels right."

He stops rowing once again—and just when I think he's about to respond, he looks next to our boat.

I also turn my head toward the several trees that cover the bank. And that's when I see it—the two old, wooden swings hanging side-by-side under one of the trees.

It never crossed my mind that he might be rowing us here.

Neither of us say anything as Austin ties the boat to a low-hanging tree, steps out onto the bank, and reaches for my hand. I hold on tightly—making sure not to fall into the water—then sit down on the same swing I was on the last time we were here.

Austin sits down on the swing next to me, and I can't help but feel him watching as I take in the beauty of the sky—the stars, the fireworks, the moon.

"What are you thinking about?" It's not the first time he's asked me that question.

"Just hoping I can remember every detail about this night."

His brown eyes soften as I face him.

"You know, I really didn't deserve you saving me that day."

"And you think we deserved Christ dying for us?"

I'm taken aback at his response, reminded of the dream I had a few nights after the accident. "That's true."

The corner of his mouth rises, and he reaches over to take my hand as we continue to gently swing. "You've been a blessing for me, Selena."

"Me?" I raise my eyebrows. "How?"

Steadying his foot on the ground to stop the swing, Austin stares at me before finally saying, "You're so passionate. And you don't care about all of the material things like other girls do."

My heart pounds faster, realizing that the look on his face is the same as it was just before he kissed me.

"You've made me realize that God works everything out in His timing. And just so you know—" he squeezes my hand— "I think it feels right, too."

My swinging comes to a complete stop. And, without even a second thought, I lean in to give Austin a light kiss— one that I will never forget.

He smiles, once again showing off those adorable dimples of his.

All this time, I have been trying to pen my own fairy tales. It's no wonder they have always had bad endings.

This summer marks the first chapter of a brand new book. Except, this time, I'm letting go of the pen and letting God write the story.

Austin and I turn our attention back toward the sky as the grand finale of the firework show goes off above the mountains.

There's something different about the moon tonight. No, it's not purple—it looks exactly the way it always does.

It's the feeling I get when a new season is approaching. I know that it's still only the middle of the summer; but spiritually, maybe, it's a new season.

A new beginning. Just like Mom said.

Discussion Questions

1) At the beginning of Selena's stay in North Carolina, Whitney asks Selena how she can have fun if she's worried about following all the rules. Later, Hayden tells Selena to loosen up because "it's summer". Have you ever believed that in order to have fun, you should break the rules? In what ways do Selena's friends from SummerThirst have fun without partying?

2) When Selena first arrives at Lake Lure, she gives in to temptation little by little through believing lies, such as, "this is my last cigarette". How does this relate to the "Everything" skit, and how does the main role in the skit overcome this? Read James 1:14 and discuss what it says about temptation.

3) Selena feels like she should look a certain way in order for Richard to accept her. Have you ever tried changing your appearance for acceptance? After reading Galatians 1:10, discuss ways you can strive for God's acceptance rather than man's.

4) At Sliding Rock, Brooke teasingly tells Selena and Audrey that the Bible says to not be "halfway in and halfway out" (see Rev. 3:16). Later, Austin tells Selena that she can't have both lifestyles. What are some ways that you have been living "halfway in and halfway out"? How can you make changes to live entirely for God rather than for the world as well?

5) Selena regrets not telling Hilarie a year ago that what she had with Josh wasn't going to last. Do you think

it's worth having a boyfriend just for the fun of it, when you know it will most likely end in heartbreak— or in Richard's words, have a "not so happy ending"?

6) During the hike that Selena goes on during SummerThirst, she's completely exhausted and wants to go home. After learning about the spiritual truths applied to the hike, what are some ways you can prevent yourself from becoming exhausted on your journey through life? Is there unnecessary baggage you might be holding onto? Read Psalm 55:22 and discuss the relief that Selena experienced after she finally released her baggage to the Lord.

7) Austin points out to Selena that in fairy tales, the characters are broken—but that's what makes the ending so satisfying. After reading Rom. 5:3-5, Deut. 8:2-3, James 1:2-4, 1 Pet. 1:6-7, and 2 Cor. 4:16-17, discuss the benefits of going through trials. Have you ever gone through a hard time, only to realize that God was trying to teach you something?

8) When Selena finds out the truth about her parents, she becomes angry at her mom—not only for withholding the truth from her, but for keeping her from having a relationship with her dad. Have you ever been betrayed by a family member or friend? How did you react? Think about when Austin saved Selena the night of her wreck. How does the dream Selena had soon after relate to Jesus sacrificing himself for us? Read Matthew 18:21-22. Is there any unforgiveness you might be holding onto?

9) Selena gives into temptation several times throughout the story—however, during the party on the first

night she was in Lake Lure, she leaves after realizing that she may not be strong enough to handle the temptation. Do you escape temptation as soon as it's offered, or do you assume that you're strong enough to handle it? Read Luke 22:40, Matthew 4:10, and Matthew 26:41. If you were put in a similar situation, how do you think God would want you to handle it?

10) Before her car accident, Selena tells Austin that the only way to get rid of pain is to keep running. She even accused God of messing up her life. Have you ever been tempted to run away from your problems? How can you give them to God, like Selena does, so you can begin the healing process rather than allowing the wound to become an infection?

For more discussion questions and devotionals related to the book, please visit www.purplemoonseries.com. If your youth group or book club is reading *Purple Moon*, contact me at tessaehall@gmail.com and I will be happy to schedule a meeting or video chat via Skype.

If you accepted Christ as your personal Savior while reading *Purple Moon*—or if you would like to—please let me know by sending me an email at tessaehall@gmail.com.

CPSIA information can be obtained
at www.ICGtesting.com
Printed in the USA
BVHW051513230123
656891BV00015B/289

9 781647 131760